THE ONES WHO NEVER LEFT

If walls could talk...

GABRIELLE MULLARKEY

SPIRAL
BOOKS

First published in Great Britain in 2025 by Spiral Books
an imprint of Spiral Publishing Ltd

1 3 5 7 9 10 8 6 4 2

Spiral Publishing, 38 Pulla Hill Drive,
Storrington, West Sussex RH20 3LS
Edited by Martin Cooper

email: jonathan@spiralpublishing.com
www.spiral-books.com

ISBN 978-1-0685670-8-7

British Library Cataloguing in Publication Data.
A catalogue record for this book is available from the British Library.

Printed and bound in England by 4edge Limited,
22 Eldon Way Industrial Estate, Hockley, Essex SS5 4AD

Dedication:

To my parents, for sharing
their love of stories,
the taller the better

Revenge should have no bounds.

From Hamlet
by William Shakespeare

1

Two days after her wedding to a man she'd known for seven months, Lucy Driscoll left London for Yorkshire to move into a house she'd only seen online. A few months short of her 30th birthday, she'd embraced the art of the impulsive.

Hugh had travelled north the day before, taking the InterCity to York, the branch line to Sowersby and a taxi the last six miles to Rook House. It was his second visit to the house. He'd been there a few weeks earlier to collect the keys.

The house had already been cleaned and aired by a housekeeper who lived locally, the last tenants having left three months ago. But Hugh had wanted to go on ahead and ensure their new home made a good impression on his new bride, telling Lucy: "I can still carry you over the threshold when you get here, give or take a dodgy disc, but might have to be a fireman's."

"An advance party is a good idea," Lucy had agreed. "But I'll pass on the fireman's lift, ta."

She was all for romantic gestures, but drew the line at being hauled into her new home like a sack of spuds by a puffing spouse clutching his back.

Besides, she enjoyed a solo drive with just her thoughts, the motorway unspooling ahead.

But now those thoughts skittered, wary of sober reality: overnight she'd become a grown-up, with a husband, house, car. All would require regular maintenance.

On the stuttery radio, Karen Carpenter sang that rainy days and Mondays always got her down.

Lucy jabbed the dial off, listening instead to the percussive rattle of the car heater.

She rolled her shoulders, her course set but her internal compass still veering wildly.

Rook House. Proper gothic name for a proper old house. It must have once echoed to the strains of house parties and industrious servants; the click of billiard balls and clatter of buckets, maids summoned by bells, dogs barking, a dropped tureen, a hissing log kicked back into the grate.

Her imagination snagging on *Downton Abbey* clichés, she leant forward to rub the frosty arc carved dimly out of her windscreen by reluctant wipers, dampness soaking through her gloved palm. A house like that must long for richly textured sound. Two naturally quiet people would never generate enough variety to meet its expectations unless they...

The phone on the passenger seat lit up with a text; she hauled it closer to read the message.

I swear there'll be hell to pay!

...I will prevail until the end

The snarling voice filled the car, shrieking from the dashboard radio. She dropped her phone into the footwell in shock and nearly swerved into the adjoining lane, a Jeep blasting a furious rebuke.

"Sorry, fuckit!" she panted, scrabbling for the phone and glancing into the back seat, where her suitcases jolted against each other.

She jabbed the radio off *again* just as the car heater gave a corresponding death rattle and expired. Great, just great.

Peering at the radio dial, she steadied one hand on the wheel while the other soothed her racing heart. What the hell was *that*? She hadn't recognised the band or the lyrics but she knew heavy metal when she heard it. She hated heavy metal. All that taking your daughters to the slaughter and biting the heads off bats.

She continued to eye the radio, daring it to start up again, dashboard still displaying the logo of the easy-listening station she'd selected, a jolly pink quaver.

Whatever.

She'd bought the Honda a week ago, dipping into her meagre reserves (*their* meagre reserves now, she supposed) because no way was she living in the boonies without a set of wheels.

"Essential for going the full rustic," she'd told Hugh. "Like, I dunno, owning a wax jacket and burning hunt saboteurs in a giant wicker man."

And they'd snickered because they knew nothing about living in the country.

She'd soon discovered that the car vibrated in protest if she exceeded 60, its wipers made an odd whistling sound like her old maths teacher and the heater – apparently now an ex-heater – did a passable impression of a rattlesnake poised to strike.

Thank God for the heavy jumper beneath her coat.

Another glance at the suitcases, her life crammed into fraying nylon.

"Why no examples of your work?" Hugh had asked soon after they met.

"I chuck as I go along," she'd shrugged.

Nothing was ever worth keeping. She was only as good as her last failure. At Rook House, her accumulated output would've been so much clutter confronting her at every turn.

She wanted her new home and her marriage to be a fresh start – assuming she carried on painting at all. Maybe she'd find a local course on beekeeping or tarot reading and forget the whole artist schtick altogether.

Growing stiff at the wheel, she pulled into a service station to check that latest text.

Hugh's tone was cheery: *"This place will blow you away! Got a treat lined up as well! Nothing went bump in the wee hours last night. Bit disappointed, tbh."*

She'd resisted the temptation to delve deeper into the online history of Rook House, which Hugh had lapped up. She would let the house guide her towards its full story when it was ready, one dropped breadcrumb at a time.

But sipping black coffee, she brooded on the leap of faith she'd taken. There was an old saying she'd read somewhere: *leap and the net shall appear*. Was that Confucius or the back of a beer mat? Possibly Confucius *on* the back of a beer mat.

Usually, she countered that sort of happy-clappy with, *leap and break your neck in the fall*.

Hugh had changed her. Or she'd changed herself to complement his 'carpe diem' philosophy.

She'd been living with Hugh Driscoll for four even-keeled months when he came bounding out of the bedroom he used as an office, displaying an "exciting opportunity" on his laptop.

Owners of an old house on the edge of the Yorkshire Moors were seeking a couple to live there as property guardians for a year. "Basically, to keep the lights on and make sure the roof doesn't fall in. Here's a pic."

She'd examined a gaunt outline of ivy-clad brick on a sullen horizon. "How'd you find out about it?"

"I browse images of spooky-looking houses as possible book covers. This one had the ad attached for property guardians."

Hugh wrote supernatural fiction and proof-read leaflets for a big pharma company to pay the bills. Or he was a badly paid proof-reader who wrote supernatural fiction in his spare time (his parents' take on it).

"Looks remote," she'd said.

"That's the beauty of it. No sirens going all night or neighbours playing drum and bass. Nothing around for miles but fresh air and a few grizzled locals."

"Any photos of the inside?"

"Nah, but it's furnished. Think of it, a chance to get the hell out of Dodge. All that scenery for you to paint. And I can work anywhere with a good signal."

She'd detected his excitement from the way he pulled at the extra-long hair growing out of his left eyebrow.

"I dunno, Hugh." An office temp, she'd just bagged a three-month assignment and there was a lot to be said for the security blanket of grinding familiarity. Plus, she knew that property guardians needed basic maintenance skills. She and Hugh hit their thumbs hanging up pictures.

"Not a problem," he'd claimed when she raised this concern. "Ad says a housekeeper comes in once a week. Bet she knows a local handyman."

"Who owns the house?"

"Not sure but it looks like some conglomerate snapped it up recently, thinking to make it a conference centre or something."

"Why haven't they?"

"Maybe cos it's haunted. Allegedly."

"Ah. I'm guessing *Hound of the Baskervilles* meets *American Werewolf in London* territory?"

"This conglomerate bought the house as part of a portfolio, far as I can tell. They're getting round to doing up the place but meantime, need someone on site to keep things ticking over. Just stories on the net say it's haunted."

"By what?"

"Couple of links here." He'd passed her the laptop. "Standard stuff. What old house standing alone in the countryside doesn't have stories attached to it?"

She'd only glanced at the links, robustly disinclined to believe in ghosts – *details* – eyes drawn to the peppercorn rent.

"Includes bills? That's not a wind-up?"

"It's God's honest, Luce. Amazing value for money when you consider what I – what we – pay for this fleapit."

Hugh's basement flat had a permanent leak of mysterious origin which the landlord had no interest in finding or fixing.

"Must be *very* haunted to be that dirt-cheap," she'd reckoned, handing back the laptop.

"Yeah, well, nothing tempting comes without strings attached." Another tug of the straggly eyebrow. "I'm prepared to take my chances to live like a landed gent. Place has been rented out for years without any tenants running screaming for the hills."

The deadline for applications had been imminent. "We could even get married," he'd added out of left field. "The ad does specify a couple."

"Is marriage a requirement?"

"Nah, I was just speaking my brains. What d'you reckon to the rest of it – the house?"

"I'll have to sleep on it."

Not just the house proposal, but the other one; the sort-of-marriage proposal, which had secretly floored her. She'd gone to bed brooding on it all.

They didn't even share a bank account. She paid half the rent money into his account every month *and* bought most of the groceries, her income exceeding his. They'd never discussed long-term commitment. Never discussed anything 'deep', really.

They liked it that way. After a rush of mutual bean-spilling on their first date, they'd settled into the comfy groove of each other with astonishing ease. They were a good fit, but neither of them cared much for future-proofing their relationship. Why rock the boat? Jeopardise a good thing? (Other clichés were available). She'd known from the off that he was impulsive. It was part of his attraction. Look at the way he'd asked her to move in with him, within three months of meeting: "If your lease is up for renewal, now's a good time to jump ship, don't you reckon? Two can live as cheaply as one, after all." (Other clichés were available).

But now he'd really gone for it: wanting to rent a gothic house and suggesting (rather than formally proposing) marriage. A two-for-the-price-of-one offer. Get it while it's going!

She was still brooding the following morning when she arrived at work to find her purse missing from her coat pocket.

She'd phoned Hugh, holding back angry tears. "I was jostled getting off the Tube, but that's par for the course, so thought nothing of it. I rang the police just now to get a crime number, but they gave off a 'shit happens' vibe. I've been such a mug, Hugh."

"But Luce, are you all right? Did they get your bank cards?"

"No, they're in the side pocket of my bag and I always wear that cross-body. Plus, my Oyster card is contactless and-"

"So your purse was just loose change and bits of fluff? Thank God."

"I lost a photo of Mum at 18. Irreplaceable."

"Jeez, sorry."

"I've had it with London, Hugh. This place is toxic. The air, the people..."

"There is an alternative. For us, I mean. Losing your purse, shitty as it is, could be a sign."

"I didn't *lose* it, I shoved it in my pocket last minute when I should've... wait, you're talking about that property guardian gig?"

"I filled in the online application just after you left this morning, Luce. Figured we'd be in it to win it and don't have to go through with it if we change our minds."

She'd lapsed into shocked silence. "I haven't changed my mind, Hugh, because I don't remember giving the green light."

"I know, sorry, poor choice of words. Why *don't* we get married, though? I want to take care of you."

"What? You're jumping from one thing to another like a hyperactive flea. And I've been taking care of myself since I was 15!"

"OK, OK, sorry. Again. You're right, I'm all over the shop recently. You know how I like to run with an idea, the bigger the better. Which brings me back to the guardianship. We're pedalling fast to stay still here. If we can't grab opportunities now, when can we?"

He'd had a point. Or two. She'd boarded the Tube that evening nervy as a cat, glaring at every space invader. Once you lost your mojo in a big city, game over.

She'd said nothing more about his haste to submit the application. Probably wouldn't lead to anything. She doubted they'd make a convincing case for keeping a large, draughty house ticking over.

While waiting to hear back, they'd travelled to Surrey to spend a weekend with Hugh's parents.

It was only the second time Lucy had met them, the first an awkward couple of days over Christmas.

Tom and Frances Driscoll took pains to withhold their disapproval of her while signalling it via theatrical levels of discretion and civility. They were so stilted and well-bred – even their golden retriever had haughty, impeccable manners – she'd come away yet again rolling an inward eye.

And yet.

That house with the sweeping lawn. Those muddy boots lined up in the porch next to the fox-shaped foot scraper, the scent of baked apples wafting through open-plan kitchen...

On the train back to London, she'd turned to Hugh. "Ask me again."

"Ask you what?"

"You know what."

He did, so he did.

When she'd said "yes", the whole carriage cheered.

Then London's grimy skyline had flickered into view and she'd said, more quietly: "You can ask me again about the Yorkshire option if you like. In for a penny. If we get it, I mean."

Because he was right. Only a fool rejected plausible alternatives to a life of grinding familiarity in a leaky flat.

Much to her (slightly uneasy) surprise, they'd duly been appointed property guardians of Rook House.

Hugh's interview had consisted of chatting on a video call to the letting agent, Emma. She hadn't even asked to meet Lucy.

As long as they got their skates on, the owners of Rook House had been prepared to wait until after the wedding for the guardianship to commence.

So here was Lucy on a chill February day, the service station dwindling in her rear-view, chugging at a steady 55 towards her new husband in an old house, the cold settling into her bones as the far north crept closer.

Mrs Lucy Driscoll. Lucy Emilia Driscoll. Variations to doodle inside inked hearts on the cover of an exercise book. Her attachment to patriarchal name-taking bothered her slightly. But not enough to regret it.

Hugh had shivered beside her on the steps of Hackney town hall in Tom's old wedding suit, a midnight-blue crushed velvet, urging his dad to hurry up with photos.

She'd hired her outfit, a trouser suit in burnt-orange silk. Her stepmother Elena had said she resembled a slice of cinnamon toast.

"Why'd you invite that cow?" Hugh had asked, perplexed.

"I didn't. She found out somehow. Her spies are probably everywhere."

In fact, she *had* invited Elena, partly to see if she'd come and partly to check whether she was still contactable at her last-known phone number.

Elena had dodged the ceremony but swept into the pub reception in a white fur coat, tutting at thinly spread food and guests, her presence a painful reminder of the unavoidably absent.

She'd dragged Lucy into the freezing beer garden to deliver her verdict on the hastily arranged nuptials, blowing smoke through her nostrils like an alpine dragon. "The pâté is off. And what you do with your *hair*, Lucy? So young, yet want to look like a duenna!"

"I don't know what a duenna is. I'll alert the food police about the pâté."

Elena had been aghast at the Yorkshire plan. "You change your whole life for a man, Lucy?"

"You're the expert on men, granted," Lucy had retorted. "Incidentally, who's your current mark? Shame I didn't specify a plus one. Could've checked his neck for fang marks."

"Same old Lucy. Tell me why you marry now, leave London now?"

In a rash moment fuelled by too many bubbles, Lucy had admitted: "Because I want a shot at living in the moment, like Hugh. It'll be good for me."

"Maybe better for *him*?" Elena had jerked her artfully streaked head towards the bar, where Hugh was laughing with his mates from university. "*He* can live in moment because he has those two to fall back on."

Another dip of the head towards the pub interior, where Tom and Frances sat glumly behind an ice bucket. Her words had struck a nerve in Lucy. "God forbid I ever fall back on *you*, Elena. I'd skewer myself on your trident."

"My what?"

"Look it up in an English dictionary. May as well open one some time."

Last word secured, she'd stomped off to reclaim her husband. Ordinarily she'd have felt small and mean, mocking a foreigner's command of English. But this was Elena, destroyer of worlds. Probably literally, given the amount of hairspray she used.

Sod her, Lucy had thought, watching Elena pluck a sugar rose off the despised cake, balance it on a purple acrylic and wolf it down.

Wolf was right. Elena was a snow wolf on the prowl, following tracks, sniffing out blood. Lucy never had to see her again.

Following her own tracks on the frost-bright motorway, she touched the gold locket at her neck and risked accelerating to 65.

2

She reached Rook House at dusk. Despite her lack of a sat-nav, it had been easy to find, wrought-iron gates yawning open on rusting hinges, red ivy turning the supporting pillars into columns of fire. The gates were set into a crumbling perimeter wall.

She idled before a cattle grid, massaging aching shoulders.

On impulse, she got out of the car, deferring the moment of no return. She was nervous. She and Rook House were about to meet each other.

Fading green twilight wove itself through purple shadows, her nose prickling at the acrid whiff of something – yellow arch-angel? – ears attuned to the distant calls of thinly bleating sheep rising to pewter skies.

No sign of any rooks.

The last few miles on bumpy moorland roads had excited her. She'd never been to rural Yorkshire.

At first glance, its winter landscape appeared barren and featureless, beyond the occasional clump of Swaledales leaning into dry stone walls. But to the artist's eye, the subtle variations in colour teemed with possibility.

She peered up at a dark dot suspended in the twilight from invisible wire. A kestrel? One of the most solitary birds.

She got back in the car and eased through the gates, noting leaf-stripped trees either side of the driveway, spindle-armed sentinels in threadbare livery.

She sensed the house waiting for her before she cleared the trees and let it flood into view, a bulky redbrick with sash windows and a baleful expression. It was far more imperious than its online photo and she was mildly dismayed to note it had chimneys, two that she could see. Chimneys would need sweeping. And that was a point. Did the place have central heating?

She parked before the solid-looking front door.

The house leant down to inspect her. Here, a sleeping rose bush rattled against a window pane; there, trailing ivy scratched ragged fingernails on blistered wood.

Her flesh puckered with goosebumps. "*Will I do?*" she asked.

The dashboard lit up suddenly and poured out another tangle of red-hot noise. She scrambled from the car in shock, desperate to escape those screaming guitar riffs.

The front door opened and Hugh hurried out to join her, wincing at the racket inside the car.

"Never had you pegged for a Judas Priest fan, Luce."

"Is that who it is?" She leant back in to jab the radio off again. "Bloody thing keeps going on and off with a mind and a playlist of its own."

Hugh skimmed her cheek and dragged her luggage from the back seat. His lips were stiff and he wore *two* jumpers, she noted with alarm. She felt slippery with cold from the inside out and craved a hot bath and a cup of tea.

"I was thinking of taking it with us when we leave," he nodded at the lion's head door knocker. He led her into a checkerboard hallway, their footsteps echoing under a high ceiling.

Peeling off her gloves, she inhaled 'old house' smells of coffee grounds, dark wood and the musk of long-gone bodies. She shivered.

"Yeah, still trying to work out the kitchen range to heat the place up," Hugh said, setting down her cases. "There's a manual but might as well be in Serbo-Croat. Mrs Bird the housekeeper is coming tomorrow to show us the ropes. She was here the day I collected the keys, but said I'd probably forget if she ran through the basics then. I did try starting a fire in the living room with old newspaper, not my best effort, but at least there's a working kettle..." He walked as he talked, Lucy following him into a huge living room.

Its walls were painted dusky pink, peeling in places. The only items of furniture were two button-backed sofas in oxblood leather. A pair of ruched dark-crimson curtains hung across the sash window. Below it, a radiator gleamed like a celebrity's veneered smile. Thank God for that.

She stared at the painting over the long stone mantelpiece.

Hugh crouched before the fireplace, blowing on embers twinkling feebly from a pyre of newspapers. "Found the old papers in a shed. There were logs too, but soaking wet from an overhead leak."

As he spoke, the embers guttered and curled into black smoke.

Lucy's eyes began to smart. To avoid the portrait over the mantelpiece, she examined Hugh hunched over like that, jeans slipping at the back to reveal the stippled tail of his spine. He was long and lean, just like the years before she met him. She longed to touch him, to coil her cold, slippery self around his vulnerable, welcoming skin.

"Belching like an unappeased volcanic god," she nodded at the smoking embers. "Doubt we'll bother with that old thing anyway if we have rads."

Hugh stood up and turned, frowning. "Wish you wouldn't."

"Wouldn't what?"

"Come over all poetic to expose my linguistic shortcomings."

"I was making an observation. Jee-sus." She turned on her heel and reclaimed the hallway, Hugh scurrying after her.

"Sorry. I'm knackered. Bet you are too. We'll eat. You did get the takeaway?"

"What takeaway?"

"It was in my last text! I asked you to stop at the Lowmorten chippy, seeing as we lack the wherewithal to cook at the mo. Lowmorten – nearest outpost of civilisation? Sent you directions."

She drew her phone from her pocket. "It's just come through now. Must be the signal."

"Signal should be fine. I've already set up my laptop and sent a successful test email to work."

"Well, I'm sorry, but I didn't get the text. Where's this kettle? I'm parched. We do have milk, at least?"

"Yeah, and a working fridge. Kitchen's this way."

It was another cavernous space, this one lined with a mishmash of pine cabinets. A squat rectangle sat in one corner, flaunting its complexity. The hinged doors must once have been bright indigo, but were now stained midnight blue by ancient burn marks. "That's a Rayburn," she said.

Hugh flicked the switch on an ancient-looking kettle. "The range thing I was telling you about. Heats the water and the radiators. Looks terrifying."

"Not as terrifying as that portrait over the mantelpiece back there. Mutton-chop whiskers, handlebar 'tache, staring blue eyes. Sure Jack the Ripper didn't live here?"

"That's Ezra Napier, Edwardian gent and most famous – or infamous – owner of Rook House. Got his mug immortalised in oils to mark his 50th. Lived here until his death. Some say he liked the place so much, he never left."

Lucy recalled the basics of her online browsing. "So he's not the bloke who returned from the First World War shell-shocked and jumped to his death from a bedroom window?"

"No, that was Phineas, Ezra's son. He's ghost number one. Ezra's wife went mad years earlier and folk living here have reputedly heard her screaming as she's dragged off to the asylum. She's ghost number two."

"And Ezra himself makes three?"

"According to popular theory."

Lucy brooded on the living room portrait. It depicted a vigorous, middle-aged man unbowed by family tragedy. "I assume it was painted *before* his wife went mad and he lost his son?"

"Not sure. Comes with the house. I was warned not to touch it. Must be valuable, though not *too* valuable or it'd be in storage."

"Surely we can turn his face to the wall? I can't sit in there under his death-ray stare."

"I'm sure no one would object." Hugh busied himself with cups. "'Fraid there's no chance of hot water until Mrs Bird inducts us into the mysteries of the Rayburn, so I'd get as many hot liquids down you as you can. Plenty of crockery, cutlery, pots and pans. Plus a clunky old washing machine. I'll show you our bedroom while the kettle's boiling."

She was startled to find the hallway now sunk in total darkness. Hugh fumbled for the light switch. "Amazing staircase, right?" He touched a carved wooden pineapple atop a newel post.

"Have we got a four-poster?" Lucy asked.

"I wish! Fantastic room, though."

She followed him up creaking, uncarpeted stairs. Outside, a wind rose, trembling the door knocker.

"Ignore it," Hugh shrugged. "Woke up last night thinking someone was knocking until I realised it was just the wind. You hear it all the time. It might explain reports of mad Belle – that's Ezra's wife – shrieking all over the gaff when it really gets going."

"Lovely."

He switched on the landing light. It stuttered in a weak bulb. Lucy pictured trapped house ghosts tapping out Morse code, begging for release. Luckily, she didn't read Morse code.

"Here we are." Hugh opened a door by its blue china door-knob and switched on another weak light. "I made up the bed with our own linen and the mattress is clean and dry."

She stepped inside, assailed by a draught. Checking the window, she pushed aside another pair of dark-crimson curtains, but the sash was firmly shut.

"More moorland air," said Hugh. "No way of keeping it out. Mrs B had the room aired as well, which was probably overkill."

"Are those elms lining the driveway?"

"Yep. Good tree spotting."

Imagining the wind on a sly circuit of the house, picking locks and sliding incognito through hairline cracks, she brushed a hand over the nearest wall, patterned with Strawberry Thief wallpaper. The paper must once have been thick and velvety, a bright crimson fruit clutched in the bird's now faded beak.

For a second, she glimpsed a ghostly palm alongside her own, smoothing down the wallpaper seams, thin white fingers stroking the nap. "*So pretty, Lucia. In an old house like this, we might find jackdaws nesting in the chimneys. They lay such beautiful eggs.*"

Her mother's voice. A submerged memory of another time and place.

"Most of the rooms have bird-themed wallpaper," Hugh said. "Been here since the 1980s, according to the letting agent. It'll all be easier to explore tomorrow in daylight."

The room's remaining features were two bedside cabinets, a chest of drawers, a dressing table with carved fruit legs and a double-width wardrobe, all in the same dark, knotty pine as the kitchen cupboards.

A faint outline in the wallpaper suggested a hidden fireplace. "Only one bedroom has an open fireplace," said Hugh, following her gaze. "But that room has no curtains or furniture. I think this must've been the master in recent years. I'll bring the cases up. We'll have tea first, then you can unpack. I've left you space in the wardrobe and chest of drawers. Tomorrow we'll go out for supplies after Mrs Bird's visit."

He was also keen to show her the attic – perfect as an art studio. That was the 'treat' he'd mentioned in his text.

Lucy was curious but wanted her first viewing to be in daylight.

So they drank tea, unpacked, brushed their teeth in the echoey, freezing bathroom (no en suites) and went to bed from mutual exhaustion with socked feet intertwined, the house rocking beneath them in the darkness, a wind-blown galleon on the high seas of rolling land.

Lucy listened to Hugh's soft snores and touched her locket. She had a wedding photo of her parents on one side and planned to add a photo of her own wedding on the other.

The room's darkness was absolute, though every now and then the closed curtains puffed gently like black sails on a becalmed sea.

She'd exhumed that memory of her mother telling her about jackdaw eggs. When Lucy was four, her father had rented a holiday cottage by the sea in Norfolk, its walls the soft blue of a jackdaw's egg, the cottage itself seeming to follow the light as it moved throughout the day.

Outside, bleached wooden decking had led down to the beach. Her father would race Lucy to the shoreline while her mother set up her easel on the decking. Their last holiday as a family.

She sank into the memory, eyelids heavy. She'd almost drifted off when a piercing shriek broke the silence of the night.

She gasped, sitting bolt upright, and poked Hugh in his shoulder. "Christ alive, Hugh, what the hell was *that*?"

Hugh sat up groggily, knuckling his eye sockets. "Can't hear anything."

A sound split the air again, its tone shrill and mocking. "Oh, that," he shrugged. "Landline downstairs." Yawning, he slid his feet on to bare floorboards.

Lucy was clutching her locket. "That's not what I heard! It was a scream."

"You've probably still got Judas Priest on the brain. I'd better go answer it."

"Who'd be ringing us at this hour?"

He plucked his phone off the bedside cabinet. "Only just gone nine. Feels later."

"I'll go down with you." She didn't want to be alone up here.

"If you like."

He led the way, throwing light switches as he went. The ring tone now sounded hysterical.

The phone, Lucy saw, was an old-fashioned dark-green thing, possibly Bakelite, crouched on a table under the stairs. She hadn't noticed it before.

She sat on the bottom stair as Hugh answered the call, her anxiety only subsiding when the shrieking ring tone fell silent. "Hello? Oh, Mum, hi. Yeah, she's here. Got here a couple of hours ago. What? OK, I'll ask her." He held out the receiver to Lucy. "Mum wants a word." He dropped his voice. "Haven't told her we're in bed. She'll only feel guilty for waking us."

"Understood." Lucy took the phone and Hugh vanished into the living room, its darkness swallowing him whole. Seconds later, a light came on beneath the shut door.

Lucy stood at the phone table with her back to the living room and its horrible portrait. *Had* she heard a scream? Her bare arms goose-pimpled under her T-shirt and the cold bled through the checkerboard tiles into her socked feet. "Hello, Mrs Driscoll."

"Now Lucy, we're both Mrs Driscoll, so it would avoid confusion to call me Frances. How was the journey?"

"Fine, thank you."

"I'm so glad you've arrived. I've seen pictures of the house and didn't like to think of Hugh there all alone. We look forward to visiting, once you've settled in."

"We'd like that, too."

"And spend your wedding present from us wisely," added Frances in a tone of mock sternness. "That's what it's for!"

"Er... we will," promised Lucy, mystified. She and Hugh had paid for the modest wedding out of their own pockets without expecting gifts. They'd discussed this at length. Lucy didn't want to feel beholden to Tom and Frances. Hugh had said he got that.

"It was very generous of you both," she said, intending to tackle Hugh.

"Oh, not at all. We thought it only fair, since you're not having a honeymoon." Frances dropped an octave. "Hugh has a degree in classics, as you know. We had high hopes. Such high hopes."

Lucy considered her response. Hugh had found an agent for his first novel and secured a two-book deal. *Among the Tall Reeds* had sold modestly while earning positive reviews. The second book was under way. "Hugh's doing what makes him happy," she murmured eventually.

"For now." Frances gave a dry laugh. "You should see all his short-lived projects cluttering up the loft. 'That boy's not a sticker', my father used to say, and I'd always defend him."

"To be fair, his writing's not a hobby or a short-lived project, Mrs Dr... Frances."

Silence on the other end. Lucy shifted feet, anxious she'd gone too far but annoyed on Hugh's behalf.

"I'm very glad to hear you speak up for him like that," said Frances at last. "A man needs a supportive wife, not just one he has to support."

"No, I didn't mean-"

"Well! I shan't keep you, dear. I'm sure you're fit to drop. No need to get Hugh back on the phone. I'll bid you goodnight."

Lucy said goodnight and hung up, puzzled and frustrated on more than one front.

She could easily deflect her mother-in-law's passive-aggressive barbs, but what was this wedding present she knew nothing about and why hadn't Hugh said anything? Had to be money.

Frances had also departed from type: goodbye poker-up-the-jacksie formality, hello whispery indiscretion. Was it a blatant attempt to sow discord while she and Hugh were still shaking confetti out of their creases? She could almost hear Elena asking: "How well you really know this man or his family, Lucy? You think a tornado marriage is romantic, hmm? More a fool rushing in."

Sod off, Elena! And it's 'whirlwind', fyi.

She opened the living room door.

"Look!" Hugh pointed above the mantelpiece.

She looked. He'd turned the portrait of Ezra Napier to face the wall.

"You're welcome," he said with a sweeping bow.

"What did Frances mean just now about spending their gift to us wisely?"

"Oh, that. She and Dad bunged us a few quid a couple of weeks ago to see us on our way. No biggie." He saw her face. "Soz – wasn't thinking. Of course it should be in a joint account for us both to access. I'll set that up. I've already set up a direct debit for the rent."

"How much is a few quid?"

"Just ten grand."

"Just?"

"To launch us into married life, as Mum put it. Luce." He laid his hands on her shoulders, steering her out of the room. "That money takes the heat off, means you can paint away to your heart's content knowing there's enough in the kitty for essentials. That's the last ace I had up my sleeve, far as top intel goes. No more skeletons in my cupboard."

She shuddered. "Not an expression I want to hear in this place. And why is your mother calling on a landline when she's got your mobile number? I didn't even know the house came with a landline."

"Nor me. Found it when I arrived, number written on the dial, so rang home to see if it worked properly. Told them to stick to modern tech from now on, but guess Mum forgot. I'll remind her tomorrow. Let's go back to bed before we both freeze."

Once again, he fell asleep first, leaving her straining her eyes in the darkness at a water-stained ceiling rose.

Had she heard a scream? It was easy to doubt herself when she felt this exhausted.

Her thoughts shifted into another groove.

Should she ask Hugh why he'd let her spend £800 on a rattly second-hand car when he had ten grand in the bank, courtesy of his parents? Tricky to broach without sounding accusatory.

Then again...

Lucy is too diffident, one school report had said.

Elena would have agreed.

Before Hugh, her only long-term boyfriend had been Luke, a trainee solicitor she'd met on one of her temp assignments.

Poor Luke, she'd thought initially. Poor closed-off, vulnerable Luke, scarred by boarding school and unable to share anything (even a chocolate mousse he couldn't finish) or tolerate non-perpendicular cutlery. She would gently mess him up, pare down his sharp edges, artless ying to his anally retentive yang. Yeah, right.

And now, Hugh. He shared similarities with Luke – a defensive wall built up at boarding school, fastidious hygiene (his own nail brush!) and a boyish vulnerability.

Opening a new review on his laptop, he'd get so nervous that he'd abandon his straggly eyebrow and pull the cuffs of his favourite old unravelling jumper over his knuckles, as though defending himself pre-emptively from attack.

She had a protective instinct towards these boy-men that irritated her and would have horrified Elena.

She finally dozed off. When she woke again, she could hear birdsong.

She looked at her phone. 8am.

If she got up now, she'd catch sunrise in the attic.

Sliding out of bed, she tiptoed out of the room without waking Hugh, grabbing her dressing gown en route.

But as she crept along the landing, she heard a sound downstairs, a slight thump.

Her own heart thumped in response.

Her first instinct was to go back to bed, shut the bedroom door and curl up against Hugh's catlike warmth.

Her second was to creep downstairs and find the source of the sound.

It was daylight, after all. And this was her home for the foreseeable. The house would do well to remember that.

The stairs groaned under even the lightest pressure. She paused a couple of times on her descent but there was no sign of Hugh stirring in response to the creaking treads.

Just as well: the timbers moving or air in the pipes, he'd say; a bird in the chimney. Things that were possible.

The door to the living room stood ajar. Had they shut it last thing? She tried to remember. Hugh had come up the stairs behind her, so he'd have been closest to the door.

She sucked her lower lip and approached the door, pushed it open and stood on the threshold.

At first she couldn't see anything amiss.

Then she gave a small cry, hand fluttering to her locket.

Ezra Napier was staring out at her from his portrait over the mantelpiece.

3

Lucy Calland met Hugh Driscoll in the National Gallery on one of her regular Saturday visits to her favourite painting, *Portrait of a Lady with a Squirrel and a Starling*.

One minute she was savouring the painting as usual, the next a bloke had appeared alongside. "Catchy title," he observed. "Say what you see. What's her deal, then?"

"Deal?" she echoed without taking her eyes off the portrait.

It depicted Anne Lovell, a Tudor noblewoman. A red squirrel sat on her lap, nibbling a hazelnut, while a glossy black starling perched on a vine just behind her shoulder. Lucy had always felt that Anne Lovell's expression of pained dignity hid some unexpressed grievance, possibly man-related.

"She's clearly pissed off about something," said the stranger. "Never work with children or animals, they say. Not exactly the *Mona Lisa*, is she? That glint in her eye would make me think twice about spilling her pint."

Lucy tactfully avoided the *Mona Lisa* comparison. So many blokes couldn't see a portrait of a woman without comparing it to the "original sacred cow", to quote her old art teacher.

"Well, the starling and squirrel are heraldic symbols on the family crest of Anne Lovell, the woman in the painting. The artist would've picked the pose and the symbolic wildlife, probably after discussion with her husband. Women didn't get a lot of say. In a way, they were props themselves."

"Gotcha," the bloke nodded. "And what's the deal with *you* and this painting?" he asked, turning to face her.

She was forced to acknowledge his gaze by returning it. He had wine-dark eyes, floppy chestnut hair, a slightly weak chin and prominent eyebrows. Almost handsome, in other words.

"I love the background as much as the foreground," she replied. "See those strong, stylised colours, dark-green leaves twisting through blue, the outline of the starling echoed in the black contours of her clothing? And the contrast of all that with her milk-white shawl."

"You a painter yourself? I can hear the passion in your voice."

"I love this painting, but I've always preferred to work on landscapes or still life. Abstract as you like."

"Do you exhibit?"

"Nah. Did a foundation year but still marshalling funds for a degree. I'm a full-time temp at the mo, so art has had to take a back seat."

She didn't tell him that the correct term was 'artist', not painter. She didn't tell him that she hadn't picked up a paintbrush in nearly two years and felt sick with longing and terror whenever she thought of doing so again.

"Come here often?" he asked next.

"Funnily enough, yeah. You?"

"Nope. First-time caller. Thought it might inspire me to look at creepy old paintings with skulls and ravens. Very Edgar Allan Poe. I write supernatural stuff. Do you read?"

"Yeah. Not horror, though. I like a good night's sleep."

"I'll show you my book online if you like." He took out his phone. "And can I come up and see your etchings some time?"

She turned from the painting. "You're very direct."

"Yeah." As he held out his phone, his knuckles brushed her arm, accidentally or otherwise, sending an electric charge through her funny bone. "You have to be pushy when you're a starving writer," he shrugged. "Shrinking violets need not apply."

She leant over his phone. "*Among the Tall Reeds*," she read aloud. "I'll look that up when I get the chance." No point in telling him that reeds were, by definition, tall.

"No pressure. Talking of starving, fancy some chips? When you've finished here, I mean."

They adjourned to a café. She ate her own chips and most of his. He squirted ketchup on the few he'd ring-fenced but she snaffled those too, dipping them defiantly in scarlet sauce.

They had a lot in common, it turned out. They were both only children and hard-pressed creatives with boring day jobs. At least he had a published book under his belt. "And you can work from home," she pointed out. "It's schlepping about all over the place for temping gigs that makes me too knackered to paint, even when I carve out the time."

"That's sad." He nodded down at his plate. "Last chip standing. Person with the saddest back story wins it. Think *X Factor* sobfest – dying nan, dog with stage-three cancer – you know the drill."

"So young, yet so cynical."

"OK, I'll start. I'm adopted. My biological ma's an ex-junkie. She was withdrawing from heroin when she had me, couldn't cope. I was put up for adoption at 18 months."

"That's rough. And since then?"

"We met again when I was 18. Nothing in common and not much to say on either side. We agreed to leave it as a one-off. My folks are salt-of-the-earth types. Sort their recycling into proper bins and voted Remain." He hovered over the lone chip. "Your go."

Deep breath. "My mother died when I was five. Run over on a zebra crossing by a drink-driver. My father remarried when I was ten to a woman half his age. He died of a heart attack when I was 15. Nothing left in the kitty because stepma has spent it all. I cut ties when I was 18, but she turns up periodically on the off-chance I'm sitting on a secret trust fund."

"Jesus H! I can't compete with that. You're a one-woman Catherine Cookson novel! The chip is yours."

"Thanks." She scooped it up, wretched with embarrassment, yet giddy with cathartic release. "I don't normally spill all my beans on a first date." Sod, why had she said *that*?

"How'd your evil stepma get her mitts on your inheritance in the first place?"

"She got my dad to sign things, put assets in her name. Probably. I dunno. I was at boarding school in Wiltshire, out of the picture till it was too late."

Luckily, he didn't ask the obvious: what sort of idiot was your dad?

She still burned at the memory of Elena's arrival in Wiltshire to deliver the coup de grace in person. "He's gone, Lucy, my David is gone. There is no money for luxuries now. You understand this? You are no longer a child. You come back to London with me and I send you to local school. All will be good."

She bit down on the cold chip, expression darkening.

"Didn't mean to touch a nerve," said the stranger. "Although the brooding thing suits. You look like a sexy Victorian governess about to rap me over the knuckles for not learning my prepositions."

"Would you *like* to be rapped over the knuckles?" Daring for her, experimental flirtation.

"Maybe I would." He extended his knuckles across the table, ready to be chastised. "Hugh."

She considered giving a false name but settled for bumping fists and admitting, "Lucy."

"Hello, Lucy. What are you doing with the rest of your life?"

———◆◆◆◆◆———

She backed away from the painting staring out at her from the living room wall, pulled the door shut and hurried upstairs, glancing over her shoulder all the way.

Hugh must have turned the portrait back to face into the room before he followed her upstairs last night. Would only have taken seconds. But why? Why mess with her like that?

She looked down at her wedding ring. Shunning traditional bands of gold, they'd settled on matching circlets of a coiled serpent swallowing its own tail. Hugh's idea. "A symbol of eternity," he'd said. "As the snake devours itself, it also regenerates."

It didn't do, her father had once said, to deep-dive into your own or other people's psyches; better to ignore your Mariana Trench and the scuttling things impervious to light. *Deep dives only lead to drowning.* Was her father right?

Not if you looked at how Elena had fleeced him. He'd neglected due diligence there. Was she guilty of the same when it came to Hugh?

You think a tornado marriage so romantic, hmm?

She shivered on the landing, tightening the belt on her dressing gown. Life was ridiculous. One day you were flirting with a man over a plastic tomato, the next, moving into a haunted house with him.

She headed along the landing towards a narrow stone staircase that spiralled up, presumably to the attic. Four steps to the left, a sharp turn, six steps to the right.

She reached a door at the top and pushed it open.

A high, slanting window flung early morning light over worn floorboards. The only furniture was a green ladder-back chair with two slats missing. The room was marginally warmer than the master bedroom, the air dusted with a sweet undertow of turps-laced rot.

On the draining board of a butler sink, she found two jam jars stuffed with calcified brushes like closed tulips, their tapered edges striped with old paint. So the room had already been used as an art studio by a previous occupant.

She touched the hardened bristles, imagining possibilities. Maybe a bird theme? Sketches of jackdaws, rooks, blackbirds: avian flocks released from sun-faded wallpaper.

Up to now, she'd always worked on a small table in cramped conditions – sometimes just a card table that could be folded away and stored under a window. Now she had all this space and time, there could be no more excuses.

But had she been any good to begin with?

Deep breath, think about all she'd gained in the past seven months: a kind husband who shared her values, a sense of adventure and the chance to do what she loved with no distractions (or those ever-handy excuses). Bound to be a simple explanation for the portrait in the living room.

So. She'd buy fresh materials. She pictured gleaming metallic tubes laid out on the draining board: phthalo, titanium, umber. When she was little and intimidated by those grown-up words uttered in her mother's richly fluting accent, she'd renamed paint colours in her head as *thrilling* orange, *patient* white, *sarcastic* green, *serious* blue. When she'd confided her charming childhood habit to Luke, he'd asked if she might be "on the spectrum".

"Luce?" Hugh barged into the room, tucking his shirt into jeans. "You found it, then? Wanted to be here to see your face. It's a great space, right?"

She indicated the window. "That's not where wotsisname Napier flung himself from?"

"Nah, too high. Phineas, son of Ezra, chose one of the bedrooms. Could even be ours."

"A cheery thought."

"Mrs Bird might know more. She's downstairs."

Lucy started. "Blimey, that's early. When did she get here?"

"'Bout half an hour ago, but she's only just come into the house. Got her own key and came through the back door as I was heading downstairs. She's been out in the shed, sorting wet from dry wood. Reckons some can be salvaged. I said I'd come find you so she could show us the ropes together."

"I'll get dressed first."

"See you down there. And I know this attic's chilly without a rad. We'll buy a heater."

He ran out again, leaving her standing in the room.

Why hadn't she asked him about the portrait in the living room? Maybe now wasn't the right time.

She patrolled the room once more, closed the door behind her and descended the spiral staircase. One thing at a time, following each dropped breadcrumb. For now, the housekeeper.

4

In the kitchen, she found Hugh talking to a tall woman with wavy silver hair. The woman turned her strong-featured face to Lucy. She wore outsize white trainers and a hairy jumper tucked into the waistband of beige corduroy trousers. "Ah, Mrs Driscoll."

"It's Lucy. Lucy and Hugh, please."

"Snowy."

"What?"

"I'm Snowy Bird," the woman said patiently. "I hope you're both settling in?"

"Early days," murmured Lucy.

Hugh shot her a look she couldn't decipher.

"You're Londoners?" Snowy asked in a suspiciously neutral tone.

"Someone has to be." Lucy moved towards the kettle. "I'm guessing no one local applied to be guardians?"

"You were the best of the bunch," Snowy replied. "So I hear. You didn't bang on about the haunting thing *too* much. Not like some. Ghouls themselves."

"Speaking of-" began Hugh.

"Now, this here range will heat everything if you treat her right," Snowy cut across him. "But I don't plan to repeat myself, so gather round. She'll take logs and briquettes. I'll tell you where to buy them in town."

Lucy paid more attention to Snowy Bird than to her tutorial, especially to her bare feet, raw as collarbones, shoved into the trainers. Had to be near freezing outside. "Did you walk here, Mrs Bird?"

"Cycled. From Lowmorten. I'll come in and do for you once a week, starting this Wednesday. The Hoover's under the stairs but I'll bring cleaning supplies. If it looks like we're running low, I'll top up. Now, think you can manage the old girl?"

"The range? Absolutely," nodded Hugh. "Could we get a fire going in the living room as well, d'you reckon?"

Snowy didn't bother to hide her incredulity. "You'd choke on the smoke. Chimney hasn't been cleared out in years. Why would you take such a daft notion when the Rayburn suits all your needs?"

"Just a notion, as you say," he shrugged. "Luce fancies using the portrait of old Ezra Napier as kindling, don't you, Luce?"

"Did you turn around the painting in the living room, Mrs Bird?" Lucy asked.

"What?"

"I'll show you." Lucy left the kitchen and crossed the hallway, expecting them both to follow.

"Well?" She gestured to the portrait over the mantelpiece. "How come it's facing a different way from last night? You turned it to the wall last thing, Hugh."

"I... yes, I did," Hugh agreed, rubbing his chin. "But... have you been in here, Mrs Bird?"

"No." She was coolly untroubled by Lucy's *j'accuse*. "So leave me out of it, if you please. Now, I've places to be after this, so I'd like to get on. First, I'll put you through your paces on the Rayburn, then I'll fetch in the inventory of goods and chattels from my bike."

Lucy's heart sank when she saw the thickly stapled inventory. "I don't understand. It's not like we paid a deposit we're hoping to get back."

"It's a record of what's what," said Snowy.

"Oh, I see. In case we walk off with an antique tea strainer?"

"Luce," murmured Hugh.

"In case items get lost or broken, Mrs Driscoll, in which case you report the loss or breakage to me and I arrange a replacement. There are no antiques worth stealing, by the by."

"Checked, have you?"

"Suppose that furniture in your bedroom might fetch a few quid at a flea market. Hard to load it on to my bike, though."

When the housekeeper finally left, bidding a curt good day, Hugh rounded on Lucy. "What the hell? We can't afford to piss her off. From what the letting agent told me, she's practically local royalty. And you've just accused her of nicking the silverware."

"So *you* turned the painting back to face outwards?"

"No."

"Which would leave me. I did it, m'lud, then accused the other two other people in the house. Why would I do that?"

"I dunno. Why would you?"

Stalemate. And their first snarky exchange since they'd moved in together months ago.

Lucy tried one last time. "Bit of a coincidence, don't you think, that a strange woman was creeping about the place using her own key, before either of us were up?"

"Hardly a strange woman. Doubt she can creep anywhere in shoes the size of Cornish pasties."

"But they're trainers, not Cuban heels. It's not like we'd have heard her."

"I think you're being a tad..." He searched hesitantly for a word, "...neurotic."

Neurotic. She'd have tolerated "fanciful", at a push. "Christ. I'm going for a walk!"

"What about break-" Hugh began.

"Stuff breakfast! Bread's mouldy anyway. After my walk, I'll drive into this Lowmorten place and buy some proper food."

She ran upstairs to grab her coat and gloves, leaving by the front door. Easing open its heavy frame and stepping with relief into fresh air, she immediately felt calmer. The sky was brightening to the east, showing its underskirt in a flash of Paul Klee blue.

She headed towards the elms, stifling a twinge of penitence. She'd blown things out of proportion.

But then, so had Hugh.

Deep beneath the trees, she peered upwards for a glimpse of kestrel or rook, envying birds their high-flying freedom. The surface of the drive was muddy but at least it was dry.

Halfway down, she turned to look back at the house. It appeared... self-contained. As if it was one more natural feature rearing from the landscape, not built for people at all.

She peered at the upper windows, tensed for the sun-struck apparition of a man raising a sash and preparing to step on to the narrow ledge-

"Simmered down, have we?"

She turned with a start to see Snowy Bird regarding her from the high brown saddle of a man's bicycle. She'd added a squashy felt hat and ratty blue fleece to her ensemble.

"Mrs Bird-"

"Snowy."

"Right. Where'd you get that name anyway?"

"Off my folks."

"Got a sister called Tawny?"

The older woman smiled. It softened her stern face. "My da's name for me, on account of finding a white hair in my jet-black head when I was a nipper. By age 20, I had a whole stripe down the middle. People used to touch it for luck. My real name's Juniper."

Which struck Lucy as equally unlikely. Weren't Yorkshire folk called things like Elsie Throttlebottom? "I didn't imagine it about the portrait in the living room."

"Never said you did. That old man likes to play tricks."

"What old man?"

"You know who I mean."

Lucy did and shivered, glancing up at the bare trees. "Where are the rooks? Do they fly south for the winter?" She knew nothing about rooks.

"Long gone. Farmers shot them to keep them off crops."

"Really? Bit drastic."

"They're entitled." Snowy spun a pedal under her heel. "You two are babes, the pair of you. I'd no idea."

"Pardon?"

"You and him. Still losing a few milk teeth to tuck under the pillow. Not long married, so I hear."

"You hear a lot. And we're both nearly 30."

They'd got a special marriage licence to speed things up. All very exciting. It had felt almost clandestine: shades of a Gretna Green elopement.

"Word was, you both had the smell of fresh paint about you, is all. Before you go taking offence, a young couple is just what the old place needs, shake it up a bit. But if you're going walkabout, stay out of the wood round the back of the house. Napier's Wood."

Oh yeah, Hugh had mentioned a wood on the property. "Why would we stay out of it?"

"Apparently, some local nut with more money than sense released a pet wolf on the moors when it got too feisty. Folk reckon it's been spotted in Napier's."

"Right." Big-cat sightings were bullshit. "Doesn't that make us vulnerable wherever we walk around here?"

Snowy hesitated. "I said the animal had been spotted in the wood. Doubt it lives there. Likelier to stay on the moors, well away from people. Bigger hunting ground too."

"OK." Classic backpedalling. "Do you know which room Phineas Napier jumped from?"

"No. And while I think of it, you might give the pear orchard the swerve too. Opposite side to the wood."

"Oh? Bigfoot lurking in there, is he?"

Snowy gave a thin smile. "Phineas is buried there, alongside his stillborn twin brother. Nasty bit of barbed wire fencing there I don't want you snagging on." She settled into her saddle. "Good day, Mrs Driscoll."

"Look, I'm sorry for my high-handed manner back in the house, Mrs Bird – Snowy. I was just a bit... unnerved about the portrait in the living room."

"Understandable."

"You said the old man likes to play tricks..."

"Odd things have happened in Rook House now and then, but nothing to worry the level-headed. Just heed my advice about the wood. Enjoy your walks but watch *where* you walk. Good day." She resettled her squashed hat and cycled off towards the pillared gates.

Lucy turned in the direction of the wood. It lay just over a ridge behind the house, from this distance a rich smear of sable on a heaped brush.

Curiosity piqued by that big-cat thing (a glaringly unsubtle 'keep out' warning for some other reason, probably), she scaled the ridge with aching lungs, crested its tussocky spine and paused on the edge of dense, evergreen trees.

Napier's Wood went deep and pulsed with silence. A gap-toothed dry-stone wall boundaried one edge. Perhaps because it bore the Napier name, she was reluctant to enter.

Another quick look and she turned her back on all that close-set greenery, quashing a strong urge to run back to the house.

Instead, she made herself walk, gritting her teeth against the irrational fear that if she peeped over her shoulder, the trees would have followed her. Or maybe a silently loping wolf.

Having left Rook House without a key, she ignored the front-door knocker and took Snowy's route to the back door, now unlocked. Hugh was eating toast in the warm kitchen.

He jumped up and put his arms around her. "I'm sorry, Mouse. I never meant to imply you mucked around with the portrait. *Must've* been Mrs Bird. Maybe an initiation test or joke. No point asking her, though."

"You're probably right. But what about that scream I heard last night?"

He frowned. "You sure it *wasn't* the phone? We were both asleep..."

"Tell me more about the history of the house. Did you know that some Napiers are buried in our pear orchard, wherever that is? Snowy just told me."

"Yeah, I knew. But you said you didn't want all the details."

She sucked in her breath. "I've changed my mind. Give me edited highlights."

5

"OK then." He sat down and gestured her into the opposite chair, pushing his plate with its last slice of uneaten toast towards her. "Well, Ezra's first wife, Belle, was the mother of twin boys, Phineas and his stillborn brother. Belle was always 'delicate' in coded parlance, which seems to have meant mentally fragile. Supposedly went off her rocker after the traumatic delivery of twins, with only one surviving. Never a patient bloke, Ezra had her put away."

"Big red flags there," sniffed Lucy, peeling off her gloves. "Starting with *went off her rocker*. She must have been grieving. Sounds like a classic case of postnatal depression or even postpartum psychosis recast as female hysteria."

"Agreed. But we're talking about a time when husbands could easily commit problematic wives. I've looked at committal records. Did you know that women could be locked away for taking long walks or reading too many novels? Anyway, Ezra decided to whisk Belle out of the picture. Showed no interest in remarrying until Phineas killed himself. By then, Ezra was middle-aged, with a pretty unsavoury rep among locals. Ended up marrying Nanette Carterton, a 30-year-old 'spinster' and daughter of a local horse breeder. They seem to have made a deal that she'd provide an heir, then be allowed to live apart. Ultimate marriage of convenience."

"What was this unsavoury reputation?"

"The usual. Ezra had form for knocking up the servant girls. It's reckoned half the county could be descended from him."

"Jesus."

"Nanette had a daughter, Marianne. Clearly, Ezra had wanted a son, but Nanette reckoned she'd fulfilled her part of the bargain and took off."

Lucy rolled her eyes. "There's irony for you. Ezra probably had strapping sons all over the place, discounted for being born on the wrong side of the blanket."

Hugh nodded. "Anyhoo, Marianne never saw eye to eye with her father and moved out of Rook House when she was 21, going to live with her mother in Lowmorten. She never married, inherited the house and land when Ezra died, and died herself in 1992 without ever coming back to live here. So ended the Napier line."

"Who got this place after she died?"

"Distant relatives. They never took up residence, either. Ezra lived here into a ripe old age and the house has been tenanted since his death. Now his remaining descendants have called time. Which brings you up to speed, Mouse." He reached for her hand. "Come on, I'll give you the official daylight tour. I'm not due to start work for a bit."

They explored the rest of downstairs first – a vast, empty dining room and a small study next to the living room, where Hugh had set up his laptop. (Lucy's was upstairs on the bedroom dressing table).

The study contained a desk and a listing swivel chair with a broken arm. It faced a window overlooking the driveway.

At first they inspected their domain in mutually reverent silence, awed to have all this space to themselves. Lucy remarked on the sole bathroom in a house this size.

"Configuration's changed a lot down the years," Hugh mused. "Originally, would've been servants' quarters next to the attic room, plus a back staircase, probably carpeted, so the family didn't have to hear or meet servants coming and going with chamber pots or hot water. As the years passed and the servants mostly left, the attic was extended into what would have been the servants' tiny bedrooms. Ezra was here at the end with just one or two faithful retainers. Kitchen would've been downstairs, a drawing and billiards room off what's now the living room. There's no lower level now, where the old kitchen used to be."

"How'd you know so much about the layout?"

"That's online too."

Next, they explored the remaining six bedrooms, all uncurtained and empty of furniture. As Hugh had said last night, most were papered with a bird motif. All were William Morris designs, Lucy recognised belatedly, a palette of once-deep greens and velvety reds chosen to match blue china doorknobs. "I thought the owners said the place was furnished," she frowned. "A lot of empty rooms here. False advertising, if you ask me."

"For the past couple of years, the tenants here have been couples on their own, so I'm guessing the owners removed anything deemed excess to requirements."

"Why no families?"

"No idea. Probably cos we're miles from any schools."

The smallest bedroom had an open fireplace and bird-free wallpaper – also William Morris – featuring old-gold and pale-green leaves in snake-like coils. "Acanthus leaves," Lucy identified.

Glancing at the faded paper, she had the strange sensation, just for a second, that the curling leaves were flowing and reforming into Rorschach ink blots, as if the pattern – maybe even the wall itself – was writhing with dark, silent life. Just like the woodland she'd peeped into.

She blinked and turned away. Staring at swirling patterns too long could induce a migraine. She'd never told Hugh about those.

He was inspecting the fireplace, its indigo tiles (the same original colour as the Rayburn) dark with old soot stains. A gust of wind whistled down the chimney, sounding like pursed lips blowing on the rim of an empty bottle. She took a step back.

Hugh ran his finger along the fireplace tiles. "Years since anyone lit a fire in here, I reckon. These stains look like brown soot. Happens when rain gets into the chimney and mixes with brick dust in the flue. You're supposed to put wire over the top of the flue to stop birds or mice getting in. And other things," he added half to himself.

"What other things?"

"Witches, it used to be." He adopted a hammy facsimile of a Yorkshire accent. "Stop 'em flying right down yer chimney, see? Same with windows you'd install at an angle so a witch would crash when she tried to fly through one."

"Is that all?" Witches were old (pointy) hat, the stuff of garish Halloween masks and nylon wigs.

"Don't let Mrs Bird hear you making fun of her accent or local tall tales," Lucy sniffed. "How do you know so much about chimneys?"

"We've got one at home that Dad's made me sweep a few times..." He stopped, seeing her mouth twitch. "What?"

"Never had Tom down as an exploiter of child labour. Did you have to warble a Dick Van Dyke number while twirling your bristles?"

"Behave." Their eyes met. They had the same thought about their welcoming bed down the landing – until he looked at his watch and sighed.

"Work calls, I'm afraid. Hope to finish by two, then have a few hours to write. Why don't you drive into Lowmorten, get those supplies and report back? I've a list somewhere that I started yesterday."

"All right." She'd be glad to get out of this room. And explore further afield.

Twenty minutes later, she drove out of the gates, watching their crimson pillars recede in her wing mirror. She kept an eye on the car radio but it remained obediently in the off position. Her phone lay beside her, showing her progress as a blue dot advancing down the winding moorland road towards Lowmorten.

Hadn't Snowy 'Juniper' Bird said she lived there? Lucy still couldn't get over that name. It was like Elena being called Mrs Fezziwig or-

A red sports car shot round the corner and nearly hit the Honda head on, forcing Lucy to swerve sharply and pitch into the verge, the red car vanishing in a cloud of exhaust fumes.

Lucy hit the brake and gasped for breath, smacking the steering wheel in shock and anger. What the *hell!*

Waiting for her ragged heartbeat to steady, she regretted her failure to clock the road hog's redge and report it.

Her phone was still on the passenger seat and undamaged, thank God – probably couldn't survive another nosedive into the footwell.

She put the car into reverse, braced for wheels to spin uselessly in soft mud. She didn't have breakdown insurance. Too expensive.

To her relief, the Honda shot backwards on to the road and her grip relaxed on the wheel.

A growl made her glance up. The red sports car had reappeared, stopping in front of her.

A woman jumped out, wearing a cream wool coat and a bright pink scarf to match her lipstick.

She high-stepped over to Lucy in black Louboutins and rapped on the car window, which Lucy wound down with difficulty. "You OK?" asked the woman, eyes a luminous hazel under electric blue eyeshadow. "Nearly clipped you there. Came back to check you're OK. Need to watch where you're going on these twisty roads."

"*I* need to watch where I'm going?" Lucy opened her sticky door and clambered out to stand toe to toe with the woman. "You nearly ran me off the road!"

"Bit dramatic," sniffed the woman, who was about her own age. "Hang on, you one of the newbies renting Spooky Towers?"

"If you mean Rook House, the answer is yes. Not that it's any of yours. And I reckon we've more to fear from local hot-rodders than ghosties and ghoulies."

"What's it like living there?"

Lucy was still angry. "We've been there, like, five minutes."

"Yeah, but you'd have got a feel for the place straightaway, wouldn't you?"

"News travels fast around here, I see."

The woman showed snowy veneers. "Oh yeah, locals will have gone door to door by now to spread the word. Height, shoe size, blood group, the usual."

"Really?"

"Hell, no! I'm just shit-hot at deduction, my dear Watson." She extended a hand. "Look, let's start over. Jude Hollenbeck. Sorry for the near miss. I was in a hurry. Got a mani-pedi booked in town."

Disarmed, Lucy removed her gloves and shook Jude's hand. "Lucy Driscoll. You're heading into Lowmorten?"

"Nah, tried the salon there once. Nice enough girl but told me it was watching her dad trimming hooves that gave her the idea to be a nail technician. I go to Sowersby."

"I take it *you're* not a local."

"What gives it away, beyond the lack of grass growing out of my ears? Joke!"

Lucy dropped her gaze to the Louboutins. "Your accent."

"Case closed, m'lord. No, I'm not local, God forbid, although my husband's a Yorkshireman. Nominally. We live a mile past your place. Henry made a pile in tech and now fancies himself a gentleman farmer. We've a couple of dairy cows and some chickens that live in climate-controlled swank pods and a local yokel pops in to check for fluke worms or what have you and to laugh at us. We *were* the talk of The Slaughtered Lamb but I'm guessing they'll move on to the loony-tune out-of-towners occupying Spook Central. I'm stopping in Sowersby for a spot of lunch. You're welcome to join me, get all the local lowdown."

Lucy sifted Jude's monologue for which bit to tackle first. "We're not loony."

"You say so." Jude glanced at her Apple watch. "Look, I've got to get going. You're welcome to follow me for the quickest way to Sowersby."

"I've shopping to do. Food supplies."

"Great. You could stock up while I get my mani-pedi and meet for lunch, say, oneish? Pub called The Blue Texel is our best bet. It's at the end of Sowersby high street, plenty of parking."

Lucy wavered. "Does Sowersby have an art supplies shop?"

"Yep. Just *off* the high street, can't miss it. Thought you had an artistic vibe about you. What about hubby?"

"He's a writer. Of supernatural fiction."

"Even better! You met Snowy Bird yet? Housekeeper at Rook House, isn't she? Quite the character."

Lucy couldn't decide if Jude Hollenbeck was naturally talkative or just lonely. Now she was heading back to her car as though the matter was all arranged.

"Wait..." Lucy began, then shrugged.

As Jude Hollenbeck turned away, Lucy had noticed a tell-tale speckle of white in one nostril. That explained a lot – including the woman's driving technique and over-bright hazel eyes. Not to mention her feverishly chatty tone.

Maybe Jude Hollenbeck was heading into Sowersby to meet her supplier?

Lucy had already changed her mind about following, but Jude was gunning her engine and waiting for the Honda to fall in behind.

Lucy chewed her lip. If all else failed, she'd be a witness to Jude running over a deer or, God forbid, a local.

She restarted her car and followed the leader. This might be a chance to find out exactly what people were saying about her and Hugh – and more about Snowy Bird, for example.

She texted Hugh illegally as she drove: "*Met a local who advised me shops in Swsby are a better bet than L'morten. Might b back later than planned, if u can bear it.*"

No immediate reply. He must already be hard at work.

6

At a quarter to one, Lucy headed to the pub nominated by Jude, The Blue Texel. It had horse brasses and a real fire in the inglenook. She sank into a wing-backed chair and texted Hugh again: "*On my way back in about an hour with food. Checking out art supplies shop now.*"

A fib. She'd found the art shop but stood outside, reluctant to enter.

She'd leave it for another day. One thing at a time.

This time, Hugh replied. "*Take your time, Mouse. All quiet on haunted house front! See you soon.*"

He was still calling her 'Mouse', despite agreeing to stop.

Her father had nicknamed her that when, aged seven, she'd played the dormouse at the Mad Hatter's Tea Party in a primary school production of *Alice's Adventures in Wonderland*, the role requiring her to snore adorably with her head on a table. School had let her keep the felt brown ears, which she'd worn for days (and nights) afterwards, though she'd reluctantly agreed to scrub off the painted black nose and whiskers.

It might've been a mistake to tell Hugh that story. He didn't always get that some memories were sacrosanct.

She leant towards the fire, sipping a decaf latte and switching thoughts to Jude Hollenbeck and drugs.

Lucy had taken a few Es at school and come to no harm. More by luck than judgment?

Hugh was anti-drugs full stop. Hardly surprising, given that his biological mother had been a junkie.

Jude approached, holding up sparkling nails, her glossy hair richly dark against her cream coat and the deep pink of her scarf. "Let's grab a table," she called to Lucy. "This place fills up quickly at lunchtime."

Lucy nodded cautiously and rose to follow her. She was in listening mode and didn't plan to match Jude's apparent candour with indiscretions about Rook House, Snowy Bird or her 'tornado' marriage.

"Well!" Jude sat back with a large glass of red in her hand. "That takes the weight off. And this-" she tipped back her glass "-takes the edge off."

Lucy said nothing, nursing a spurt of white-hot anger as she sipped her own glass of mineral water.

Her mother had been killed – murdered – by a boy racer full of vodka shots. Of course, the law didn't see it that way. The law took a 'nuanced' approach to an evil bastard bouncing a young mother off his windscreen. Four-year sentence, out in two. That could just as easily have been Jude.

Sometimes Lucy browsed the details of her mother's death online, purely to keep her wound fresh and aching in all weathers. Other times she trawled social media platforms, braced to find the murderer, now a bit grey around the gills but otherwise ageing like Jude's pricey wine, grinning from an Insta account. So far, nada. It was the smallest of small mercies. "I never even saw her," he'd claimed in court, whimpering with self-pity. "She stepped out right at the last second. Gave me no chance."

Victim-blaming, the evil pus bag.

"You found the art shop?" Jude asked.

Lucy nodded. "The Paintbox. Looks like it has everything I'll need."

"What mediums do you work in?"

"Acrylic mostly. Some charcoal. What do you do?"

"As little as possible! Used to work in fashion PR in London. Met Henry just before Covid and he convinced me to run for the hills."

"Do you miss London?"

"Sometimes. The way you miss a boyfriend who'd ghost you for months, only to get back in touch as though nothing had happened and take you out for a night of fabulous dancing, food and sex. Then ghost you again. London was bad for me in lots of ways." Jude rubbed her nose absently and signalled a passing waiter for a top-up. "But old habits die hard."

Their meals arrived. A famished Lucy tucked into fish and chips. She felt guilty leaving Hugh back at base on rations.

Jude cleared her pasta carbonara with noisy gusto. Lucy hoped it would mop up the two glasses of red she'd downed in swift succession. "We could have bandy tart for afters," suggested Jude. "Share one slice between us, since you can use it to lag pipes."

"Sounds delicious," said Lucy doubtfully.

"It is. Delicious stodge anyway. More of a pudding than a tart. Made with ground almonds, around 20 eggs and several 'secret ingredients'. Originally boiled in a cloth bag on a pot-bellied iron stove with bandy legs. Snowy Bird might rustle one up if you ask nicely."

"She warned me to stay out of the wood at Rook House. Said there might be an escaped big cat living in there. Know anything about that?"

"It's bollocks!" snorted Jude. "I tell you what's probably in that wood. Poisonous mushrooms. Doesn't want you accidentally topping yourself on her watch, or else..." Jude held up a pink-tipped finger to signal a further thought. "She *could* be warning you off because her son goes moonlight poaching in there. Pinky Bird. Lives with his mother on the turn into

Lowmorten. He might have set traps in your wood."

"Do any of the Birds have bog standard names?"

Jude waved her little finger. "Wears a signet ring on his pinky. Mysterious bloke. Fingers, including bejewelled pinky, in lots of pies. Allegedly." She rubbed her nose again.

"You called Rook House Spook Central, Jude. So you know the history of the house and the Napiers?"

"Everyone around here does. What've you discovered so far?"

Lucy recounted what Hugh had told her.

"Yeah, vicar in Lowmorten used to give talks on the subject. I toddled along to one." Jude found a stray shallot under her serviette and popped it into her mouth, eyes glittering at Lucy. "I'm dying to know – *have* you seen or heard anything weird yet?"

Lucy shook her head, thinking of the portrait in the living room and Hugh's throwaway remark: *some say he liked the place so much, he's never left.*

What if Ezra was the only ghost haunting Rook House? His direct descendants had died out. He might be watching over his sole surviving legacy, his gloomy old house.

Jude couldn't hide her disappointment. "And you don't mind living there?"

Lucy shrugged. "Hugh thinks the place could inspire him. Personally, as I said, the living are more dangerous than the dead."

Jude still didn't take the hint. But she did insist on paying for their meals. "How long have you and Hugh been married?" she asked, flicking her Apple watch over the card reader.

"A while," replied Lucy evasively.

"Not long, then. Still popping the bubble wrap, euphemistically speaking?"

"Something like that." Was it so obvious that she and Hugh reeked of fresh paint? "Thanks for treating me, Jude. Er, my turn next time."

"Tell you what, you can repay me by coming to dinner at our place. You and Hugh. Intelligent life at last. We're at The Grange. Give me your number to put in my phone and we'll pick a date. Always wanted to meet a real live writer."

"OK." Lucy fumbled for her phone.

Jude cocked her head and regarded her with a faint smile. "Don't think you're big on girly friendships, are you, little Luce?"

As Lucy stiffened, Jude laid a sparkling hand on her coat sleeve, nails glittering like a row of metallic paint tubes. "Let's see how we go about changing that."

Waiting for Lucy's return, Hugh made a fresh round of toast and listened to the wind running scales up and down the roof. It never seemed to stop, tuning up continuously for a performance that never arrived.

Emma the letting agent had made light of the soughing wind and everything else. On the drive from Sowersby station, she hadn't even blinked when a red car shot round a corner and nearly forced them off the road. He'd had time to notice that the car was a Porsche Cayman and its driver a woman who'd flipped him the bird.

"Who was *that*?" he'd wondered.

"Oh, some local," Emma had replied vaguely. "It's the tractors you have to look out for, appearing suddenly from concealed entrances."

Now he took his toast into the hallway and stood there, dropping crumbs on to checkerboard tiles. The house needed roughing up a bit, reminded of its true function. He was master of this domain, keeper of closed doors and unshared secrets.

On his first night here, he'd stood alone in the dark on this same spot and let the place sink into him, picturing its emptiness before he arrived, a house standing firm against the elements, night after night, full of wasted noise. If a haunted house creaks and shudders in the night with no one to hear it, does it make a sound?

He hadn't told Lucy about the scrap of paper he'd found among the old newspapers wrapped around logs in the shed: a yellowing scrap with waterlogged cursive in spidery brown ink that still bore the legible words: "A man should take a life as easily as rubbing a caddis fly between his palms and think nothing of it."

He'd tucked the scrap into the back of his spiral-bound notebook, shuddering with the sort of anticipatory pleasure you felt when sitting down to watch a good horror film.

For a split second he'd wondered whether Lucy's arrival would sunder the link he'd established with the elemental forces in the house. It felt like a house that had been built to embody something raw and powerful. Something that wanted to include rather than repel him: *come on in and close the door.*

Lucy wasn't raw or powerful and he'd liked that about her from the get-go.

He'd approached her on the spur of the moment in the National Gallery, transfixed by the dreamy look on her face as she gazed at that weird old painting.

Chatting up strangers in art galleries – not his style at all. But those limpid brown eyes, the mass of black corkscrew hair...

She was a portrait he could study indefinitely. Turned out she was half-Italian. A cloud dweller, open to new ideas. Open to him. He'd fallen, though not too deeply. Even when he was in a swimming pool, he liked to be able to put one foot on the bottom.

His parents weren't best pleased with his choice of 'career', or any of his recent decisions.

He'd cringed when taking Lucy to meet them at Christmas.

Lucy, God love her, hadn't commented on his mother's hawk-like vigilance – "no, dear, that's a sherry glass, *this* is a brandy balloon" – or veiled questions about her 'background'.

On Boxing Day, his father had invited him into his greenhouse, a rare occurrence that heralded a manly talk, and pretended to repot a sickly geranium while saying of Lucy, "that girl's vulnerable."

"Are you criticising her or me?"

"Just advising you to take things slowly. She's certainly very pretty, but delicate. Shallow roots. Might wither at the first nip of frost." His father never could resist a botanical metaphor.

"I'll chuck some compost over her, add water when needed."

A sharp look from his father. "You told us she lost both her parents while very young, the mother in particularly tragic circumstances."

"Yeah, and? Lucy doesn't like to talk about her past. She believes in looking forward, not back. We both do."

"She's probably repressed then. Has she ever seen a therapist?"

"They're the snake oil hustlers of their day, Lucy says."

Tom had wiped soily fingers on a cloth hanging off a rail. "Does she now? I'm all for stiffening the sinews and summoning up the blood, but bottling things up never does any good. Comes out other ways."

"Is that why Ma's always on the sauce?"

"You're out of order, son. I'm just saying, Lucy has no clear direction or career path and, from what you've told me, no real capital or equity."

"You're dissing her for not having a pension pot and a 35-year mortgage?" Probably to be expected, looking back. Tom was something big in financial planning.

"She's nearly 30 but drifting."

"Like me?"

"We're talking about the girl."

"*The girl* has a name!"

"Son." Heavily paternal hand on shoulder, probing eye contact. "We only want what's best for you. Just promise us that you won't rush into anything. She's a sweet girl but damaged. Tread carefully."

"Leave me to worry about Lucy and I'll leave you to worry about Mum."

"Very well. But you're our son. I'm speaking out of concern."

He recalled the way his father had rubbed his fingers while banking the final word, as if crushing a caddis fly.

He was so tired of disappointing them. It was partly why he'd proposed to Lucy. In for a penny.

Now he returned to his study off the hallway and sat at his desk to stare over his laptop at the driveway and think about his first chapter.

He wasn't just slightly blocked, as he'd told Lucy, he was bunged up, fretting over his agent's recent claim that his new idea might be too *The Woman in Black* with a dash of *The Changeling*; maybe *The Turn of the Screw* thrown in for good measure.

But how could you avoid being influenced by the classics? And why hadn't Carol Pelham – agent to 'the stars of tomorrow' – mentioned her misgivings before now?

Having read that writing by hand could unblock the constipated creative, last month he'd bought a spiral-bound notebook, a hand-tooled number with turquoise suede cover and cream, gold-flecked pages that were stiff and shiny as meringue. Beautiful to stroke and sniff, he'd printed words like bird tracks on virgin snow.

But words were the problem; so far, imaginary names for Yorkshire pubs, including The Chummy Ox, The Tranny Fox and The Clammy Lox (two out of five on Tripadvisor for its smoked salmon breakfast). And bumper stickers for writers:

"My other book's a classic", "If you're close enough to read this sticker, why aren't you reading my bloody book?"

"What about a novelty book in time for Christmas?" he could imagine Carol asking, grasping at the latest proffered straw. "Bumper stickers about different professions. Now that's an idea I could flog."

As if a novel was a widget or a packet of crisps.

But God, what if he couldn't repeat the trick of book writing? What if all this was just a waystation on the road to creative oblivion? Read that and weep, Carol Pelham.

He jumped up with relief when Lucy's car puttered into view beneath the elm trees.

7

Pink-faced from the cold, she struggled through the back door and plonked bags of shopping on the kitchen table. "I got enough provisions to last a couple of weeks."

"Including the vino?"

"Yep, red, like you wanted."

"Great. I could murder a packet of crisps."

"There's a salt and vinegar in here somewhere." She dug out a packet and tossed it over.

He dived in with relish. "Meant to remind you about the joint bank account, Luce. Think we have to bring proof of ID to a branch, though I'm hazy on deets. I'm paying the rent by direct debit."

"Then of course I should contribute."

"The ten grand is to take the heat off, remember?"

"All the same..."

He stood behind her, circled her waist and nuzzled her neck. She was deliciously warm, despite coming in from the cold. "Mouse," he said throatily, skimming salt-flaked lips across the soft hair on her nape.

She drew gently away. "That local I told you about meeting? Turns out she's a neighbour called Jude. We've swapped numbers. Wants to have us over for dinner."

"Did you get your art stuff?"

"I was conscious of our bare cupboards, so I'll make a return trip for the art stuff. Think I'll take a bath after I've unpacked this lot, put the plumbing through its paces. Be down then to crack on with food."

"OK." She'd better hurry. A few crisps wouldn't touch the sides. "You want me to turn the portrait of Ezra Napier to the wall again tonight?"

She hesitated. "Let's leave it. I don't plan on spending any time in that room if I can help it."

She went upstairs.

The bath was a roll-top affair with extravagantly scrolled brass taps. The water ran hot from shuddering pipes as she set her towel and bottle of bath foam on the closed toilet lid and started to undress.

He'd called her Mouse again. Was he doing it deliberately or just forgetful? For a while, when they'd first moved in together, he'd called her his "muse" and then his "moose". A short step from there to "Mouse", once he'd learned of her acting claim to fame.

She slipped into the bath with a sigh of pleasure, thoughts still circling Hugh.

Even-keeled, that was how she saw him. He ticked along, prone to the occasional bout of artistic self-doubt but basically easygoing. And impulsive, of course. In a good way.

But ultimately, did a parental safety net allow him to bounce back from the consequences of impulsive decisions? Was Elena right in claiming he had less to risk?

She slid under the water, going for total immersion. It was like pulling a duvet over your head to shut out the world. She held her breath with her eyes shut. Her PB was more than 20 seconds. By then, you could see darkness blooming behind your eyelids as you sank down towards your Mariana Trench. Where dark things scuttled that never saw the light.

Abruptly, she sat up with a splash and a gasp, letting water stream off her face.

She reclined again more carefully, nose and chin cresting the water, allowing her mind to empty like water swirling down the plughole. *Don't think, be. Just for a few moments. Leap and the net shall appea*r. *Carpe diem*. She closed her eyes and floated.

A noise on the landing.

She inched upright and stared at the closed bathroom door. She hadn't bothered locking it. "Hello? That you, Hugh?"

Then, very faintly, she heard scratching against wood. Like someone scrabbling at the door to get in.

She jerked to her feet and reached for the towel on the toilet lid.

Think dog – nice, friendly dog. She'd stayed in a B&B once that was home to a red setter that used to scratch and whine at the bedroom doors of guests, eager to be petted. "Don't encourage the old show-off," the landlady had laughed.

Wrapped in her towel, Lucy stepped out of the bath on to cold, slippery tiles. The scratching went on.

She looked in the mirror, wiping steam away. Her own pale face and no one else's looked back, shoulder-length hair lank with water.

The scratching persisted.

But as she crept towards the door, she realised the sound was coming from behind her, distorted as it bounced off tiled walls.

No, wait. Was it *under* the floor?

She got down on her knees and tapped the floor, its tiles solidly ceramic. As were the cream-coloured tiles covering the walls, each decorated with a pale-green sea horse.

Then she noticed a sheet of yellowing wood behind the sink where floor met wall. The wood looked out of place. She ran her fingers along its edges, discovering it had been glued firmly in place. She put her ear against it.

Scratch, scratch, scratch. Like fingernails. She toppled back.

Scrambling to her feet, she grabbed her clothes, flung open the door and ran towards the bedroom, dripping.

Hugh appeared at the top of the stairs, gazing at her in surprise. "I came to ask if you wanted toasted cheese. Where's the fire?"

"Come with me." She tossed her clothes into their bedroom, took his hand and led him back to the bathroom, pushing the door wide open with a bare knee. "I heard a noise." She crabbed her fingers into claws. "Like someone scratching behind that piece of board behind the sink."

He cocked an ear. "Can't hear anything."

"It's gone now."

"Sure it wasn't the plumbing? We haven't used the bath before."

She frowned. "Yeah, I'm sure. Just as I'm sure I didn't turn around the portrait on the wall!"

"All right, calm down."

"You'll be calling me a hysterical woman next!" Her teeth chattered as she knotted the towel over her breastbone. "I know what I heard! It wasn't the pipes and it wasn't my imagination."

"All right, well, you probably don't want to hear *this*, but could be a mouse or a rat in the wall cavity. Might be stuck in there. Sometimes they die and that creates another problem – flies or roaches that flock into the space to eat the body."

"Right. Thanks for that. Lovely."

"I'm just saying, doubt these walls are cavity-insulated. Things will get into the gaps. Did you hear a clicking noise? That'd be deathwatch beetles. They love old houses."

She glared at him. Was he *trying* to get under her skin? "No, I didn't hear a clicking noise. Why's that particular spot covered up with a chunk of unsightly wood?"

"Result of half-arsed remedial work?" His hand touched the trailing edge of her towel where it barely skimmed her thigh. "That's one hell of a sexy outfit." He waggled his eyebrows.

"For God's sake!" She swatted his hand away. "You'll be asking me to dress up as a French maid next and chasing me round the house!"

"We haven't... you know... since the wedding. And here we are, a big house all to ourselves..."

"Thought you were writing."

"I've come up against a temporary roadblock. It gets dark early and there's no telly. How do you expect us to while away the hours?"

"Charmed, I'm sure."

The water made a thin rippling sound in the bath. She stalked over and pulled the plug without looking in, almost as though she feared to see an Ophelia-like shadow of herself floating there, gazing up with open eyes from beneath the water.

"I only meant... oh, forget it," said Hugh.

She turned to face him. "I do want to make the most of a romantic old gothic house, Hugh, but not because we don't have a telly!"

"I put that badly. Cheese toastie's still on offer when you come downstairs. I won't impose on you with my repulsive urges a second longer."

She ran after him down the landing. "Hugh, why did you propose to me? Was I just there, like Everest?"

"What? Of course not! How could you think that? What are you saying? That I talked you into it?"

"You made it sound more practical than romantic, is all."

"Didn't know you expected a string quartet and a flypast by the Red Arrows."

"Oh, for God's sake-"

"I'm not listening to any more of this." He stormed off down the stairs.

She stomped back to the bedroom and slammed the door.

Like a pair of five-year-olds, she winced. Somewhere in the background, Elena was laughing.

8

She slept badly, Hugh snoring on the adjoining pillow. He could nap on a tightrope. He hadn't offered to sleep downstairs, and she had no intention of bunking down on a living room sofa under the Napier gaze, watching dark-pink walls merge with oxblood leather into the colour of dry-aged steak.

Never go to bed on an argument, to quote beer mat philosophy.

Why not, though? When she'd lived with Elena, she'd used many an early night to seethe and plot her counter-offensive.

But marriage was different. Rows felt different; anger easy to chew on, remorse hard to swallow. Or maybe just rows with Hugh? That accusation about his proposal being practical had taken her by surprise, never mind him. She'd always regarded his impulsive streak as romantic. But maybe he just tumbled from one decision to another, making it up as he went along, calculating the immediate benefits to himself. For instance, he might've reasoned that the owners of Rook House would prefer a married couple to take over as guardians of the house, despite the ad not stipulating it.

And he might have asked her to move in with him initially because she paid for the groceries, sorted the laundry, brought him endless cups of tea while he frowned over a laptop, and provided sex on tap.

No! That was Elena corrupting her thoughts.

She dozed off around 3am, waking just after eight to find

Hugh's side of the bed empty, though still warm.

Hearing running water in the bathroom, she got up, dragged on her dressing gown and went downstairs.

Mrs Bird was in the kitchen. "Oh, Snowy," she said in surprise, glancing at the wall clock.

"It's Wednesday," said Snowy, dropping a pile of briquettes into a basket by the Rayburn. "I said I'd come by Wednesday. Like to get an early start. Kettle's on. I can do you an egg if you'd like."

Lucy sat down at the scarred pine kitchen table. "Haven't got any eggs."

"Brought some. I've good laying hens at the moment. Boiled or poached?"

Lucy chose boiled.

"One for his nibs, too?" Snowy nodded at the ceiling. "Assume he's gracing us with his presence or does he go straight to it, the writing?"

"He has a day job he has to clear first. He's starting at nine this morning, I think." Lucy pushed her finger through a groove in the pine. "Do you know the Hollenbecks? They keep chickens too. I met Jude Hollenbeck yesterday on the road to Sowersby."

She'd expected Snowy to purse her lips and mutter about incomers with more money than sense, but Snowy merely replied, "they've Rhode Island reds. Nice temperaments but easy pickings for foxes. Told Judith I'd get my son to drop by and build a proper coop next time he's passing."

"She told me they've got a state-of-the-art swank pod for their chickens. Surely it's fox-proof?"

"Likelier to have mood music and soft lighting than a padlock," noted Snowy.

"Are she and her husband well thought of?"

Snowy plonked a saucepan on the range. "They spend money locally. That's always well thought of. Only thing folk object to is the way she tears about the place in her little red chariot. Ben Hur in high heels, my son calls her."

"Pinky?"

Snowy turned with a shrewd gaze. "Jerome by name, Pinky by nickname. His fame goes before him, then."

"Jude told me, that's all." Lucy hesitated. "Said your ancestors might even have worked for the Napiers."

"Yes, my great-gandy Mickey – my great-grandfather – was here as an under-gardener in Ezra Napier's time."

"Did he know Belle Napier?"

"Maybe. Briefly. Mickey left Rook House not long after she was sent to the asylum in York. He got himself a hardware shop in Lowmorten and married one of the maids from here. She left service to run the shop with him. Butter a few slices, would you, while I watch this egg."

"I try not to look at the portrait of Ezra," Lucy murmured, rising to oblige with the bread. "I'm thinking of taking it down."

"Work away." Snowy paused. "I'll tell you a story in passing about that painting, not because I lend any credence to it."

Lucy tensed. "OK. I'm all ears."

"After Ezra died, a fellow from York was the first tenant here, a newspaper editor. Packed up the portrait of Ezra and put it in the attic. One night, fire breaks out in the grounds and half the outbuildings go up in flames, fire brigade arriving just in time to save the house. Marianne discovers the portrait of her father is AWOL and rumour spreads that Ezra started the fire in a fit of pique at being shut in the attic. So Marianne puts the portrait back in the living room. Just as insurance against further disturbances, if you like. And it's been there ever since."

Lucy reached into a cupboard for the butter dish. "Ezra

Napier didn't like having his face turned to a blank wall, either."

"Here's the truth of it," said Snowy. "That fire started because the daft-fool newspaper editor left a bonfire of weeds unattended. But you can't keep a good mummy's curse down. Right, this egg's almost done."

"But there *have* been further disturbances," Lucy demurred. "I mean, the stories about Belle screaming, and the apparition of Phineas jumping from a window. Or did they start while Ezra was still alive?"

Snowy cocked her head, thinking. "Not sure. Like I say, keeping the portrait here is no more than tradition."

"Or *superstition*," suggested Lucy.

"This looks cosy," remarked Hugh, stepping into the kitchen fully dressed, damp hair sticking up over one ear. He pulled out a chair.

"I'm boiling an egg for your wife. I'll put another on."

"Thank you."

Lucy glanced at him almost shyly. "Snowy's great-grandfather worked here as a gardener in Ezra's time."

"Really? So he knew the old man?"

"In passing, probably," replied Snowy. "While working here, Mickey would've lived in one of the old estate cottages. They're long gone now. But I was just telling Lucy that Mickey left here long before Phineas died, let alone Ezra. He and his wife ran a hardware shop in Lowmorten. The family sold that years ago, mind you."

"Did *you* know Mickey?" Hugh asked.

Snowy's eyebrows shot up into her hairline. "How old do you think I am, Mr Driscoll? I was born in 1961, so we're not talking Blitz spirit and powdered egg! I knew my grandmother."

Hugh looked sheepish. "Lucy said she heard a weird noise in the bathroom yesterday. Scratching."

This time, Lucy swivelled round to glare at him.

Snowy went still with Lucy's egg on the end of a spoon. "Scratching?"

"Well, yes," Lucy admitted. "But Hugh, you said it might be a mouse or, or a squirrel."

"I never said squirrel!"

Snowy plonked the egg on a plate by the saucepan. "A mouse *is* the likeliest explanation, but it's nowt to worry about. Now, I'll have to get on shortly. All right to do your egg yourself, Mr D? I'll fetch my cleaning materials from the cubby and start with the bathroom, if you've both finished up there."

Lucy hadn't but said nothing. She watched Snowy sail from the room and slid buttered bread on to plates. "You can use the same water for your egg." She tensed. "Why'd you tell her the scratching was spooky while telling *me* it was nothing to worry about?"

"I said weird, not spooky, and I was laying it on a bit thick to draw her out, that's all. You going up to your studio today? You've got to start some time."

"I still need materials from that shop in Sowersby."

He got up and stood behind her, circling her waist and nuzzling her neck, his default seduction technique, she'd noticed. "I'm sorry about yesterday, Luce." His nose nudged the locket clasp on the back of her neck and snuffled her dark curls. "I asked you to marry me because I love you and want to spend my life with you. I'm sorry for what I said yesterday. You're right and I was out of order, misjudged the moment. Forgive and forget?"

It was a good, straight-from-the-heart speech. She turned to face him, bumping foreheads. "Yeah, of course I forgive you. I'm sorry too. We're still finding our feet here – and with each other, when you think about it. But stop making out I'm imagining things. Only wish I was," she added absently.

9

Finishing her breakfast, she went upstairs to get dressed, light with relief that Hugh had made the first move. Maybe he'd had more practice at being the bigger person, coming from a normal family. She was scarred by years of siege warfare with Elena.

Snowy was still clattering about in the bathroom. Lucy sat on the bed with her laptop on her knees, searching for images of the Napier family.

She found a few photos of Ezra looking much as he did in his portrait: stern and forbidding, his eyes even more penetrating in black and white.

And here was his son Phineas in uniform, about to go off to war, his eager, sensitive face unaware of the horrors to come. God, he was just a boy. Nineteen, she read in the photo caption. He was what Elena would've called "asking for trouble handsome". Doubtful the poor bloke ever got the chance to find out.

Marianne appeared in photos from archives of the local county show, stout and smiling, presenting rosettes or petting prize cattle on the nose. She had Ezra's profile but none of her brother's delicate grace.

There were no photos of the fleeting Nanette and only one poignant, sepia snapshot of a youthful Belle, stiff and corseted beside a japonica vase, eyes downcast beneath a pile of soft, dark hair. Here was the template for Phineas's easily spoiled beauty.

As if to echo that fragility, the vase beside Belle held a single, pale rose wilting on the stem.

According to Hugh, Ezra had only remarried to bag himself an heir. But that didn't mean he'd been faithful to Belle before she went 'mad'. When had he started 'knocking up' the female servants?

Next, Lucy looked up the church in Lowmorten where Jude said she'd attended a talk on Rook House.

"Checking the times of services?" asked Snowy from the doorway.

Lucy glanced up, her screen visible from Snowy's vantage point.

"Not unless I turn C of E," Lucy replied. "I'm sorta Catholic. Currently lapsed."

"Ah." Snowy advanced into the room. "If you're interested, there's 10am Sunday Mass at The Sacred Heart in Sowersby. I do the flowers there."

Coded info that Snowy was a fellow left-footer. "Thanks, might check it out. D'you think Ezra was having – relations – with the servants while married to Belle?"

Snowy blanched. "You shouldn't read all that online stuff. Answer is, I don't know."

"Why did Marianne never marry?"

"She was rumoured to be of the Sapphic persuasion."

"Did Ezra know?"

Snowy shook her head. "Doubt *Marianne* fully knew. She had 'friendships' but kept them discreet. She probably left Rook House because Ezra was pestering her to marry as soon as she came of age. Her husband was to take the Napier name so the line would continue. My ma looked after Marianne when she was getting on," Snowy continued. "Marianne talked of the times she'd sit on the counter of Mickey's shop eating pear drops and he'd tell her about the old days at Rook House. She took to my family more than her own, Ezra being colder than a winter walk on the fells, and her mother preferring horses to children."

"Sounds like she had a lonely childhood," observed Lucy. Took one to know one.

Snowy about-turned towards the door, then paused. "Don't dwell on them too much – the people of this house. I'm just getting the Hoover out. What about the attic? I hear you've an art studio up there?"

"It's clean as a whistle at the mo," said Lucy. "Haven't started work there yet."

"Hope you don't go in for portraits," said Snowy, and went on her way.

Once Snowy left at noon, the house returned to its watchful silence. Lucy drifted from room to room, following the light as it moved. At lunchtime, she told Hugh about her talk with Snowy and asked: "How's the book going, really?"

"How's the painting going?"

"I haven't bought materials yet. You're well into your book, allegedly."

He didn't answer.

"We should go for walks together," she said. "We could both draw inspiration from the landscape."

"Thanks for the tip."

She watched him open the fridge and pull out the bottle of red he'd started last night. He'd never drunk this much in London, as far as she knew. But then, she'd been in an office while he worked from home. Maybe he'd slipped out regularly to the pub round the corner. Quite often she'd come back to find him sprawled on the sofa, opening glazed eyes to greet her, and she'd attributed his fatigue and hazy expression to a hard day at the keyboard.

She wasn't teetotal or anything, but after a few benders in her 20s and the associated crippling guilt, she'd lost her tolerance for booze, not to mention the lingering hangovers.

Besides, alcohol was a trigger for migraines, alongside food she avoided or ate in moderation. Even her coffee was usually decaf.

"You're doing a cat's bum thing with your mouth," Hugh noted, slopping wine into a mug on the draining board.

"Can't help my resting bitch face. I'm just saying, a walk would shake the cobwebs."

"Mrs B's already done that with her trusty Hoover nozzle."

She rose to put their dishes in the sink. "I'm sorry if I was glib just now. I know you're doing your best – with the book, I mean."

Wrong thing to say. "Thanks for having every faith in me."

"Although... is it wise to drink before the sun's over the yard arm?"

"Dunno. Let's put it to the test." He swigged from the mug. "Yep, can feel the wisdom flowing through my veins. Chin chin."

Her heart plummeted. So much for his kiss-and-make-up speech earlier.

At a loss how to respond, she grabbed her coat and phone and set out to explore the pear orchard.

Perhaps because of Snowy's warning, she felt a stubborn urge to see it for herself, just like the deep and silent wood.

To reach the orchard, she crossed the last remaining bit of 'garden' that belonged to the house, a neglected tangle of briars and shaggy laurels that had once been a kitchen garden, the pear orchard accessed through an arch in a brick wall.

The orchard was a gnarly old place, thick with sleeping trees. She edged past the wire fence Snowy had mentioned, pausing to photograph scuddy clouds of sheep wool snagged on its barbs.

But her heart wasn't in it. She looked skywards instead, searching in vain for a kestrel.

Clouds brewed, along with her tears. That wary mind of hers skittered away from the present and took refuge in the distant past: the time after her mother but before Elena.

For those few, precious years, she and her father had refined the art of pretending to be enough for each other. He'd taught her to ride a bike and watched anxiously as she graduated to roller skates, weaving around dogs and pushchairs in crowded London parks. He'd indulged her short-lived passion for fidget spinners and a boy band she now cringed to recall. Glancing at a scrap of white wool fluttering from a spike of barbed wire, she remembered his patience when she threw a hissy fit because her veil didn't match the lace detail on her first holy communion dress. "We'll go back to the shop and get another one," he'd soothed, picking up the mangled white tulle and smoothing it out with a nervous smile. An atheist by upbringing and instinct, he'd raised her as a Catholic out of respect for her mother.

She'd put him through the wringer and then some. Not deliberately, of course. Simply by being a kid missing her mum.

But part of her wondered whether she'd driven him into the arms of Elena; better a woman, any woman, than facing the years ahead with a capricious child growing into a bolshie teen.

If only Lucy had been better behaved, she and her dad might've carried on being enough for each other. Or at least pretending that was the case. And wasn't pretending part and parcel, perhaps even the most essential part, of making a relationship work?

Scrubbing her eyes with the heel of her hand, she surveyed the ragged trees and wondered which ones marked the final resting places of Phineas and his unnamed, stillborn twin.

No plaque or memorial indicated the spots. Or had they been buried under the same tree?

She walked beneath the branches, her tread shivering dew off sodden boughs. Although the sun rode high in a pale sky, the orchard slouched in shade. Wherever Phineas and his twin lay, it was a fittingly sombre spot.

She trailed back to the house. In the kitchen, Hugh was boiling the kettle.

He turned to her, expression beseeching. "Mouse, I... sorry, I mean, Luce. I'm sorry for snapping. Again."

Another lurch in her ribcage, this time upwards. It was like being on a see-saw, dizzying and faintly nauseating. And yet, she couldn't turn away that look or the appeal in his voice. "I know, Hugh. Me too."

They went to bed.

Twisting her hair through his hands as the house rocked beneath them on its rolling seas, he yanked the gold locket so that its links snagged in her hair. She kept very still.

He smiled hazily. "Let's have an afternoon snooze, Luce. A post-coital siesta. Leave us fighting fit for the evening." He kissed her forehead and burrowed into the mattress, asleep within seconds.

She stared at the ceiling rose.

When he'd kissed her, she'd got the full force of his wine breath.

She lay there wide awake, listening to silence whisper at the window.

No more displacement activity. She drove back to the art shop in Sowersby the following morning to choose her weapons.

The owner, a man in a polka-dot bow tie, was helpful without being pushy. She came away with easel, sketchbook, pencils and charcoal, a trio of canvases, a selection of brushes and a box of fresh acrylic paints. Hugh had said no more about accessing the £10k, so she'd used her own money.

Her purchases weighed down the back of her car with a desire to be used that both excited and unnerved her. Could she do her investment justice?

On the way 'home', she detoured into Lowmorten for her first recce.

The small market town on their doorstep was just as it appeared on Google Images: gritty and unpretentious, the outline of a squat church rising from the brow of a hill.

She sampled a coffee in a place called The Little Red Cooking Pot, buying a croissant as a treat for Hugh.

Driving out of town, curiosity drew her towards the church. She parked in front of a plain, functional building of grey stone encircled by a graveyard.

Opening a waist-high wooden gate, she approached the church door along a path winding between old gravestones.

A shadow under a yew tree caught her eye and she went in for a closer look. The tree shaded a tapering black obelisk topped by a marble urn. Stark white lettering on the urn spelt out 'Ezra Napier, scion of this county'. No dates. Almost as if he was still alive, she shuddered. No pear orchard interment for him.

"You're one of the guardians at Rook House."

Statement, not question. She turned to meet the watery gaze of an elderly man in a dog collar.

"How did you..."

"You've been seen driving in and out of the gates. Very little escapes local notice." He extended a hand. "Rupert Dayton."

Lucy shook his hand. "Are you the vicar who gives talks on the history of the house?"

"I used to. Always keen to meet a present inhabitant."

She gestured towards the obelisk. "Nice and understated."

"Ezra commissioned it himself. Marianne is buried elsewhere – she became a Catholic late in life – and poor Belle was buried in the grounds of the York asylum where she died in 1906."

Lucy had a sudden thought. "Is Phineas in the pear orchard because the church wouldn't bury a suicide in consecrated ground?"

"Oh no, not at all, Mrs..."

"Driscoll. Lucy Driscoll."

"The law against burying suicides in sanctified ground had long been rescinded. I believe Ezra just wanted his sons nearby."

"D'you think Rook House is haunted, Reverend? And if so, by Ezra?"

"I think the truth often gets in the way of a good story."

"The truth being?"

The vicar stroked his cheek. "Ezra Napier was so domineering in life that some people believe he overcame death itself. But belief isn't fact."

"Pretty odd statement from a man of the cloth," she said without thinking.

He laughed. "You got me there. But belief and *faith* are different things."

Tomato, tomayto, she thought.

"It's all too easy to hang labels on what we don't understand," Dayton continued. "We shouldn't judge Ezra Napier by modern standards. He was born into wealth, power and privilege. That must've made him arrogant and uncaring of others. Over time he's come to embody the idea of a moustache-twirling villain."

Nurture over nature. Was that an excuse or an explanation for a wicked man's flaws?

"Ezra was of the 'pull yourself together' generation," Dayton insisted, Lucy getting the impression he was a bit of a fanboy when it came to old Ezra. "He wouldn't have understood the nature of his son's mental fragility after returning from war."

"So no namby-pamby PTSD on his watch, even though he'd never been to war himself, presumably?"

"All about appearances. A Napier was expected to uphold certain standards."

Lucy snorted. "Where did those sit with sexually harassing defenceless housemaids?"

Dayton replied delicately: "Quite. Marianne would've agreed. She was well aware of her father's... proclivities." He changed tack. "What do you think of the portrait in the house? Some people have found it... disquieting. One tenant even claimed that if you look at it long enough, Ezra smiles at you."

The hairs jumped to attention on Lucy's arms, chilled by the idea of Ezra Napier smiling. Recalling her own experience in the acanthus room, half-convinced the pattern on the wall had begun to writhe, she murmured: "You can imagine all sorts if you stare too long at an image."

"It's possible," conceded Dayton. "Same goes for a so-called haunted house. Residents might project their own fears and even longings on to shadows, sounds, hearsay."

Lucy raised an eyebrow, but Dayton plunged on: "It's been very nice to meet you, Mrs Driscoll. Perhaps I'll see you at matins this week? One doesn't like to presume..."

"Thanks for the, er, offer. But I should probably come clean and tell you that I'm a left-footer, just like Marianne."

10

Hugh was pacing the attic in Lucy's absence when the lion's head knocker slammed on the front door. He almost jumped out of his skin. What the hell?

He scooted down to open the door before the noise went off again like a gunshot.

A woman stood on the doorstep, a glossy brunette with her hand still on the lion's mouth. "Soz if I made an unholy racket. Don't think your knocker does subtlety." She waved behind her. "I've parked there, if that's OK."

He peered over her shoulder. The Porsche Cayman. Right. So this was the woman who'd flipped him the bird.

"Jude Hollenbeck, your nearest neighbour." She extended a slim hand glinting with rings. "You must be Hugh. I met your charming wife Lucy the other day."

He cleared his throat, conscious of gawping. "Yeah, I'm Hugh. Luce mentioned bumping into you. Nice to meet you. Want to come in for a cuppa? I'm a poor substitute for my wife, but..."

"Sure I'm not disturbing? Lucy mentioned you're a writer."

"I'd welcome the break, to be honest."

No need to tell her he'd been taking a breather from the boring day job.

She stepped inside, looking around. "So cool! Never been here before. I'm awash with tea, ta. Prefer to hear about your latest book or is that strictly verboten? Like mentioning the Scottish play in a theatre?"

"It's still in the early stages." He hesitated. "I can show you the centre of operations if you like. This way."

He meant it jokily as he led her into the study, spotting the sticky wine glass just in time and tucking it out of sight behind his open laptop.

He plonked down on his swivel chair. "This is where the magic allegedly happens, give or take videos of skateboarding cats."

She perched on the edge of his desk, putting him at eye level with her smooth, tanned knees. "Hope you don't mind. Alternative is sitting on your lap."

"Good point." She seemed to have few boundaries or inhibitions. Refreshing or alarming, depending on your point of view. He pulled the cuffs of his ratty old jumper over his knuckles.

"So – your latest book?"

"*Very* early stages."

"Supernatural, Lucy says."

"In a nutshell, yeah."

She laid a pink-tipped hand on his unravelling cuff. "Could you bear to share the briefest of brief extracts with little old me? No pressure."

Tempting. She was part of the wider, semi-literate public he should be aiming for.

He turned to his screen, shut down several incriminating tabs and called up the opening page of *A Trick of the Dark*. "Working title," he explained. "Val McDermid's written a book with a similar one, so I'll need a rethink."

She listened to him read with her eyes closed, opening them when he'd finished to ask, "am I sitting on real walnut?"

He sighed inwardly. "Probably."

She slid off the desk. "Mind if I take a shufti? I promise to stay downstairs."

"Work away."

She returned ten minutes later, reclaiming the desk edge. "Love that old range. Always wanted one. That portrait's something. Ezra Napier, I presume? He'd win best in show with that handlebar."

"Yeah, that's him. Luce isn't keen."

"Your writing, by the way," she said, crossing her legs and leaning back. "Now I've had a proper think, reminds me of someone... I *want* to say Algernon Blackwood, but could be someone else." She took a mobile phone from her pocket and slid it over the desk. "Put your number in there and I'll text you the name when my fog clears."

Disarmed by the Blackwood reference, he obliged and handed back the phone. "I've added a link to my most recent book on Amazon if you'd like to help a starving writer and even add a review. No pressure."

She clicked on the link. "*Among the Tall Reeds*. Let's just say you had me at 'starving writer'."

The back door opened. "Hello!" Lucy called.

"In here!" Hugh called back, eyeing Jude's crossed legs. She seemed in no hurry to slide them off his desk.

Lucy opened the study door. "Oh, you're both in here. Saw you'd parked up, Jude."

"I've just been distracting your poor hubby," Jude mock-groaned. "He's even regaled me with his opening paragraphs."

"Oh? He hasn't asked me to be his beta reader."

Hugh pulled a face at her sulky tone. "Only cos you know me too well."

"Do I?" She tossed a paper bag on the desk. "Got a pastry to keep the brain cells perky via a sugar rush."

Jude slid off the desk. "Sorry for dropping round unannounced.

Should've texted or phoned but I was driving past and got an overwhelming urge to look inside the fabled Rook House. Who wouldn't? Also gives me an opp to extend that invite to dinner we talked about, Lucy. Henry and I were thinking, this Friday? Seven-thirty and no need to bring anything but your good selves. I'll send you a map." She turned to Hugh. "Thanks for the guided tour. Hope I didn't interrupt the flow too much."

"Nah, you're good."

Lucy escorted her out, returning a moment later. "How long was she here?"

"Dunno. Half an hour? Told her to poke around downstairs if she wanted. Barely spoke to her. Think she came to get a good look at the Rayburn."

Lucy hooked a stray curl behind one ear. "Finally bought art supplies. I'll hoik them up to the attic."

"Need a hand?"

"I'll be fine. She genuinely loves the book, by the way. Told me on the way out. Said that if she'd told you directly, you might've thought it was empty flattery."

Hugh felt a swell of pride. "She only heard a few sentences. Can't say I'm staking its prospects on a woman whose reading material probably consists of *Closer* mag and the back of her moisturiser jar."

"Bit snobbish," Lucy murmured. "You up for dinner with the Hollenbecks? Nothing to bring but our good selves. Probably terrified we'll turn up with Chateau plonk du Tesco instead of a cheeky vintage from our tour of Tuscany."

"Looks like we'll have to brave it," he groaned. "Might be fun to see how the nouveau riche other half live."

They sniggered. This felt like a normal, back-bitey exchange in a normal, unhaunted house. "Thanks for the pastry."

"You're welcome. It's a chocolate croissant." She turned to go.

"Luce? You haven't heard that weird scratching in the bathroom again?"

"No." But her face flamed a deep scarlet he didn't see.

"If you did, you'd tell me?"

"Yeah, of course. Must get on. I'll catch you later."

As Lucy drove them away from Rook House on Friday evening, Hugh felt a flicker of childlike excitement, envying Lucy her driving licence. Living in London, he'd never bothered to learn, despite his parents' offer to pay for lessons. On that note, how had Lucy afforded lessons while penny pinching to survive Elena's extravagance?

He was curious to meet Jude Hollenbeck again. Had she been flirting with him? Hard to tell. What might've happened if he'd brushed against one of her smooth, swinging kneecaps?

The Grange was just over a mile from Rook House, accessed through electronically controlled gates. A camera swivelled to inspect their approach and the gates buzzed open.

The driveway was even longer than the elm tunnel at Rook House and lined with triangular shrubs in silver pots.

"Bloody hell," said Hugh when a slab of concrete and glass shouldered through the evening gloom, its flat roof sprouting a dark quiff of grass. "Maybe they reckoned a couple of Howitzers poking out of gun turrets were a step too far."

Lucy laughed. "Probably designed the place themselves, so play nice."

Jude appeared from the side of the house as they parked beside her Porsche and a black SUV. Hugh unclipped his seatbelt. "Smoked-glass windows on a Chelsea tractor. Very drug baron."

So far, so predictable.

"Welcome, welcome!" Jude was in full hostess mode, wearing something pink and fluttery in layers. Her face was pink too, Hugh noted, as she went in for the double-cheek kiss. "Behold our humble abode."

"It's... pretty rad," said Lucy, nodding at the tufted outline. "Is it one of those eco houses where you grow veg on the roof?"

"Nah, that stuff's called wavy-hair grass, planted for aesthetic purposes. Meant to soften the outline. You be the judge."

The front door led straight into a huge living room. Hugh paused to take it all in. African tribal masks on lime-washed walls, uncomfortable-looking chairs (possibly knock-off Le Corbusiers), glass coffee table mounted on tree stump, kilim rug.

Designed by committee, by the looks of. Still, if you had money and a total lack of imagination, that was fair enough.

"Hubby's through that archway," nodded Jude, taking their coats. "Dinner might be a while. I foolishly let Consuela go for the evening and now I have to work out the cooker knobs for myself."

They found Henry Hollenbeck shaking a cocktail mixer behind a glass-bricked bar, Miles Davis meandering from recessed speakers in the ceiling. To Hugh's surprise, Henry was a lean, balding man in a tracksuit. Hugh had expected a fat bloke with hair plugs.

"One olive or two?" Henry asked his guests.

"I'm driving, so no booze for me," said Lucy.

"Spoilsport." He turned to Hugh. "You look like a two-olive man. Sit down and I'll bring it over. *Darling*, can you rustle up a libation for our designated driver?"

Hugh noticed Henry's faint Yorkshire burr. A local, then.

One drink became two, with no aroma of the promised dinner. Hugh sank into a squishy pink sofa, Jude perched alongside. With Henry fussing at the bar and Lucy wandering the edges of the room, Hugh noted with a mixture of alarm and excitement that Jude's fingertips were climbing his inner thigh.

Lucy held up a framed photo of two teenagers sulking on a yacht. "I didn't know you had kids."

"Henry's," clarified Jude, moving away unhurriedly from Hugh. "Live with their mother in Cyprus, the attractions of which beat straw-chewing or stick-whittling in the English countryside. Thank gawd."

"So, what's it like living in a creepy old haunted house?" Henry wanted to know, finally plonking into a squishy armchair. "All grist to the writer's mill, I'm sure."

"It's certainly atmospheric," replied Hugh. "Lucy's heard odd scratching noises behind a wall, haven't you, Luce?"

"Oh?" Both their hosts stared at Lucy with interest.

"I..." Her face glowed. "We decided it was a mouse or something stuck in the wall cavity."

"Or a ghost with scabies," snorted Henry.

"Hugh's an excellent writer," Jude told her husband. "He read me an extract from his latest novel the other day."

"My wife has an English degree from Oxford," Henry eye-rolled. "Might as well put it to use now and then."

Hugh's surprise showed. "I went to Oxford too," he said. "Magdalen."

"Somerville," said Jude. "God, I could murder a fag. Gave 'em up when I moved here," she explained to her guests. "All part of the new, improved, bucolic me. Can't say the craving's gone. Half-crazed with it sometimes."

"That would explain your driving technique," said Lucy, the only one still standing. She laughed to show it was meant as a joke, twisting the gold locket at her neck.

Hugh said quickly, "to be fair, Jude, you did swerve like Schumacher on a chicane and flip me the bird when the letting agent was driving me to Rook House."

Henry guffawed. "Busted, darling!"

"I *do* apologise," said Jude with mock penitence. "On the other hand, I'm sure locals rejoice in the rich pickings I provide via roadkill."

"Why doesn't Rev Dayton give his talks any more?" Lucy asked in a pointed change of subject. "You told me that he used to, Jude."

"Well," said Jude, lowering her tone, "he came out of the vestry one day and there was old Ezra in the front pew of an otherwise empty church. Poor old Dayton fainted clean away, took it as a sign to lay off the amateur history stuff."

"Really?" blinked Hugh.

"She's winding us up," said Lucy with a honking laugh that made Hugh's fillings jangle.

Jude threw back her hair. "Yeah, word is, the bish took a dim view. Not that Dayton ever said he believed in the Rook House ghosts." She struggled out of the sofa's jaws. "I'll go check on dinner. Back in two shakes of a dead fox's tail."

"I'll help her dish up," Hugh decided a moment later, rising to hurry after his hostess despite having no idea of the kitchen's whereabouts.

He found it eventually, a space the size of an aircraft hangar, dangerously bright with knives and cleavers. Jude was grappling with a shiny double-oven.

"Sorry for that dig about your driving," he said. "Apologies on behalf of my wife too."

Jude blew caramel-dark hair off her hot cheek. "Pass me that oven glove, would you? I can take a joke, you know. I've had to. Henry's gruesome twosome could do a show at the Fringe about me."

He passed her the glove and felt her hand through it, thin and birdlike. Their eyes met.

By the time dinner was served, the chicken was dry and the

green things shrivelled to black, but at least the food was hot and they fell on it with gusto in a beige and ecru dining room.

Henry asked Hugh whether he played golf. Hugh said he'd often thought about it, ignoring Lucy's side-eye. Henry said he could put in a word for him at the golf club, although there was a waiting list for new members. Hugh said he'd be very grateful. At which point, Lucy nearly choked on a green bean.

Hugh frowned at his plate. Lucy knew he'd rather have root canal treatment without anaesthetic than trudge round 18 holes dressed like Rupert the Bear, but why insult their gracious host?

Henry revealed that The Grange had been designed by a fellow member of the golf club. "Bloke had a hand in the Shard so I wasn't going to look a gift horse in the mouth."

"You don't think locals see it as a carbuncle?" Lucy asked.

Henry shrugged. "Who cares? I didn't come back here to live in a crofter's cottage with water running down the walls."

"Noticed the camera above the gates," Hugh said. "I bet you have a state-of-the-art alarm system too."

"No need." Henry pointed his knife at Jude. "You'd hear her at your place if someone came in and got their mitts on her shoe collection."

Jude raised a full glass of red. "To new neighbours and new possibilities." Her eye meeting Hugh's again, she knocked back her wine in one go.

Henry raised his glass next. "To Rook House! And to those who never left it!"

A second of silence ticked by.

"God, is this one of your chickens?" Lucy asked suddenly, peering at her plate.

"Don't worry, they're in their swank pod round the back," replied Jude. "Next door to Stacey and Erica's heated stall."

"She named the cows after my daughters," said Henry. "Draw your own conclusions."

He found and lit a fat cigar, leaning back in his chair. No giving up filthy cravings for *him*. He blew smoke into Hugh's face. "This writing lark, Hugh. Make a decent living from it, do you? If not, why bother?"

Hugh bristled, suspecting this was payback for Lucy's "carbuncle" comment. Henry knew that Hugh wasn't raking it in or he wouldn't have taken the gig at Rook House. "I'm not in the JK Rowling bracket, obviously, but I pay my way."

A strange snort from Lucy. He glanced at her irritably. What was *that* for?

Henry frowned. "You only need four things to succeed in life, whatever caper you're in."

"Here we go!" warned Jude. "The four pillars of wisdom according to Henry Hollenbeck! Feel free to take notes."

"First two-" Henry aimed a couple of fingers at Hugh, flicking ash on the table, "-are energy and effort. Without those as your baseline, end of story. After that..." He added two more fingers to his pistol aim. "You need a hard neck and luck. Don't matter if you're knocking out metal rivets or the next Jeffrey Archer."

Hugh reached for his wine glass. "No room for talent or ability, then?"

"Overrated," barked Henry. "And a matter of opinion when it comes to the artsy fartsy scene. One man's masterpiece is another man's pile of bricks or unmade bed. What's that crap called again, Jude?"

"Conceptual. Though I believe 'crap' is the layman's term."

"I'd have said grit and determination play a part," said Lucy. "Hugh has those in abundance."

"Filed under 'e' for effort," replied Henry. "For which you need energy. You take the knocks, get back in the saddle and plod on to the next watering hole. In your case, agent. Play your cards right, your horse will never be thirsty again. Otherwise, like I said, why bother?"

"My husband never met a metaphor he couldn't mix," sighed Jude. "Now shut up, Henry, and mix some fresh drinks instead."

Over dessert – soggy tiramisu – talk turned to Snowy Bird. "Quite the woman," said Henry. "From what I hear."

"In what way?" asked Hugh, struggling to feign interest. Aside from that fleeting moment with Jude in the kitchen, the company had turned out to be as disappointing as the food, Henry's snide comments matched by Lucy's lack of tact. He suspected that the invitation to dinner might've been Henry's idea all along; a chance to get a close-up look at the deluded writer and mock his aspirations.

"Just that Snowy Bird's one of your formidable local types," Henry opined. "Able to strangle an injured pheasant with one hand and demand a bypass round Lowmorten with the other. Reminds me of our late Queen."

"Is a bypass on the cards?" Lucy asked.

Henry scratched a cheek. "In the wind, as they say. Point is, nothing gets done around here without the Snowy Bird seal of approval. Even The Grange needed the imperial nod. Doubt she'd have flung herself in front of a JCB once we got planning permish but, as the pencil-pusher from the council put it, 'Always best to have key locals onside.' Snowy's a key local."

"Did you know her maiden name was Lamb?" Jude asked her guests.

"No!" gasped Hugh. "Snowy Lamb? That's priceless. If I used that in a book, no one would believe it!"

"Think the locals just take their names from the first fauna and flora they clap eyes on."

"Foxy Roadkill is still available," laughed Henry.

"Maybe her son Pinky should be called Snowy," said Lucy, twirling her glass. "I reckon he could be the local coke supplier."

Jude gazed at her. "Where'd you hear *that*? Bloke barely has an opposable thumb."

"I thought you said he had fingers in lots of pies?" Lucy batted back.

"Never said he was Yorkshire's answer to Pablo Escobar!"

"Oh? Got the impression you knew him pretty well."

"Don't recall saying that, either."

"But when we met for lunch, you said-"

Jude rose abruptly from the table. "Seconds for anyone before I offer the rest of this sad pudding to the dog we don't have?"

11

"Well, that was interesting," observed Lucy on the drive 'home', navigating the unlit switchbacks with care. "You can tell they're both bored to tears by country life but seem resigned to it. They've made their comfy king-size bed, now they have to lie in it."

Hugh, flushed with too much drink, muttered: "Why'd you make that carbuncle crack? And go to town on winding up Jude?"

"That's a bit rich. You and Henry came close to butting heads."

"No, I bent over backwards to be polite. Despite that dickhead provoking me."

"That why you let him think you'd ever be into golf?"

"I was being a good guest. Why *did* you wind Jude up about that Pinky bloke?"

"Think she may be on the old marching powder, that's all. Saw a white trail in her nostrils the day I met her. Plus, she told me that Snowy's son was a local operator, so I joined the dots."

"Huh. You ask me, if anyone's the local supplier, could be Snowy herself. Clue's in the name."

"That's a childhood nickname. Come on, can you see her giving Walter White a run for his money?"

"Yeah, I can. Cooking up crystal meth alongside the York-shires in beef dripping. Perfect cover. Don't look at me like that. It's no more cracked than your theory about the son. Which is my point."

Lucy jounced through a pothole. "I noticed you were happy to go on about being a writer without reminding them that I'm an artist."

"Are you? Not since we moved here. Done *any* work in that studio yet?"

"It's not like writing, Hugh."

"Oh yeah, I forgot. A lot more involved in looking at a bloody apple and copying it. You don't need to defend me to the likes of Henry Hollenbeck, by the way, going on about my grit and determination. And why's this car so bloody cold?"

Her foot pressed the accelerator, knuckles white on the wheel. "Because I bought an old banger before I knew your parents had dropped £10k in your lap! You know, the £10k that helps you pay your way."

"Look, I told you, that money-"

A creature reared up in the dark moorland road, yellow eyes burning like lamps. Lucy swerved to try to avoid it. A sickening thud, followed by a bone-crunching thump as a body landed on the bonnet. Lucy hit the brake and screamed.

Hugh leapt out of the car, Lucy gasping and shaking as she stared at the body.

Hugh's outline filled the glow cast by her headlights, his shadow elongated and thrown behind him in long black fingers. He opened the door on her side. "A rabbit," he confirmed shakily. "Already dead and leaking blood when someone dropped it."

"Or chucked it at us?" she trembled, gazing at long, fur-lined ears and a golden eye staring up at her, filmed with death.

"I think you nearly flattened someone crossing the road in

front of us. They got as big a fright as we did and dropped Bugs before scarpering."

"Or *tossed* Bugs."

"You were giving it some welly on a narrow road. In the dark."

She glared at him. "What exactly are you accusing me of?"

"Luce..."

"Yes?"

"Nothing."

"You're saying that if anyone should be a careful driver, it's me?"

"What are we going to do about Bugs?"

"Put on these and chuck it at the side of the road." She drew off her gloves and tossed them out of the door. "If it belongs to a poacher, they may come back after we leave."

Hugh looked startled. "Why would it be a poacher?"

She thought of Jude's claim about Pinky Bird's activities in Napier's Wood. "Who else would be running around in the dark waving a dead rabbit? See if there's still a snare round its neck."

"I won't if you don't mind." He pulled on the gloves and dragged the rabbit off the bonnet with a squeal of trailing blood. Seconds later, he climbed back into the car, tossing her gloves into the dark verge. "I'll wash the car in the morning."

She put the Honda into gear. "Anyone who comes across it might chalk it up to Jude's speeding. Poor thing."

"People have to eat, Luce."

"Come off it, Hugh, it's not the 18th century; labourers starving because cruel landowners have enclosed the land. There's a 24-hour Tesco in Sowersby."

"You're shaking," he noticed. "You OK to drive?"

"I'm fine." She didn't want to linger in the rural night a second longer than necessary. "Put your seatbelt on."

Was it a poacher she wondered, and if so, was it Pinky Bird? They were nearly back at the gates of Rook House. It seemed even likelier that Snowy had concocted that big cat story to leave Napier's Wood clear for Pinky. Which made Lucy angry. Napier's Wood was on their land. Should she tell the letting agent her suspicions? Or Hugh?

She glanced at his grim profile. They'd probably said enough for tonight, that crack about her driving taking the final biscuit.

Why didn't *he* learn to drive if he was such an expert? Stupid git. Sensing her foot creeping down on the accelerator as she approached a bend, she drew it back in time, loath to give him further ammo.

When Snowy arrived the following Wednesday, they said nothing about the rabbit incident and she didn't broach it. After Snowy left, Lucy recalled that they still lacked a contact phone number for her. Plus, Snowy had her own back door key and never knocked.

"We'll have to tell her that's not on."

"Yeah, stick your head in the lion's mouth, why not?" Hugh said helpfully.

Lucy was still dodging the attic and engaging in displacement activity. Hugh had his skateboarding cats and a turquoise notebook he stroked like some exotic animal pelt (she'd spied through a gap in the study door) while she flitted through the house on socked feet, avoiding giveaway creaks.

At one point she even read the guardianship agreement, drawn up between Hugh and the letting agency "on behalf of our client, Gymbr Holdings".

She Googled Gymbr Holdings but got nowhere. Shady set-up, when you thought about it. Was it one of those shell companies? To what end, though? Maybe the plan to turn the house into a conference centre was a money-laundering scheme.

She'd lied to Hugh about hearing the scrabbling sound in the bathroom again. She'd heard it on two subsequent occasions as she brushed her teeth before bed.

She still couldn't fathom *why* she'd lied – was it because she couldn't bear to see a shadow of doubt cross his eyes as he weighed her words?

Both times she'd sensed the sound before she heard it, switching off her electric toothbrush to stand in the cold bathroom and pay close attention. The scrabbling had seemed louder, as though claw-like fingers were getting closer to breaking through the wall.

Now she drank her last cup of tea at 5pm rather than risk a bathroom visit in the middle of the night.

Hugh, meanwhile, was piling up the empties behind the back door.

What you really know about this man, Lucy, hmm?

On Thursday, the electric heater they'd ordered online arrived. She carried it up to the attic and made herself stay there, working up a sketch of the sheep's wool she'd photographed on barbed wire.

She sketched lightly in charcoal on virgin paper, cross-hatching the darker parts, recalling the words of Mr Griffin, her school art teacher, that an artist should strive to "detect a contrast between light and dark without necessarily having the whole vista in front of them".

Easy for him to say, he'd exhibited at the Royal Academy. Lucy hadn't even exhibited to Hugh.

She switched to making a thank you note for the Hollenbecks, sketching a half-remembered outline of The Grange. She'd drop it off next time she was passing.

Thursday evening, Frances rang again on the green Bakelite phone, Hugh answering.

Lucy heard the low rumble of exchanged fire as she chopped parsnips in the kitchen.

Hugh came in and rolled his eyes. "Pickled again."

"Oh?"

"Dunno if you've already guessed but Ma's what Dad likes to call a 'functioning' alcoholic behind her back. Caveat being, she's the only one who thinks she's functioning. Even he doesn't believe it."

"Oh," was all Lucy could repeat, brooding again on nurture versus nature.

Frances and Hugh weren't biologically linked, yet he was also fond of his drink.

Maybe he'd watched Frances taking crafty nips at the school gates from a silver hip flask. Monogrammed. "She always been like that?"

"Long as I can remember. Some sort of breakdown in her 20s. Never discussed, naturally. Officially she's a happy homemaker with no regrets." He plucked a clean wine glass off the draining board, Lucy staring hard at a parsnip. "I remember one time they both came to uni to watch me in a play," he continued. "Mum nearly missed the whole thing, clinging to a stool in the union bar. Overheard a few people call her 'the drunken Driscoll'. Dad's stuck his head in the sand for so long, he's become another dysfunctional Driscoll. You didn't hear any of that from me, perish the thought."

Truth be told, Lucy was dismayed to hear any unvarnished truths about Hugh's parents. She preferred to think of them as reserved and stand-offish but essentially wholesome. Still, she was touched by Hugh opening up to her like this. "I'm so sorry, Hugh. That must've been tough for you, growing up."

He paled. "Don't need your pity, Luce."

Her dismay deepened. "It's sympathy, not pity. Seems like Frances has had a tough time of it, too."

"Anyhoo, she was ringing to firm up arrangements for her and Pops to come visit. Told her they can't stay here, so I'm leaning towards a room at The Rusty Nail in Lowmorten. Four out of five on TripAdvisor."

"We should scope it out first," said Lucy. "The food menu, I mean."

It would be a chance for them to get out of this house and relax, maybe even talk about things big and small. Just talk, full stop. She was ashamed of her outburst on the drive back from The Grange; well, at least some of her petty broadsides before The Rabbit Incident. If she knew anything about Hugh, he was feeling the same way. He just found it harder to admit.

On Friday morning, with the weather fine, she took a sketchbook outside, found a dry stump to perch on and made charcoal sketches of stone and tree bark, planning to add colour back in her studio.

She returned to the house for lunch, calling in at Hugh's study.

No sign of him, laptop shut.

In the kitchen, a note under a fridge magnet revealed he'd "gone out for a walk to clear sinuses like you suggested".

She tutted. Yeah, but she'd meant *together*. And he'd given no timeline. Had he gone out ten minutes or an hour ago? When would he be back?

She was buttering a heel of bread when the back door opened. She turned, butter knife in hand. "Hugh, I – who the hell are you?"

12

The stranger advanced into the kitchen, looking around. He was about her own age; tall, broad-shouldered and thick-haired, wearing Doc Martens, a long dark coat and jeans anchored by a belt with a silver star in the buckle.

They both regarded her snub-nosed knife and he said with amusement, "happen that would cut an atmosphere and not much else. Didn't mean to startle you, like. I'm Pinky, Snowy's son."

She spotted the signet ring on his little finger and relaxed her grip on the knife. "Do all the Birds come and go as they please without so much as a door-knock?"

"Pretty much. Could've used my own key front or back." He drew a bunch of keys from a coat pocket. "Not that I've visited in a while."

Lucy was annoyed. "I'm not happy about that. Can you leave your keys here, please?"

"No problem." He set them beside the butter dish, smiling at her. A Pyrrhic victory. He probably had copies.

"I didn't even hear you drive up."

"Fancied the walk. Parked up outside t'gates."

She took a deep breath. "To what do I owe the pleasure?"

His smile faltered. He was darkly handsome, she thought, surprised by the thought. It summoned up a stock image from romantic fiction.

"I wanted to explain about rabbit t'other night. Your hubby here? Then I can do the honours in one go."

"He's gone out. We thought the rabbit might've been you. Were you poaching in our wood?"

"Well now, it is and it isn't your wood," he replied mildly. "So 'poaching' is a strong word."

"A mighty strong word," she agreed, gesturing to his silver buckle. "I see there's a new sheriff in town."

"Point is, Mrs D, I never meant to scare you like that. Didn't see your car coming before I stepped out. Had a look at your bonnet just now and can't see a dent."

"Luckily."

"Mind you, that car's probably worth more as scrap."

"You've taken a while to come and say this," she pointed out. "Why now?"

"Don't want there to be any – misunderstandings – about my future activities."

"Right." She wondered whether Snowy had found out about the dead rabbit and sent him round. "Is it safe for us to walk in the wood?" she demanded. "Traps have been mentioned."

"If you must go walking, you're perfectly safe, yes. I prefer to use a ferret and purse net to chase rabbits out of the burrow, then freeze them with a light. That's why I work at night."

"You catch them for food?"

"Sell to an organic meat producer," he nodded. "Pheasants are top dollar, rabbits more of a sideline. I'm no bother to you, Mrs D. If you hear lampers in Napier's Wood, though, or see their lights, let me know. They can be nasty, pesky buggers, ruining land and even coming down this way on quad bikes, scaring the life out of tenants."

"I see. What about escaped big cats?"

He smiled again. He had excellent teeth. "Oh, that. Talk of it a while back. Ma's taken with the idea but there's no substance to it."

"Based on your extensive experience of being in the wood at all hours?"

"If you like." He extended a hand. "Let us be friends, Mrs D."

"It's Lucy." She looked down at his square-fingered, capable hand, then gripped it. His handshake was firm and lingering. He smelt of sandalwood, its strength a little overpowering. "Can I ask a favour of you, Mr Bird?"

"Pinky."

"Pinky." She outlined the "favour".

His navy-blue eyes widened. "I'm not a plumber."

"I only want you to take down the piece of wood and a few tiles behind the bathroom sink. Like I said, we've heard this weird scratching behind the wall, maybe in the wall itself. I want to make sure it's not an infestation of some kind. That's within the remit of our responsibilities as guardians."

He rubbed his jawline. "S'pose I could throw my eye over it. Now I'm here."

Up in the bathroom, his doubt returned. "Reckon those are the original tiles put in by old Ezra. He wouldn't take kindly to them being mucked about. One or two might crack if dislodged."

"Then can you recommend someone to do it?"

"Probably." He got down on all fours, just as she'd done the first time she'd heard the noise, and pressed an ear to the yellowing wood behind the sink. He put his finger to his lips to indicate she should be quiet. Lucy held her breath.

"Nope," he frowned after a few moments, springing to his feet. "Can't hear owt moving about in there."

"If it's a mouse or something, maybe it's asleep?"

"I *could* take a closer look, s'pose. Have to check first with owner and you might be liable for accidental damage."

"I'm OK with that."

"Wait here."

He bounded down the stairs, pulling a phone from his coat pocket. She stood on the landing rather than loiter in the bathroom. She could hear him talking into his phone behind the closed kitchen door.

He returned, tapping the phone against his hip. "Owners said to go for it if you've heard a noise more than once; best check it out before summat chews through wires or pipes. I'll get my tools."

"Wait, you'll do it now?"

"No time like the present. I've probably enough tools in the truck for an initial look-see. Unless you were planning to take a bath?"

"No, now is fine. Wait – how come you've got the phone number for Gymbr Holdings?"

He smiled at her pronunciation without correcting it. "Off Ma, what with her being the housekeeper here."

"Oh, yes, of course. So. Carry on."

He gave a mock salute. "Yes, milady. Back in a jiff. I'll knock on the back door this time."

She followed him down the stairs, hugging her elbows. After telling him about the scratching, she'd been primed for him to say: "Oh, *that* old noise. The infamous scratching of Rook House. Pay it no regard."

His dismissal would have been reassuring proof that a noise couldn't hurt her.

She plucked her phone off the kitchen table and texted Hugh: "*Where r u? Pinky Bird, Snowy's son, has turned up. I've asked him to check out that old bit of wood in bathroom.*"

No need to be more specific. She didn't want to refer to the scratching directly.

A swift reply: "*I shoulda said on my fridge note – decided to walk into Lowmorten, check out its pub grub like u said. Might be a while.*"

She stared at this missive in frustration. He was going to The Rusty Nail on his own after what she'd said about sampling the menu together?

Pinky knocked loudly on the kitchen door and came in carrying a battered metal toolbox.

"Here we are again." Wide grin. "Let the dog see the rabbit. As it were."

She hovered in the bathroom doorway as he set to work. "Do you want a cuppa or anything?"

"Nah. Best get on with it."

She watched him prise away the ugly piece of yellow wood. "Old glue," he grimaced. "Doubt this were done in Ezra's day."

Next he chipped away the tiles that lay behind the piece of wood, exposing a bare wall darker in some places than others.

"There's your problem for starters." He poked a finger into the wall and plaster crumbled away. "Damp's wet the plaster, see? Happening a while from looks of. You'd need one of those damp detectors to pick it up." He scraped away more plaster with his fingernail, setting Lucy's teeth on edge. "There's a gap of sorts behind this wall."

Lucy blinked. "You mean the wall cavity itself?"

"No, a bigger gap." He tapped the wall. Lucy wondered, briefly, if he was winding her up.

"What's t'other side of this wall?" he asked.

"A bedroom." The acanthus room with the writhing wallpaper. "Why?"

"Let's go see."

She led him into the acanthus room. It was bitterly cold. "S'pose you turn off rads in rooms you're not using," he observed, blowing on his hands.

"No. One of the rules of guardianship is that we heat each room until the start of April." She touched the single radiator beneath the uncurtained window. It nearly burnt her hand.

Pinky hunkered down, examining the wall opposite the fireplace, and tapping again.

He eased to his feet and went out to the landing, moved about briefly and returned moments later to the acanthus room. "I reckon there's a much bigger space between the bathroom wall and this room than between the other bedrooms." He looked puzzled. "Easier to know what's what if we break through the wall from this side towards the bathroom. If you're up for that, I'll have to use a sledgehammer."

"God, I don't know..."

"Your shout. Well, the owners' shout, I s'pose, but that damp on the bathroom side could be just the tip of a nasties' iceberg."

"You mean a family of mice?"

"Put it this way. I once took down a bath panel that was 'rippling a bit', quote unquote. You shoulda seen what poured out. Cockroach City, Arizona."

"Don't!" she shuddered, recalling Hugh's wind-up about deathwatch beetles. "Look, if you break through the wall, can you repair it afterwards?"

"Hang on." He was feeling along the wall now, fingers splayed over twisted fronds of acanthus. "There's a door here, been papered over!" he said with excitement. "No more than four feet high. Pretty thickly papered over. If I can uncover this, no need to go knocking down walls. Could be a real room waiting to be found. Bloody hell!" He stepped back and grinned at her. "I feel like Howard Carter discovering the tomb of King Tut!"

Lucy didn't feel the same way but shared his relief that the wall could remain intact. "A door? To a room?"

"Pretty small room, but yep. I could rip off paper here with your say-so and take it from there."

She nodded. It felt foolish to balk at this key juncture. What might they discover? Dear God, not a skeleton or the mummified body of one of the poor servant girls!

But somebody had concealed a small doorway behind a thick layer of wallpaper. Whatever lay on the other side backed on to the bathroom and was the possible source of a weird, unnerving scratching.

As Pinky tried, experimentally, to peel away the stubborn wallpaper, she had another thought. "Your mother told Hugh that this wallpaper was added in the 1980s or thereabouts. So the door would have been known about pretty recently."

"You're right there." He frowned at the wallpaper. "Not coming off easily, even without another layer underneath. I'll fetch a steamer from home. But just cos someone knew the door was there, doesn't mean they went inside any room it's hiding. Or door coulda been papered over on the orders of Marianne before she died in the 90s. She had this place rented out after she inherited. Maybe the kids of a tenant were mucking around with the door, trying to get in or break the padlock, so she ordered it covered up. Back in the day, might even have been a piece of furniture pushed against the wall as an added deterrent to poking about."

To keep people out or something else *in*? Lucy looked back at the place where he'd indicated the door's location.

"I'll run home for that steamer. I'm as curious as you are."

"All right. Thank you."

His footsteps fading as he bounded down the stairs, Lucy sat in the acanthus room with her back against one side of the tiled fireplace, knees drawn under her chin, worrying her gold locket.

The room was still bitter, though she knew the radiator would still be scalding to touch.

Lunch forgotten, part of her wanted to flee and hide in the attic with the door shut and the winter sun streaming over her papers and scattered pencils. But another part didn't want to leave this room to its own devices.

As she picked at loose skin round her thumbnail, a sound made her freeze. *Scratch, scratch, scratch.* Terror seized her by the throat. She shifted on her haunches. *Scratch.*

She twisted round. The plastic loops on her jeans belt were rubbing against the tiles of the fireplace each time she made the tiniest movement, creating a softly localised *scratch, scratch, scratch*.

She was so relieved, she laughed out loud.

Then she blinked. It was hard *not* to stare at the curving green-and-gold pattern on the wallpaper and, as she stared, to imagine the fern-like leaves were reflowing into serpentine coils that matched the ring on her finger, feathery blades locked in incestuous embrace.

Her eyes seemed unable to blink now. Little flashing lights followed. No! This was how one of her migraines started – staring at an intricate repeating pattern until it merged with a flashing brightness.

But she couldn't seem to stop.

As she stared and stared, the outline of the door shouldered forward through the paper, pushing aside veined acanthus leaves. And then came a snub protrusion pressed up against green and gold. Maybe a doorknob.

She clambered to her feet and inched forward, head starting to pulse with distant pain. When she touched the wallpaper around the 'knob', it fell away in heavy strips at her feet and she stepped back with a cry.

There *was* something there, an exposed shard of dark wood. She touched the wood and more wallpaper subsided at her feet. The room behind the wallpaper wanted her to come in. Her alone.

Working in a trance and ignoring the pain flashing behind her eyes, she tore through the rest of the paper as if through butter, until the Hobbit-sized door revealed itself.

It was a crude, flat piece of wood and the doorknob wasn't a knob at all, but a sloe-eyed bolt of tarnished silver. She stooped and fumbled with it, trying to shoot it back, the sharp edges catching her fingertips. This freshly localised pain made her stop and think.

Shouldn't she wait for Pinky's return? *No*, said a voice inside her aching head. He'll want to be the first to light a match and discover 'wonderful things'.

Not that she had any matches. Maybe a torch was in order? But she didn't want to stop – didn't want Pinky to come sailing through the back door while she was still rooting through a kitchen drawer for the heavy rubber torch she knew Hugh possessed.

She fiddled with the stiff bolt again, pushing it back, bit by finger-pinching bit, until it yielded all the way. The door, she realised, opened inwards, if it could be opened at all. The wood was warped by time and concealment, its surface pitted with old wallpaper paste. She doubted that anyone had opened it in years, probably not even in the 1980s.

Excitement gnawed at her gut, but the same teeth bit through her soft tissue, causing acid reflux. And her head – Christ, she'd pay for this later, assuming the headache became a full-blown migraine.

Her stomach was only recoiling from the smell, she told herself: the smell of old, decayed wood and musty plaster. Of yet more loss this house had sealed within itself.

The door still wouldn't budge. She hunkered at the knees and braced her shoulder against it, grunting. The door opened inwards with a silent suddenness that tipped her forward, bumping her head on the lintel. She half-fell into a dusty, dark space, clambering upright too quickly and grazing her head again on a low ceiling. "Ow!"

She stooped and swivelled, terrified the door would swing

shut behind her, maybe this time with an ominous creak. But the door stood ajar, offering a glimpse of the acanthus room in weakening daylight.

She about-turned again. Light from the bedroom leaked into the darkness. It was freezing in here, colder even than the room she'd left behind.

She scuttled forward on her haunches, aiming for a square of wall paler than the rest – that must be where Pinky had removed the bathroom tiles on the other side and scraped away the plaster.

A gust of air blew across the back of her neck. She raised a hand above her head and touched a rough sort of air brick vibrating gently.

Oxygen, ventilation. She knew what that might mean.

The wooden floor was littered with splinters. The space was empty, though she could smell something coppery, like rust, or blood.

Another gust of air blew past her through the air brick, flinging the door shut, sealing her in complete darkness.

She opened her mouth, not so much to scream, as to gasp instinctively for air, only to feel a hand on her arm, bony fingers denting the flesh under her jumper and someone breathing close to her ear.

Braced against the door, instinct told her to claw the hand away, but it held her there with easy insistence, and then the voice began.

It was no more than a whisper and she couldn't make out individual words. They ran into each other and thickened like the buzz of bees in a distant orchard. Gradually, a few words did take shape: *want... you hear?... coming, coming... a fly... my boy...*

Was the voice coming from inside her own head? Her own terror forging and coiling words out of freezing, dark air?

Darkness was blooming inside her and pouring through her, behind her eyes and filling her lungs, the darkness of fire-scorched leaves writhing through her like black blood filling her veins. *He's coming.*

She couldn't breathe, she couldn't breathe...

And then it was over.

13

A rising mist caught Hugh off-guard as soon as he left the house, gossamer-fine skeins of white thickening against his face. He slowed his step, denuded branches poking here and there from the veiled elms like skeletal supplicants pleading for alms.

Then, just as suddenly, a shimmering arc lifted above the trees, haloed with dazzling, defined white. Its sudden perfection made him uneasy, though he recognised the feature – a fogbow, aka a white rainbow.

He felt guilty for chucking a note on the fridge and doing a runner, but he'd had to get out of the house without delay or explanation. Away from his so-called work in progress.

He looked at his phone. It was a two-mile walk to Lowmorten along a grass verge on a corkscrew road. He'd have earned a hearty meal at The Rusty Nail by the time he arrived. A real-ale pub, it said online. His dad would like that.

He was still smarting over their row on the drive back from The Grange. It had struck a nerve when Lucy brought up the £10k as though he was keeping it all to himself. Not true. She only had to ask when she wanted a few readies. But they hadn't discussed it since.

Hadn't discussed anything, really. He'd blabbed about his mother's tippling and regretted it the second he saw gleeful pity in Lucy's eyes. At last he'd given her something to prove that his own background might be almost as fucked-up as her own. Rookie mistake.

Beyond the gates, fog still drifted. Hearing a car behind him, he stepped deeper into the verge.

The car slid out of wraith-like fronds. Jude stopped and wound down her window. "You should be wearing hi-viz in this weather. Hop in before you get frostbite or splatted by a hay baler."

He complied with relief.

"And your shoes," she observed as he claimed the passenger seat, "might as well be paper hankies. Bet your socks are soaking too. Didn't you do any research before you came to these here perished parts? Where to, anyway?"

Now they were alone together, he thought better of Lowmorten. "Just walking to clear my head. Where you headed?"

"Nowhere I can't go later."

She slid about on the road, following twists and turns bathed sickly yellow by her fog lights. Hugh sank into cream leather with his eyes shut, allowing his mind to drift in sync with the fog, the car's warmth spiced with Jude's rich perfume. He knew that something was about to happen between them and felt drowsy with anticipation.

The car stopped. "We're just about here, I reckon."

He opened his eyes, staring out at nothingness. "Where's here?"

"Follow me and I'll show you."

He got out and watched her walk to the rear boot (the Cayman also had a front boot, he knew), swapping heels for wellies, her cream coat for a long, padded jacket.

"You should've been a girl guide," he observed, shivering in his jeans.

"How'd you know I wasn't? C'mon."

She led him through a hole in a spiky hedge, up a slope and along the edge of a sagging barbed wire fence, stopping at a child-sized gap. "Here we are. Accessible if you stoop. Just mind you don't cut yourself."

"Are we breaking and entering?"

"Nah. It's your own pear orchard, but this is a back way in." She nipped through the gap and waited for him to follow.

The fog rolled away suddenly on the other side to reveal a tumbling vista of black-branched trees. He trailed in her wake towards a gap-toothed stone wall. She plonked down and lit a cigarette.

"That's a lot of pear trees," he noted pedantically, sitting beside her and tucking his bare hands under his armpits to keep warm. He imagined the scene in autumn as a Lucy still life: honey-coloured fruit punctured by wasps and blackbirds, yellow seams bursting with pulpy ripeness.

Jude inhaled with her eyes shut. "God, that feels good." She held the cigarette out to him.

"I shouldn't."

"I won't tell if you won't."

He took the aromatic cigarette. Yeah, it did feel good, especially out here in the burningly cold air. "How come you've forsaken the evil weed but Henry still clings to his Cubans?"

"Oh, I made the mistake of declaring I felt a new me coming on and now I have to stick to it for a while. We've got a bet going that I won't last to the end of this month, Fendi handbag at stake." She retrieved the cigarette and nodded to the dark-ribbed trees. "Phineas Napier is buried under one, along with his stillborn twin, who was buried first, obviously."

"Yeah, I read about that."

His phone buzzed. He drew it from his pocket, glanced at it, then tapped out a text and slid the phone back into his pocket.

"Who's that?" asked Jude.

"Luce. Wanting an update on my whereabouts."

"Pulling on the leash?"

He bristled. "Hardly."

She drew on the cigarette again. "I come here to think sometimes. Don't ask me about what."

Hugh glanced under the trees again, but now all he saw was a pile of split yellow fruit with rotten hearts, mashed by careless treading and left to spoil in the long grass. He saw his non-starter of a book.

"I got fired yesterday," he said. "I had a day job to pay the bills but missed a couple of deadlines. Turns out I was on borrowed time and didn't know it. Plenty chomping at the Cuban to replace me. Haven't told Luce yet."

"Don't they have to give you three warnings and all that stuff?"

"I was a freelancer."

"More time to write, then."

"I'm blocked."

"Try a high fibre diet." She sucked her cigarette once more, blowing an imperfect smoke ring as white as the recent fogbow. "Sorry."

"I love Lucy, but..."

She stopped his self-pity with a kiss. Her mouth tasted of blackberries more than nicotine. She looked up at him, eyes deep and cool as wine vats. "Henry's at his stupid golf club. We've got The Grange to ourselves for a while, if we hurry."

Jude dropped him off later at the gates of Rook House. They hadn't spoken since leaving The Grange or made further arrangements. He was ashamed of what he'd done, while fairly certain the concept of shame was alien to Jude. He could hardly judge her for that.

His head was starting to throb from the line of coke they'd

shared. His first in years. If memory served, he'd have one hell of a coming-down headache.

Halfway up the tunnel of elms, he heard a beep and turned to see an old Ford truck rattling his way. It pulled alongside and a beefy bloke leant out of the cab. "Mr D, I presume? I'm Snowy's son, Pinky. Hop in."

Hugh obeyed (Jude had dried out his socks at The Grange, but they'd grown freshly absorbent in the last few minutes). 'Pinky' told him about the damp spot behind the bathroom sink and the discovery of a possible door in the wall of the acanthus room.

"Wait, an actual door? To a secret room?"

"That's what we need to find out. Ran home to fetch a wallpaper steamer. It took longer than I thought. Left your missus on point."

Hugh stepped through the back door and called out for Lucy. No answer. "Maybe she's up in the attic. It's pretty well soundproofed up there."

Pinky took the stairs two at a time, then paused on the landing. The light was fading fast, but he pointed down at the floorboards. "See those?"

Hugh peered. "Don't see anything."

"Palm prints pressed into the wood. See how the light just catches the outlines of fingers?" Pinky walked carefully alongside prints that Hugh couldn't detect. "And they end at this door."

"That's our bedroom."

Hugh went in. Lucy was lying on the bed. When he shook her gently, she didn't respond.

He shook her more forcefully, noticing seams of dark dust veining her jumper and jeans. What had she been doing? "Lucy, love, it's me and Mr Bird."

Finally, she stirred, stretched and yawned, rubbing her eyes. "Had the strangest dream..." She sat up when she saw Pinky behind Hugh, blushing richly. "Oh, I- you've come to mend the damp patch?"

"We agreed I'd uncover the door in the wall first." Pinky was already striding towards the acanthus room, Lucy and Hugh scrambling after him.

Lucy pushed past Hugh. "I never meant to... oh."

They were all in the acanthus room now. Lucy stared at the wall in amazement, Hugh gazing at her in puzzlement.

Pinky went over to the wall. "Right, reckon I should start about... here." He touched the spot where he'd plucked unsuccessfully at the wallpaper. Otherwise, the paper was completely intact.

Lucy licked her lips. "But where is...? I mean, I could've sworn a lot of that paper had already come away. But – it's all in place."

"Apart from the bit I tried to peel away," shrugged Pinky, moving his hand higher. "Look! Now the light's moved, you can see the outline of a wardrobe that musta been shoved against the wall, just where I said. I've got the steamer in the truck. I'll grab it and make a start."

"No! Thanks, but I've changed my mind," gasped Lucy. "We don't want anything disturbed. Do we, Hugh?"

Hugh frowned. "But if it's a door..."

"Pinky would have to steam off all that thick old wallpaper and then replace it. That'll cost. And for what? An old store cupboard or something that's long forgotten about."

Hugh thought about his dwindling financial resources. "I see your point."

Pinky looked annoyed. "You were right keen before," he told Lucy.

But she was gazing down at the floor.

To Hugh's further bewilderment, she dropped on all fours, placing her palms carefully on the boards. "Do you see these?" She looked up. "Hand prints. Very faint but just visible. Someone crawled out of this room on their hands." Her body trembled as she shuffled forward on her knees, out of the room and on to the landing.

Pinky followed, saying, "I noticed prints out here just now. They stop outside your bedroom door."

"Fascinating as all this is," said Hugh, "I'm more concerned about this damp issue in the bathroom. I agree with you, Luce, no point ripping off perfectly good wallpaper to find some forgotten old cubby. Can't be anything like a priest hole because this house isn't old enough."

"It's your call." Pinky headed for the bathroom. "I *could* get someone to come round and assess the damp in here, give you a quote and fix it, but as per guardianship agreement, you're looking at the first £300 of repair costs. I checked."

Hugh grimaced. "We've only been here five minutes."

"Old house," shrugged Pinky. "Old enough, I mean."

Lucy had clambered to her feet and followed both men into the bathroom.

Hugh was shocked to see the stacked tiles and the water-darkened plaster behind the sink. What a mess the bloke had made already!

"And the scratching?" he asked Pinky. "Take it you didn't find anything to account for it?"

"Not yet," replied Pinky. "But that's partly why we wanted to open up the space between here and the room next door, to rule out any... anomalies. Mrs Driscoll – Lucy – may have forgotten that."

"I haven't forgotten," insisted Lucy. "I just have a feeling the scratching will stop now."

"You've a feeling." Hugh glanced at her in frustration. No wonder she was garlanded in dust, especially round the knees. How long had she been crawling about, investigating ghostly palm prints? "I suppose that's something."

He stalked towards the stairs, gesturing for Pinky to follow.

Pinky touched Lucy gently on her elbow, nodding down at her dangling hands. "Notice you've reefed a few fingertips," he said softly, his fingertips touching her own for a second. "How'd that happen?"

"Oh." Lucy raised her fingers and peered at them. "I opened a tin of salmon after you left. Must've nicked myself."

Pinky nodded, then followed an impatient Hugh down the stairs. In the kitchen, Pinky glanced into an overflowing swing-top bin, telling Hugh: "So if you're both agreed, I'll send someone more qualified round to throw their eye over the damp issue in the bathroom."

"Yeah, go for it, seeing as it's now such a mess. You'll let us know?"

Pinky nodded.

"Sorry if Luce has wasted your time," Hugh muttered, chastened by the man's expression. God, he could glower for a Brontë novel. "Give our best to your mother."

Pinky did something extraordinary then. He leant into Hugh's neckline and sniffed, Hugh recoiling. "What the hell are you doing?"

"Camel Blues," remarked Pinky. "As in, cigarettes? Not a lot of those sold around here." He smiled. "And you seem high on more than life, I noticed when you got in the truck."

"What?"

"See you around." He left through the back door, Hugh banging it shut behind him. The bloody nerve! But he was also alarmed.

Back upstairs, he found Lucy on all fours on the landing, walking forward on her knees, fitting her palms into shapes he couldn't see.

She looked up at him. "I thought maybe I was..." Then she caught her breath and glanced off to one side. "Nothing. It doesn't matter." She pulled herself together and upright.

"Did you have a good walk, blow away the cobwebs?"

"Yep." Now it was his turn to glance away. "Didn't make it to the pub in the end. Kept that for another day." He edged towards the disarrayed bathroom. "Think I'll have a quick shower. Got cold and damp on the walk back."

14

On Sunday, Lucy went to 10am Mass in Sowersby, seeking the comfort of childhood smells, bells and incantations. She asked Hugh if he wanted to come, hang around Sowersby and meet up afterwards, but he insisted he was working on his book. "Take all the time you need," he told her.

The Sacred Heart was balm to the weary soul, stiff with waxily fragrant flowers. Snowy's handiwork, presumably. Taking a seat at the back of the half-full church, Lucy saw Snowy up ahead, squashed felt hat dipped before the altar.

Lucy tried to sneak away at the final hymn but Snowy cornered her in the car park. "You keeping well, Lucy?"

"Yes, ta." She knew she looked haggard. "The church flowers are spectacular, a real credit to you, Snowy."

"That's a nasty bruise on your forehead," Snowy observed.

"Oh." She brushed her hair over the ripe mark uncovered by the wind. Hugh hadn't even noticed it. "Wasn't looking where I was going." That old chestnut. "Still getting used to all the nooks and crannies of the house."

"About that..." Snowy sucked in her lower lip. "Pinky was telling me about some old door behind the wallpaper in a bedroom."

"Something and nothing. We decided to leave it undisturbed and concluded that there must be similar niches all over the house."

"Possible," conceded Snowy. "At one point there was a log store beside the living room fireplace. Big enough to stand up in, with a door at the back that led into a passageway. It meant servants could restock the logs from the passageway without disturbing the family."

"You know a good bit about the house."

Snowy's smile spread as grudgingly as winter butter. "I know some things. And I think something is troubling you."

"Like what?"

"You tell me."

"There's nothing to tell."

Snowy waited, patient as hoar frost watching for early buds.

Lucy looked up at the sky and mumbled about the faint outline of handprints on the floor between the acanthus room and the master bedroom.

"Yes," said Snowy. "Pinky mentioned those too."

Next, Lucy studied a cloud that resembled a long-necked swan. "While I was waiting for Pinky to come back with his steamer, I must have lain down on our bed and drifted off. I dreamt I *did* find a room behind the wallpaper, that I unlocked the door and explored inside, but crawled out in panic, half-choked from lack of air. And I know that *was* just a dream because the wallpaper's undisturbed. But... then I saw palm prints on the floor and my fingers were skinned as though I'd nicked them on the door bolt."

She raised troubled eyes to Snowy's. "What does it mean? *Did* I dream about the room, I wonder?" She touched her forehead absently. "Or was I in there? I, I thought I heard a voice as well, but I couldn't make out what it was trying to say."

Snowy put a hand on her arm. "Come with me," she said in a tone Lucy had heard before – from Pinky, enquiring about her reefed fingers. "I'll take you to mine," said Snowy, "and we can have a proper talk out of this mithering cold."

• ⸪ ❖⬩◉⬩❖ ⸪ •

Lucy stowed Snowy's bicycle in the Honda's boot (unavoidably sticking out) and drove to a slate-roofed cottage on the outskirts of Lowmorten.

Despite its sloping walls and thick black beams, Lucy reckoned the cottage's chocolate-box appeal was deceptive, its small, single-glazed windows and odd angles bound to make repairs or redecorating difficult. It was also poky (what estate agents called "charmingly bijou"), the front door opening into a sitting room that flowed into a small, cluttered kitchen.

Still, it was a sight more homely and welcoming than The Grange. Or Rook House. Lucy would've lived here in a heartbeat.

"Pinky's out," said Snowy, hanging Lucy's coat on a hook over her own. "He'll send a plumber round early next week. Sit down and I'll make us a brew." She lifted a Brown Betty teapot off a 'souvenir of Windermere' tile on the kitchen worktop. "Grab that tin, second shelf on the left and help yourself."

Soon, Lucy was seated at the kitchen table enjoying an excellent cup of Darjeeling and a slice of the famous bandy tart. "What's in the secret recipe?" she asked.

"Oh, you've been briefed. Nowt secret as such, more a case of local family variations. I put in grated dark chocolate and a nip or two of plum brandy." She tapped her nose. "Perhaps more than a nip. Almonds tend to disguise it."

Lucy looked down at her plate. She usually swerved such a rich combination of triggering ingredients. Still, too late now. Besides, she felt her toes and fingers uncurl for the first time in perhaps weeks, the realisation a mild shock.

"You touch that locket a lot," Snowy observed.

"Belonged to my late mum."

"What's her name?"

The present tense caught Lucy unawares. "Rosa." Had Hugh ever asked her mother's name? "She was Italian."

"What was she like?"

"It's hard to remember. I was only five when she died." *She had blue-black hair that tickled my neck when she leant over me. I'd wrap my fingers round it and bury my face in its fragrant depths. She smelt of oranges and strawberry penny chews.* "A drink-driver killed her." She stumbled over the bare facts of a boy racer who "never saw" the woman on the zebra crossing before he hit her. "He got a short prison sentence and a slightly longer driving ban. So it goes." A tear splashed out. "Sorry."

Snowy handed her a box of paper tissues. "And your dad?"

"Died when I was 15. Heart attack. I sort of lived with my stepmother after that. We don't see eye to eye."

"You've had it hard and I'm sorry for it," said Snowy. She hesitated. "Coming to a place like Rook House, carrying what people call baggage..."

Lucy's head snapped up. "I didn't imagine the portrait on the wall being turned around or make up some lurid dream about an undiscovered room because I'm suggestible and messed up and need therapy!"

Snowy touched her hand across the table. "'Course not. Let me show you something."

She bustled away to open a cupboard, returning with a tin box lacquered in red and gold.

She raised the squeaking lid, lifting out a small square of off-white linen.

Unwrapping it revealed a tiny cross made from woven strands of wood. "It's very delicate, so I won't touch it," said Snowy, cheeks pinkening. "Belonged to my great-grandfather Mickey Nellis. Him that worked at Rook House as a gardener. There are letters inscribed along the arms of the cross. They spell out 'lignum sanctum'. Know what that means?"

Lucy shook her head.

"Holy wood," explained Snowy. "Or sacred wood. It's made of guaiacum wood, a tree believed to grow from a remnant of the very tree Our Lord's crucifixion cross was cut from. A priest gave it to Mickey when he learned that Mickey worked for Ezra Napier. Mickey didn't have much choice in who he worked for on account of being born with a foot turned inward. Couldn't go to the mills or the mines dragging his right kicker like that. Hereditary. Pinky was born with the same foot but they can fix it now, soon as the bab pops out. One thing Mickey did have was the green thumb. Ezra's head gardener took him on when others wouldn't."

"What are you saying? That Ezra was so evil, anyone working at Rook House needed the equivalent of garlic and a crucifix for protection?"

Snowy re-covered the little cross with the linen. "I'm saying that a priest certainly believed in taking no chances. As to your dream, Lucy, it disturbs me. A hidden room – I don't know. But your mind conjured it from somewhere. Perhaps..." She looked at the bruise on Lucy's forehead. "When you were sleepwalking?"

"And I what? Walked smack into a wall, thinking I was inside a room? I've never sleepwalked in my life!" Though she did wonder: could the onset of a migraine trigger a hallucination? It had never happened to her before, but then she'd never lived in Rook House before. She bit her lip. "I'm beginning to think it's really possible I was *in* that room behind the wallpaper!"

Snowy sighed. "To be honest, the sleepwalking theory would give me greater comfort." She paused. "They do say old houses speak to those they take a shine to, even show them things. On that front, I've not been completely honest. A few tenants *have* reported scratching in the bathroom on and off down the years, but nothing more. Even heard it myself once when I was cleaning – oh, going on six years ago? Sounded like-"

"Fingernails!" finished Lucy in a hoarse whisper. "Like – like when a person who's trapped scratches in vain for a way out."

Snowy shut the lid on the lacquered box. "Best not dwell on such things."

"Why not?" Lucy glared at her. "You're the one who said of Ezra, 'that old man likes to play tricks'. And now you've shown me a talisman that your great-grandfather kept to ward off evil. Why have you never investigated the scratching properly? Or the alleged screams of Belle Napier?"

"Because no one who reported the scratching heard it more than once. And, as far as I'm aware, there are no credible reports of a tenant hearing Belle screaming."

"What about the rumour that Phineas is a ghost there too?"

"That I give no credence to at all."

None of these answers satisfied Lucy. "D'you think Ezra rather than the house is showing me things? That he's on my wavelength?" She shuddered at the notion.

"Lucy." Snowy leant across the table and seized her hands. "I want you to leave Rook House for your own sake and the sake of your marriage. That place isn't good for you."

Lucy withdrew her hands. "I can't!"

"Why not?"

"Because."

"I'll speak to the owners on your behalf," said Snowy. "They'll find another couple quick enough."

"Tenants who won't show any curiosity or ask questions?" Lucy shook her head. "Hugh would never agree to it and we've nowhere else *to* go, unless his parents take us in. We want to stay here."

"I can help you rent another place local, if that's your sticking point." Snowy appeared anguished.

"But Rook House has that perfect art studio," said Lucy. She pushed her hands through her hair, colour rushing into her cheeks. "And I've had an idea for a painting, even while we've been sitting here talking. It's been tickling my mind for a while, waiting for the right moment to emerge. I need space to complete it."

"But Luc-"

"Look, you can tell Pinky I've changed my mind about not excavating behind the wallpaper. I *do* want to see what's there." She stood up and stepped around Snowy towards her coat. "Thanks for the hospitality."

"You could do that," said Snowy, "but what good will come of it?"

"It would solve a mystery," Lucy frowned. "At least one of them."

"Hardly. An empty room, if it exists, proves nowt. The Napiers are long gone. Don't summon them back. Live in the present. Make plans with Hugh. Plans away from that house."

"You said we were just what Rook House needed, a breath of fresh air!"

"I say a lot of things. Plenty I regret in the great scheme of things."

Lucy seized another handful of her fizzing curls. "I need to know what's going on in that house. It's eating away at me. Am I the catalyst? Or do I just have an overactive imagination?"

"Curiosity killed many a cat. Ask me, you've latched on to Rook House and its so-called mysteries as a form of *self*-therapy. Maybe a distraction from your own past."

"That's ridiculous."

But Lucy sat back down at the kitchen table and curled her nails into her palms. "I heard scratching noises, Snowy, and then Pinky found the outline of a door to a hidden room, and... and..."

"Forget all that," urged Snowy. "I should never have said what I did about old Ezra playing tricks. What's your plan for when you're back in London?"

"You're trying to manage me. It won't work."

Snowy stuck to her guns. "How'd you meet his nibs?"

"Hugh?" Lucy glared at her. "In a bar."

"And your parents? How'd they meet?"

Lucy paused. At least she could be honest about some things. "At the Trevi Fountain in Rome. Dad was on a weekend break with a couple of friends. He saw Mum from a distance, sketching the fountain. He shook off his friends a bit later and rushed back to see if she was still there, bringing a bottle of cold lemonade because she was sitting on a little folding stool without shade. He told me that story after she died. He was older than her, quite serious. Debonair, probably. He flew to Rome three times in three months and, on his third trip, asked her to marry him."

"What did her family make of the dashing older Englishman in a hurry to marry their daughter?"

"She was brought up by a reclusive 'aunt', who may or may not have been her mother. Aunt Gianna never showed any inclination to visit England, not even for Mum's funeral, and died four years ago. I never got to the bottom of it, but Dad hinted once that Mum was the illegitimate daughter of the Visconti somebody or other. He'd paid for her upbringing and education on the understanding that she was to be cut loose at 18. But..." Lucy shrugged. "Who knows?"

"So she was an artist too?"

"A frustrated one, like me." She gave a brittle laugh. "She'd had no formal training but she did have talent. She worked on a little desk in the hallway between kitchen and sitting room in our London flat. It was a thoroughfare, really. She'd snatch a minute here and there when she could." Lucy brooded. "I suppose motherhood got in the way. The pram in the hallway edging out the desk in the hallway."

Snowy touched the side of her Brown Betty pot. "I'll brew us another."

"From the time I could toddle, she'd take me to the National

Gallery. To share her love of art, I think. We'd always stop at her favourite painting, *Portrait of a Lady with a Squirrel and a Starling.* I don't know why it fascinated her so much, but I return to it myself, hoping to see her fascination reflected back to me." She blushed at over-sharing and stood up. "I won't have another cuppa, ta. Will you ask Pinky about helping to find this hidden room?"

"He'll have to check with the owners. He's already had to report the bathroom issue."

"You implied it wouldn't be a problem."

"I only meant it wouldn't take Pinky long to do the job."

Lucy shrugged on her coat. "If there *is* a room, it has to mean something."

Snowy bit her lip deeply, then raised a finger. "Wait now just a moment. I've a little something to take back with you."

15

Hugh had been surprised by Lucy's religious revival, though she claimed that attending Mass was more to do with exploring the local area. "Come with me," she'd said. "I'll drop you in Sowersby and we can meet up afterwards for an early lunch."

"No can do. At a critical point in the book. Don't want to lose momentum."

He'd no idea if she was buying his lies.

As soon as she drove off, he abandoned his swivel chair and paced about, brooding.

The house felt different recently – restless, watchful. He'd been more at ease on his first night here alone, companioned by the wind.

Maybe his guilt was getting to him. And he did feel guilty about sleeping with Jude.

Jude *was* bored out of her skull. He was just the latest distraction.

"History of substance abuse in my family," he'd said as she deftly chopped up a line of coke on a bedside cabinet.

"Lighten up. This is just to get us in the mood. No one's asking you to stick a needle between your toes."

"Do you usually need a recreational stimulant to get in the mood?"

"Yep. I do a line – discreetly – half an hour before Henry takes his little blue pill."

"Too much info."

"Welcome to a marriage of convenience. Not that there's any other kind."

Her cynical wit was arguably bleaker when she was high.

Not that it proved a passion killer. Far from it. He found her exciting. She was nothing like him or Lucy. She didn't feel any pressure to find a purpose, pursue a passion, justify her existence. She just *was*. Like a giant redwood. He envied her.

Sex had been meandering and prolonged. At one point she'd read a text over his shoulder, yet that hadn't spoilt his enjoyment.

Sex with Lucy was quiet, intense, furtive, as though they were burrow animals clinging to each other within earshot of a predator. And she just lay there, leaving it all up to him. Probably the fault of that Luke bloke, her only serious ex. Plus the Catholic upbringing.

Alongside his guilt, he had that Pinky bloke to worry about: "You're looking at £300... Camel Blues, as in cigarettes?... High on more than life, I noticed."

Bloke had enjoyed twisting the knife with every word. Was he dangerous or just petty? A blackmailer? He'd be disappointed if he thought Hugh had deep pockets.

He left his study and headed to the kitchen for a vino top-up.

Must remember to brush his teeth before the holy roller returned.

He splashed wine on the worktop as he poured, lurching slightly. Maybe chew on a sarnie to line his stomach?

He opened a drawer to search for the bread knife, alighting on the typed inventory. He pulled it out, flicked to a random page while drinking and grew immersed in a quest to find a casserole dish that was listed but never seen.

After rattling through all the kitchen drawers and cupboards, he gave up, tossed his empty glass in the sink and wandered outside to the woodshed.

The only nasties lurking in there were several hundred spiders and cords of damp wood still wrapped in desiccated newspaper.

He pulled out a few sheets of yellowing pages, searching for other handwritten notes concealed within their layers. Nothing.

But right at the back of the shed, he *did* find something intriguing.

The smell alerted him first. He picked up a thick, malodorous pile of fabric, expecting it to dissolve in his hands.

Instead, the folds flopped open to reveal a rusting axe head.

But the fabric wrapped around the axe was more interesting. Shaken out, the folds became a khaki greatcoat, single-breasted, with two side pockets. He counted four brass buttons (some were missing?) and felt a tickle of excitement. This was good stuff, army issue.

Had it belonged to Phineas? He'd been a second lieutenant in the Great War – Hugh had checked – leaving Cambridge University at 19 to join the Cheshire Regiment (strangely, not a Yorkshire one), as soon as hostilities broke out.

Nineteen! At that age, Hugh had been necking cans of Dark Fruit on stairwells and hoping some hottie would ask to stroke his man bun.

Although the smell was enough to choke a navvy, he slipped the coat on, sleeves stopping short of his wrists, hemline skimming his knees. Despite a patch of damp starting to rot one seam at the back, most of the coat was in good nick. He was thrilled with it.

How had old man Ezra felt about his son's rush to war? Probably blamed Kitchener and the rest for taking the best of his boy and leaving a shell-shocked wreck behind. "Where have all the flowers gone?" and all that.

For Phineas to survive the war and then top himself! You read about it, though: people who'd gone through unimaginable horrors, only to check out when the worst was apparently over.

Memory chased you, caught up in the end and exacted its price. Or had Phineas feared his mother's insanity was catching when the shell shock took hold?

Hugh swaggered into the house and up the stairs, enveloped in manly folds. The coat did pinch a bit under the arms. Phineas, if he was the previous owner, had clearly been shorter and slimmer than Hugh.

On the landing, he swivelled on his heels to face an invisible row of Tommies drooped over bayonets in a lice-filled trench.

Put that light out, Corporal!

Yessir!

Faint strains of *Tipperary* over the sandbags. Duckboards, barbed wired, tinned bully, letters from home, socks from sweethearts.

Maybe he should write a war novel? That would impress his old man. Least he could do as he hadn't fought in an actual war. Not that Tom had either, but he had done a stint in the army cadets at school, running up and down Slapton Sands with 25kg on his back.

That was what it took to be a real man, appaz. Well, that and becoming big in financial planning.

Right, stop thinking about his parents and their eternal disappointment in him. Time to check what Lucy was up to in the attic. She wasn't exactly secretive but, given his own reluctance to share his work, she'd become coy about hers. What was she hiding up there?

He climbed the stone spiral staircase, coat swishing behind him, and pushed open the attic door – it didn't lock. The door swung shut behind him on a silent hinge.

The room was bathed in weak sunlight, draining board scattered with pocket treasures collected on walks and pickled in layers of newspaper. He counted off a magpie feather, a dirty spiral of wool with the texture of a Brillo pad, an orange leaf crumbling to pastel dust, a pebble striped by weathering.

The open sketchbook propped on her easel displayed skeletal trees sketched in charcoal. Not his thing.

He sat on the ladder-back chair, flicked out the coat edges and noticed virgin canvases stacked against the wall, unopened paints by the sink.

Was this it so far? He'd had to carry a day job while trying to write. Yet she'd had all this – time, space, the shifting light off the moors – and done sod all with it, relatively speaking.

Her laptop was on the edge of the draining board.

He drew it on to his lap. He knew her password because she wrote all her passwords in the back of a red, Morocco leather address book that she kept (with sweet naivety) under a box of Tampax in their bedroom chest of drawers.

He went straight to her browsing history: still lifes of peaches, skulls and lustreware, but also portraits of women with birds.

Here was some rosy-cheeked girl with a small bird nestled into her shoulder.

And there was Frida Kahlo wearing parrots as epaulettes.

Was Luce going down the portrait route after all? She seemed to be just dabbling, dreaming away her days up here. Well, two could play at that game.

He put the laptop back in place, leant against the chair's remaining slats and shut his eyes.

Sun washed over him. The wine took effect. He must've dozed. When he came to, the sun had moved, carving a new passage over the floorboards.

Someone was coming up the spiral staircase.

He sat up, rubbed his eyes and pushed back the cuff of his jumper to check his watch. How long had he been out of it? He yawned and stretched, the chair creaking under him. "Hope you don't mind I'm up here," he called as Lucy approached.

The footsteps stopped on the staircase turn. He sat up a little straighter, noticing that his heart rate had increased. "Luce, that you? Pinky?"

Ole Pinko might've snuck back in, knowing he was alone, to twist the knife deeper about what he knew. Or at least suspected.

Just as Hugh leapt off the chair to investigate, the footsteps resumed. They were dragging steps, he heard now, slow and slapping against stone. Unless... unless they were hands... someone crawling up here on hands and knees.

He turned to pick up the chair – noticing dispassionately that his hands were shaking – and hurried over to the closed door, wedging the chair beneath the knob.

Just in time too. Now he could hear breathing outside the door. It sounded very close to his ear, as though the breather was next to him *in* the room... he jumped and looked over his shoulder, but he was alone in the attic.

Was it Phineas, angry at the requisition of his coat? Hugh tore it off and threw it on the floor where it sat as though threatening to rise and fill with its owner's shape.

Stop it! Someone outside the door was playing a trick, that was all. Pinky! Had to be. Putting the spooky moves on.

For starters, Pinky had supposedly 'spotted' the outline of handprints on the floor the other day. He probably hazed every new tenant – just as his mother probably *had* tinkered with the portrait of Ezra. Messing with southerners: a time-honoured Yorkshire tradition, up there with suet puddings and sly wit.

Hugh put an ear to the door. *In, out; in, out...* the tempo of his pounding heart louder than any supposed breathing.

He knelt and pressed his eye to the keyhole. Nothing, nothing there, thank God.

In, out; in, out... but the breathing was coming *through* the keyhole now; he could feel its fetid air gently fanning his straining eye.

Suddenly a bloodshot eye bulged against the keyhole, staring into his own. An eye he recognised. Piercing, scornful. Blue. Last seen glaring out of a portrait over a long stone mantelpiece.

Hugh fell back on his haunches, his mouth an open 'O' of silent terror.

The thing outside the door spoke. But he couldn't make out the words, only the intent behind them. It wanted to come in. It wanted to come in now, this very second and there'd be no discussion about it. Did he understand? Did he? *Do you, do you, do you?*

Silence, giving him time to consider the demand, a twisted take on wedding vows. Do you take this ghost to be your ghost, into your flimsily defended room?

Meanwhile, like the moorland air Hugh had grown used to, Ezra Napier searched for a way in with guile and stealth, feeling the edges of the keyhole and the door with probing, not-there fingers. Searching for access through the keyhole of Hugh's hammering heart.

He curled his fingernails into the palms of his balled hands and urged 'It', silently and fervently, to go away.

He'd return the coat to the back of the woodshed. He'd be respectful. If only that breath and that piercing blue eye, there and yet not there (his still-functioning rational senses told him), would never trouble him again. If only Ezra Napier would slink back into his portrait and stare out as a harmless, two-dimensional mute.

He must've sat like that for God knows how long when he heard footsteps again and jerked suddenly upright, eyes flying open.

He was still sitting in the ladder-back chair. He was still wearing the coat. And he'd clearly been asleep for a while.

A nightmare! What – so he'd been asleep the whole time?

But the footsteps were still coming. Now they were outside the unlocked door. And he was trapped up here at the top of the house, a lone sitting duck. His hands gripped the chair.

"Hugh?" called Lucy. "Hugh, are you in there?"

PART TWO

16

Lucy drove away from Snowy's with a niggling headache but fresh resolve. In urging her to leave, Snowy had clarified the reason for staying. The painting. *And* renewed her urgency to uncover that hidden room. What if the two were connected? What if Lucy had shrunk away from her paint tubes and canvases so far because the mystery in the acanthus room was calling to her, demanding that she alone solve it?

Then again, could there be something to Snowy's theory that Lucy's fascination with the old stories of an old house stemmed from the loss of her parents?

She rolled her shoulders.

If they were going to stay put, she and Hugh would have to pull together, stop bickering over every little thing. It might be yet another cliché (marriage was full of them) but their true north should reside in each other, wherever they lived.

Because marriage was an ongoing struggle to meet another human halfway without wanting to throttle them or sob into a pillow. And she was annoying in her own right. Probably a royal pain in the arse at times.

She drove between the pillared gates of Rook House and turned from this unpromising line of thought to her embryonic idea for a painting: *A Portrait of Rosa with a Rose in One Hand and a Rook on her Shoulder.*

It had been darting around her mind for a while without

coming into focus. Faces beguiled her in real life but she'd always shied away from the intimate gaze of a portrait sitter. Now, though, she itched to create a homage both to her mother and to her mother's favourite painting, adding a fresh twist. It would make her stay at Rook House worthwhile, whatever happened between her and Hugh.

She'd just cleared the tunnel of elms when an image flickered in her peripheral vision. She turned her head slightly, sensing a figure standing above the ridge.

She stopped the car and reversed, a shaft of low sunlight hitting her right between the eyes. Pinwheels of brightness caught her unawares and a sharp, warning pain needled her skull. She rocked back in her seat, hand raised in a fruitless warding-off gesture.

When she rolled the car forward a few inches to escape the sun's glare, the figure was melting away into evergreen trees. It was tall, man-shaped. Was that Hugh going for a walk? He'd never mentioned exploring Napier's Wood.

She stopped the car, got out and hurried towards the ridge, eager to catch up and join him on a walk. It might be easier to talk about everything out in the fresh air; his drinking, his book, his parents coming. Also, she'd read recently that the best way to avoid arguments was to talk while walking side by side, avoiding challenging eye contact. Might be worth a go.

Cresting the ridge, she stooped to grip her knees, breathless. The treeline wavered in front of her, pulsing with virulent brightness against the winter sky. Another warning sign that a migraine might be imminent.

And that caused a deeper, uneasier thought. She'd experienced similar sensations just before she 'saw' the doorway to the hidden room behind the acanthus wallpaper.

She drew her phone from her coat pocket to text Hugh and double-check his whereabouts. No signal, which was odd at this height.

She slipped the phone back into her pocket alongside car keys, frowning.

She'd wanted to remind him of the wood's potential hidden dangers. What if Pinky had lied about the absence of traps? Supposing Hugh blundered into one among the close-set trees?

The wood looked darker than ever, deep and alien. Why no birdsong? After a second's hesitation, she pushed an overhanging branch aside and plunged in, crunching over a carpet of darkly glittering needles.

Wind rose suddenly and rocked the canopies. As she walked, she looked up and felt dizzy, as though the trees were spinning around her while she stood still. The sun flashed its warning beacon through sifting branches. The wind soughed again and a great ball of golden light bloomed in front of her like a distress flare.

She focused on gazing downwards into dark earth instead of up at the pitiless sun. Why was it riding higher in the sky than just a minute ago?

Her stomach clenching around the remains of bandy tart, she glanced over her shoulder to find she'd already lost her bearings. The trail had dimmed behind her, the earth rustling forward to cover her tracks.

Still, the wood covered only a couple of acres, she knew. It had to end somewhere. If she could find her way back to the boundary wall... Or better still, find Hugh.

She gulped down a swelling tide of anxiety and walked on.

A twig cracked off to the left and she stopped, touching her locket. Was something circling her, stalking her? She tried to shake off the idea. If the wood really was dangerous, the owners would have sealed it off, reluctant to risk a law suit.

She glimpsed a flicker of movement and fabric ahead. "Hugh?" Upping her pace, she nearly went sprawling over a tree root. "Hugh, I'm behind you. Wait up!"

The image flickered again as she steadied her hand against a gnarled old trunk, the wind picking up and carrying an answering voice. She strained to hear it.

Hugh... I'm behind you... Wait up!

Hairs prickled all along her body. The echo sounded faintly mocking as though another, richly dark voice was seamed through it.

Now she paused, thinking better of advertising her presence. Someone was messing with her; someone who knew this wood better than her. Pinky? He hadn't struck her as cruel. What about those lampers he'd mentioned?

Another glimpse of fabric and this time, through the trees, she saw the back of a man moving ahead of her. Tall, broad-shouldered, with thick hair. "Pinky!" she shouted.

The man paused with his head trembling slightly, like a dog scenting something rare and possibly interesting on the breeze. Then he flexed his shoulders and walked on, slowly, with a pronounced lurch.

Because, Lucy now saw, his right foot was turned inward and dragged a little behind him. He was wearing some sort of dun-coloured shirt, sleeves rolled up to the elbows as though it was the middle of summer, a leathery waistcoat, and baggy, grass-streaked trousers tucked into thick boots.

She reached out a hand towards the vision, tripping over an unseen root and hitting her head as she plummeted to the ground with awful silence, like a tree falling in the wood with no one to hear it.

Mickey was waiting for me in our spot, a rough shelter he'd built from boughs laid across each other to conceal us from prying eyes. It always made me think of the bower-eaves in *The Lady of Shalott*.

I arrived hot and sticky from summer heat, glad of the wood's coolness, my heat rising again as Mickey's arms crept around me and his coarse stubble tickled my neck.

"How long this time, you reckon?" he asked.

I made a practised guess and glanced at my wrist to confirm it. Mickey possessed a groundsman's sense of time, slow and seasonal, depending on my gold timepiece for the ransomed minutes. "Sent Darrow back to the house for my parasol," I told him. "I brought no hat on my walk and ladies shouldn't burn."

"Only for this," he said, kissing me. "What *about* Darrow, though?"

"She'll look towards the sunken lawn, where she last saw me. Then go back to the house and wait on my return. We've a good while yet." Darrow was a find of mine, a rare ally.

Mickey sighed and kicked a fallen branch away. "But what if her failing to find you rouses others to look?"

A familiar impatience displaced my eagerness. He always did this, wasted precious moments in fruitless anxiety. "Darrow understands my wish for privacy and time alone in my own grounds. She won't seek me out with any great thoroughness and will tell anyone who asks that I'm enjoying a solo walk. Besides, the old stories keep many out of these woods."

"Stories is all they are." Finally, he began unpinning my hair, sending one of my star-headed pins spinning to earth to lie winking among the pine needles.

"Later," he murmured as I made to retrieve it. "Let me, if I may?" His dark eyes darker than glasshouse damsons, his hands hovered over my bodice.

I nodded, helping him open the front of my corset and draw off the chemise beneath. So many ridiculous layers! And beneath them all, not a soft, creamy dessert, but a boiled ham of a woman, red and perspiring from the exertion of getting here without being followed. I shivered with relief as the final layer fell to the ground.

Mickey kissed me again. "Tain't right, all that trussing-up. I've seen a partridge hung from a belt with fewer fetters 'bout its neck."

"Don't think on it too much." Or anything else. I helped him out of his own layers and stroked the wiry black hairs on his bare arm, then laid my cheek against his rough knuckles and kissed each one in turn.

These were hands that could turn mulch one moment and tease a deep blush of colour from the depths of a flower the next.

I was not 'in love' with Mickey Nellis or any other man. Why would I be?

But he afforded me stolen pleasure and more than congenial company. Within our bower I had a man to command.

We lay down on the woodland floor and stared up at the branches woven overhead, a rustic echo of the gilded cage I'd escaped for a short while.

A thought as dramatic as it was self-pitying. Mickey touched one of my quivering eyelids.

"You said not to think on owt. So don't brood on him, Belle. Not now."

I caught his finger and sucked it. The first time I ever saw him, these square fingers were probing the inner furls of a pale apricot rose with exquisite delicacy. I'd shuddered with undiscovered pleasure as the deepest, hidden blaze of colour flared from the heart of all those overlapping frills. He had cut the rose and held it out. "For your dressing table, marm, before they all turn for the season."

After we lay panting and sated among the pine needles, I rolled away and said, "we could still run away together. If we set our minds to do so."

I often said it after the deed, to test the water; to discover if the act made him want me for keeps. How far did my power extend?

He ran a questing finger down my bare backbone. "We been over this, Belle. Where'd we go? Besides, he'd not be far behind."

"I could get a divorce."

"He'd never grant it. The shame an' that. Besides, what life would we have? You a lady and me – well – this."

"Are you sure it's not your religion getting in the way? Marriage to a divorced woman..."

"We never talked of marriage. Never ever."

I lay my palm against his chest, relishing being unfair. To both of us. "If you really wanted me, you'd move heaven and earth to make it possible."

He regarded me sadly. "So you'd come live in a hut not much bigger than a hen chook? You're too high-born and delicate." He plucked a twig from my tumbled-about hair. "You're already wed and dipping low to be with me, we both know it. Have you ever scrubbed a pot, slapped out a wet woollen, soothed a colicky bairn, danced away from a beak at your ankles? And I couldn't see you do any of those things and rest easy, knowing I was the cause. Don't you see, love?"

"You underestimate me, Mickey."

"I'm being practical, like. I can't farm my own land, even if I wanted to. Not with this blighter." He flexed his unfortunate foot. "I'll always be in the keep of a man like Ezra."

"You're weak!" I muttered. "A coward!" Then I felt ashamed. "I don't mean it. But this is all I have now. This!" No longer afraid to be dramatic, I waved a hand at our hard woodland bed and abandoned clothes. (Later, he'd brush me down, carefully, ensuring I'd look half-presentable stepping out of the wood to go 'home').

"Why can't you up and leave his nibs anyway?" he asked, making it sound like the most reasonable and straightforward course of action in the world.

"On my own?" I quailed at the thought. "Do you know how hard it is for *any* woman to do that without a man at her side?

I might be 'high-born' as you call it, but he owns everything around here, including me. I don't possess a penny of my own, Mickey. I'm just as friendless and alone in the world as you. More so. You have family here. Cousins and so on."

"What of yon London? Your grandfather?"

"The man who sold me at auction to begin with? Oh, please." Angered by his attempts to find me a way out that didn't include him, I said savagely, "I hate that house almost as much as I hate *him*. I wake up at every creak in the night expecting to see Jacob Marley at the foot of my bed. Better than *him*, I suppose. Wish I could lock my door, but he won't let me."

"Who's this Marley? Is he local, like?"

His jealousy was vaguely thrilling. "He's from a book. You can read?"

"Aye, I can read, your highness. If I've a mind to."

"I didn't mean... I'm sorry. You're not afraid to be yourself. I admire that."

"Who else would I be now?" He gazed away into the greenery. "Still, what we're doing *is* a sin, Belle. I've talked it over with a priest and-"

"You've done what?" I sat up and glared at him.

"He's bound by his oath to say nowt, but he reminded me that what I'm after doing is a mortal sin, the gravest of all."

"You've always known that, Mickey, and it hasn't stopped you."

"Because the flesh is weak and you look the way you do." He gazed into my eyes. "You're sure you can't catch my bairn from our antics? Not to labour a point but you said you could only catch a bairn at certain times of the moon's wax and wane. Was I deceived in that?"

"You weren't."

Ezra desperately wanted a son. He'd shown me a calendar on his desk that told him the best days to try for one.

His determination was horrible. He'd even joked about the Wetherby stump, some damp old tree stump in a forest by which a married woman was "sure to catch a bairn if she sits on it three days before Michaelmas and calls out the name of her true love".

Such stories exerted a powerful hold, even on educated men.

I'd seen a stable lad cross himself when a horse threw a shoe on Ash Wednesday. And Mickey had told me of a farmer who'd only lend his best ram to a neighbour if the smoke blew straight up from a chimney instead of drifting to the side.

They were all mad up here if you asked me, my husband madder than most. He was worse than all of them put together. He only knew how to possess, use, break, discard.

But once I gave him a son or even two, I'd have fulfilled my function. Perhaps he wouldn't care (or care to know) if I 'carried on' with the help – same way he did and at least Mickey was a willing participant – as long as I was discreet. We could live separate, parallel lives.

"I can see you chewing on summat," said Mickey. "Not sure I'll like what you spit out."

"I was only thinking of ways we *could* be together like this in the future, without talk of marriage or fear of being spied on. We could rent a room in York. Live there as man and wife for part of the week, Darrow our go-between, as she more or less is now. I don't think she'd object if I drew her into our plans. I could pay her."

He looked edgily over his shoulder. "Don't. About being spied on."

"It's worth consideration, surely." My voice came out high and harsh, brisk with facing up to facts.

Colour marched up to his forehead. "Thing is, I would like to get married one day. Properly, like. To someone... someone..."

"Other than me? Of course. Because you want a family with a woman of your own class and religion. You're no different to other men in that respect. I'm simply saying that we could still be together, separate from all that."

Because men organised their lives like that all the time, even men of Mickey's class. A wife at home soothing the colicky bairns and an arrangement on the side with the barmaid of The Rusty Nail. "Don't we deserve the right to *try* to keep something for ourselves, Mickey?"

"You deserve to be treated better by the husband you have." He scrambled for his clothes, suddenly bleak. "And by me. That priest, he told me not to come back looking for absolution if I continued my sinful ways."

"And how's that going for you? Banking on a deathbed confession to get you off the hook? Five Hail Marys, an Act of Contrition and St Peter turns a blind eye at the pearly gates? I believe that's an option in your religion, an eleventh-hour reprieve to wash away a lifetime of sin."

"You have to repent for it to count," he said woodenly, sensitive to criticism of his Popish beliefs. They were surprisingly steadfast in the area (and bumped along happily enough with local superstitions).

"I'm sorry," I said, catching his arm. I meant it. "I'm sorry to sound the way I do. Don't think ill of me for it. Please, Mickey."

He patted my hand then, never one to brood or think much at all, really. He was a kind man, intelligent enough and a good lover, but he was also incurious. I wondered whether he forgot about me within moments of leaving this place. If only I'd had that luxury. I endured my imprisonment at Rook House by counting down to our next meeting.

He stood up, tucking his trousers into the top of his boots. "You'd better get back to your own pearly gates, love, afore he raises a search party, no matter what that maid of yours does to hold off enquiries. Come on now, I'll walk you to the edge of the wood."

17

Lucy drifted back to consciousness, face down on the woodland floor, staring at the root that had caused her downfall. Her head ached wretchedly and one knee was badly grazed under her jeans. She could feel the blood sticking to denim.

She got to her feet with slow and steady care. The wood had lost its violent, luminescent green, but a darkening sky growled and spat rain.

At least she could hear birdsong and, when a rustling alerted her to turn, she met the incurious gaze of nothing more threatening than a squirrel.

She blundered onwards, completely lost now. Her head throbbed, the sky flinging gritty handfuls of rain into her face, the ground softening treacherously around callused knuckles of tree root.

"Hey!"

The voice was so sudden, she whimpered with fear.

A figure stepped into her path and she nearly screamed.

"Hey, hey, didn't mean to scare you half to death," said Pinky Bird, taking a step back when he saw her reaction. "You OK? You're not, are you?" He glanced down at her leg. "I see you're limping."

"I... fell. Wasn't looking where I was going." She tried to laugh but only a slightly manic titter emerged.

"Let me have a look at your leg."

"Honestly, it's fine. A graze on my knee." She glanced down too, mortified to see a dark stain soaking her kneecap. "Flesh wound," she grimaced.

"No need to play the hero. I've a clean hanky somewhere I can tie round that." He rummaged in the pockets of his long, dark coat. "Should see you right till you get home. Got antiseptic wipes back at the house?"

"Never mind that, what are you doing in the wood?" she asked, sharpening her tone.

He paused. "Could ask you the same question."

"I asked first. Were you following me?"

"Nope. Why would I?"

"I heard and saw someone – someone who looked a lot like you." She frowned, the details of her 'dream' already fading. "Though you were wearing different clothes."

Other snippets were starting to elude her, slipping away as the here and now of throbbing head and knee intruded. She drew her phone from her pocket to check it hadn't cracked when she fell.

"I was taking a walk this way," Pinky replied, watching her.

"Thought you only came out at night, like the stars."

"I've been walking this land long before you came here, Mrs D, and I'll still be walking it long after you're gone. I don't owe you any explanations."

"Same here!" Her eyes filled with a rush of tears.

"Hey," he said gruffly, "don't take on. Let me walk you back to the house, 'case you fall again on that knee. You've a talent for being in the wars. See there?" He pointed at nearby tree trunks. "Plait moss. Grows thick right down to the root and can be slippy."

Without warning, he picked up her hand and spread her fingers across his square, warm palm. "At least these have healed up nicely since t'other day. When you reefed them on that tin of salmon?" he reminded her, navy eyes bright with meaning.

He held on to her hand and she let him, savouring the warmth and largeness of his clasp, the ridge of his pinky ring resting on the flesh between her fingers.

When his thumb began to stroke her fingers, she gave an involuntary gasp, yanking her hand away. "I must get back."

"Then, like I said, I'll go with. No ifs or buts," he said firmly as thunder rolled in from the dark west, rainfall beating on their shoulders with hard little knuckles. "You've a nasty bruise on your forehead as well. Gets dark as Hades in here on a day like this and you've no idea where you are. Correct me if I'm wrong."

She didn't, shrugging.

"But first, let's sort that knee." He produced the clean hanky he'd promised, an actual cotton one, kneeling before her like a chivalrous knight. "Roll up yon trouser leg, milady."

"Bet you say that to all the girls."

"Only the ones I meet in deep, dark woods."

She inched up the leg of her jeans without making the wound worse. He peered at her kneecap. "It's stopped bleeding anyway. Don't worry, I'll be gentle."

She could've done without anything so directly flirtatious, glancing down at his thick chestnut hair as he deftly bandaged her knee. "There." He stood up. "You'll have to walk back with your trews at half-mast like a Freemason but can't be helped. Be sure to bathe it soon as you get in."

"I will." Resistance was futile, she decided. Besides, his company was welcome in the increasingly dark, wet wood. She shivered.

He peeled off his coat. "And put this over your own. It's not as damp as yours yet."

She accepted the coat with an ungracious eye roll, but as they set off, she leant instinctively into him, hoisting his coat every now and then off her shoulders to stop it trailing on the ground.

It carried his sandalwood signature. Once or twice she inhaled surreptitiously, camouflaged by the gloom.

At last the boundary wall appeared. "I can find my own way from here, ta," she told him, handing back the coat. "Have to retrieve my car anyway. Thanks for the loan of this, and for the hanky. I'll wash and return it."

"No need. I get a load at Christmas and birthdays, along with socks and deodorant sticks. You get the gist."

From his mother, she wondered? Or unimaginative girlfriends? Boyfriends?

He insisted on seeing her safely into her car. She thanked him again, hesitating. "Look, no need to tell anyone about my little stumble – your mum, I mean. I'm a bit embarrassed, truth be told."

"As you wish. Goodbye, then."

She watched him stalk off up the ridge (he still hadn't explained his presence in the wood, not really), then drove the final few yards towards the house with a lot of self-conscious gear-crunching, wincing when she bumped her injured knee on the steering column.

Her head still ached but the danger of a full-blown migraine was receding and her whole body thrummed with a sensation deeper than pain. She flipped down the mirrored visor and saw dark pink roses in her cheeks under wildly mussed hair. Her palm still felt the imprint of his stroking thumb and she tutted at herself. Sod. It. She couldn't afford to go all Cathy over the local Heathcliff!

He intrigued her, though. What did he *do* all day? And did he have a steady partner or a reputation as steamy as Ezra Napier's? Jude hadn't said, so either she knew little beyond the gossipy basics or – or she was seeing him herself?

He was just the handsome 'bit of rough' someone like Jude might go for to alleviate rural boredom, although that was probably unfair to both of them. Besides, there was nothing rough or basic about Pinky Bird.

Dammit, she'd let him get under her grazed skin!

Once she'd parked outside Rook House, she smoothed her hair and waited for her cheek rosettes to fade. Then she walked round to the side of the house and pushed open the unlocked back door, depositing the apple tart Snowy had gifted her on the kitchen table. "Hugh?"

She peeked into his study. "Hugh?"

He wasn't in the living room, either – they never sat in there anyway.

Same story in their bedroom and the bathroom.

That left the attic. Would he go up there uninvited? It wasn't as if the attic was off-limits, but they shared an unspoken agreement that it was all hers. She'd never dream of ferreting about in the study when he wasn't there.

She hobbled up the stone spiral steps to the studio door. "Hugh?" she called, hand on the doorknob. "Hugh, are you in there?"

She opened the door.

"Luce!" He was sitting bolt upright in the ladder-back chair, wearing some grubby old coat. He blinked owlishly, face puffy with sleep.

"I gave Snowy a lift back to hers after Mass," she explained. "She repaid me with a delicious-smelling apple tart. Talking of smells, that coat really hums."

He looked down at it. "Yeah, it's a bit ripe. Found it in the shed outside. Came up here on a keyboard break to look out the window. Must've nodded off." He searched her face. "You don't mind me being in here, do you?"

"No, of course not."

He stretched and yawned. "I think we'll ditch this coat if it's not on the inventory. Reckon we'd have noticed it under 'smelly vintage clobber.'" He finally spotted the hanky around her exposed knee. "What happened?"

"Went for a walk and came a cropper, the usual. Stand up and let me get a good look at you in that coat before you take it off."

He complied grudgingly.

"Give us a twirl, then," she teased, and he obliged again, tamping down his irritation. The coat was his find alone.

"Do you think it belonged to Phineas?" she asked. "Looks like army issue."

She advanced and prodded the left shoulder, sending up a puff of dust and coughing. "Look, you can see where the epaulettes were torn off on each side that would have shown the owner's rank. Let me see the collar."

He yanked off the coat and bundled it into her arms. "Knock yourself out."

Apparently oblivious to his frostiness, she peered inside the collar. "Name tag's been ripped out as well. Where's the belt?" She wrinkled her nose and held the coat at arm's length. "Don't see any belt loops. Maybe I'm thinking more of a trench coat."

"Honestly, Luce, how would I know if it ever had a belt? If it did belong to Phineas, maybe Ezra took the belt away before Mad Boy Phin hanged himself with it. Why don't you paint him dangling off the banisters, give Ezra's creepy old portrait some competition?"

She stared at him. "What's with the attitude?"

"I'm hungry. Where's this apple tart?" He wasn't going to tell her he'd been royally spooked and now felt a total div.

She threw the coat over the back of the chair. Hugh could deal with it later. "If you come downstairs, I'll dish it up, m'lord."

------ •═◆❂◖◗❂◆═• ------

"So you went for a stroll through our wood and fell arse over elbow just in time for Pinky Bird to pop out from behind a tree and do his boy scout bit."

"That's the gist of it, yeah."

Hugh had cleared two slices of apple tart, Lucy sticking to black coffee, the bandy tart still heavy in her gut.

She sipped the last of her coffee. "Although..." She debated whether to tell him about her latest 'episode'. Recounting it might help her recover the details of her 'vision' in the wood.

"Although what?"

She decided to go for it, starting with the newsflash that she suffered from migraines. "It can be more than one trigger I have to watch out for. Sometimes it's alcohol or caffeine, other times heavy or rich food I'm not used to."

She swerved any reference to her first episode, the one that had started with the swirling acanthus leaves, reluctant to bring up the hidden room again. "And sometimes, just the angle of bright sunlight hitting me between the eyes can have an effect. That's what happened in Napier's Wood just now. My head started to throb, I tripped and hit my head on the ground. Think I was out of it for a few minutes, maybe only seconds. That's when... yes!" Something was coming back to her. "I thought I saw Pinky up ahead just before I fell over, but it wasn't him, it was... it looked like his ancestor, Mickey. You know, the one who worked here as a gardener for Ezra?"

"How would you know what Mickey looked like?"

She explained about the inward-turned foot. "Bloke I saw was dragging his foot in a laboured way. And then I think... I think he met someone. Belle!" She gave a shout of triumph. "That's it! He was having an affair with Belle and they used to meet in that wood, away from prying eyes."

"O-K," said Hugh, voice heavy with doubt. "So, while you were spark out, you dreamt you saw this bloke in the throes of a passionate affair with the lady of the manor? All a bit *Lady Chatterley's Lover.*"

"Like I said, I saw Mickey just *before* I fell. Maybe. Yeah, I think so. It wasn't a vision as such. I dunno." She was starting to feel tired. "I *must've* dreamt all of it, come to think. How else to explain it?"

Hugh sat back. "Snowy had just told you about Mickey's foot, so that could've been on your mind when you saw little flashing lights and hit your head. You probably did see old Pinky up ahead just before you fell over, but while you were out of it, that got turned into a story of Belle having it away with the strapping gardener."

Lucy shrugged. He hadn't asked if she was *OK* after hitting her head.

"I'm just saying," said Hugh, "your subconscious probably went off on one about Belle treating herself to a bit of rough off the estate. Could've happened, who knows? That's a nasty-looking forehead bruise, by the way. Want me to put frozen peas on it?"

She shook her head rather than point out she'd had that particular bruise for a few days.

Now she thought about it, maybe she should've gone to A&E after her latest head bump. She'd read that you should always get checked over if you knocked yourself out. Or was that only the case if you started seeing double when you came round?

"So yeah, that must be it," Hugh nodded, brow furrowed. "Your imagination took a swerve into Lady Chat territory after you banged your nut. Classic of the genre."

"At the time, seeing a bloke with a dragging foot seemed so real."

"Would do. Don't you still see your mum in a crowd sometimes?"

She stiffened. "Yes, but that often happens to bereaved people. Your mind takes a leap into wishful-thinking territory from glimpsing a hair colour or the way a person walks. *This* experience or whatever you want to call it, was different." Another fragment of memory bobbed to the surface. "Wait – yes! – I heard a voice in the wood, mimicking my own voice and words back to me. That was definitely before I fell and hit my head."

"Could all be related to the onset of a migraine. There's still a lot they don't know about the brain."

"I didn't get a full-blown migraine."

"But you did hit your head."

Lucy was becoming frustrated. Pinky might've been less sceptical. He'd probably also have insisted on A&E, and driven her there.

She gathered up their plates. "Anyway, that's all by the by. Something else you should know from my talk with Snowy. She reckons we should cut our losses and leave."

Hugh was immediately on the alert. "What brought that on?"

"She admitted to hearing the scratching herself behind the bathroom wall, and reckoned old houses speak to certain people. Got the impression she thinks we might be lightning rods for spooky goings-on."

"Right." Hugh chewed his thumbnail for a long, brooding moment. "Have you considered that she or Pinky might want this place at a knockdown price? One haunting too many and owners drop it into the bargain bin."

"But you said the new owners already got it on the cheap."

Ignoring her, he ploughed on, "Snowy's job is to up the ghostly ante while pretending to have our best interests at heart. Odds on she did muck about with the living room portrait."

"Sounds like an episode of *Scooby-Doo*. What would they do with this house once they had it? Still take a fortune to do up."

"Pinky could have a fair bit stashed away from snaring bunnies and supplying coke."

"You discounted the coke theory. And he was keen to find that hidden room, remember? Why would he take a sledgehammer to his own investment?"

"To check out what's there, with us paying for the repairs!" Hugh made it sound obvious. "Bloke's got it all worked out."

Lucy kept quiet regarding her recent insistence to Snowy that she'd had a change of heart and now *did* want to explore behind the wallpaper. "If we did pack up and leave, Snowy said it wouldn't be a big deal to replace us."

"I bet she did!"

Rosa with a Rose and a Rook wavered tantalisingly in Lucy's vision. "Do *you* want to leave, Hugh? I mean, the book-"

"The book will come." He looked at the Rayburn. "What's the alternative, Mouse? Creeping back to London with our tails between our legs, admitting we couldn't hack it? And thing is..." He swallowed, tugging his jumper cuffs over his knuckles. "Thing is..."

He paused for so long that dread began to mount from the pit of her stomach to the top of her throat. *Just spit it out!*

"I've been let go at work. Cutbacks."

"Oh God, when did this happen?"

"Other day. Been waiting for the right mo to tell you. Not that there *is* a right mo."

"I'll deffo look into getting a part-time job, then. That caff in Lowmorten is looking for staff."

"No! We've still got most of the ten grand. Let's fulfil our creative destinies first, then worry what comes next."

"Or, we could eke out that money a lot longer by adding to it as we go along."

He went quiet for so long, brows knitted and expression pensive, that Lucy grew restless again. "Hugh? Did you hear what I said?"

He turned to her, bright-eyed. "That thing about being

lightning rods has just given me an idea. I reckon we should hold a seance. Ask whoever else is here *why* they're here."

"You're not serious?"

"Apart from anything else, might help with my book."

"It's too dangerous."

"Pish posh. It's just a harmless way of tapping into an atmos and we'd take all proper precautions."

"I don't want any part of it."

"Thanks for at least considering it."

"I don't know anything about the occult or want to."

"Occult!" he scoffed. "I'm talking about using a Ouija board, stuff that school kids muck about with. Read up about it first, that's all I ask. We'll take it from there."

She hesitated, keen to head off the latest gathering storm. She'd had enough drama for one day and he'd already been funny about that smelly old coat. "But you said a minute ago that you suspected the Birds of making out the place is haunted to get it on the cheap. Which is it? Can't be both."

"Disagree. The Birds could be riffing off superstition, but that doesn't mean people living here before us haven't experienced things." He hesitated. "Or even seen things. Look, sleep on the seance idea, OK? At least give me that, the benefit of due consideration."

The same consideration he'd urged when suggesting they move here. Look how that was panning out.

Still, she nodded to ensure another few hours of relative peace.

Hugh beamed, ready to be magnanimous when she bent his way even slightly. "Thanks, Mouse. That's all I ask, that you keep an open mind. Something we'll both have to do if we're to carry on living here."

≈☙≈

18

"I'm afraid that's the final word on the matter," said Snowy a few mornings later, stacking a fresh pile of briquettes by the Rayburn. "Pinky won't be scraping off any wallpaper in search of hidden rooms. The owners were adamant. The damp problem seems accessible from the bathroom side."

"I see." Lucy sat at the kitchen table, knotting her hands round a mug of cooling cocoa. "I thought you said it wouldn't be a problem if we wanted to go ahead with opening up the space between walls?"

"I was mistaken."

"Did Pinky talk to the owners or did you?"

Snowy glanced at her sadly. "I gave you sound advice the other day, Lucy. It pains me that you won't take it."

It pained Lucy, too. For some reason she hated to disappoint Snowy. At least Pinky hadn't told his mother about their recent encounter in Napier's Wood. In retrospect, Lucy felt obscurely ashamed of her clumsiness, her brief tearfulness and the moment of intimacy that had followed.

"I told you, Snowy. I can't leave here now, having just mapped out an idea for a painting. I need the attic studio. I might never have a space like that again. Don't worry, we won't go poking about where it's not allowed."

"Good. The plumber's coming in a couple of days about the bathroom's damp issue." Snowy took an old-fashioned, blocky smartphone from a pocket. "Give me your mobile number and I'll send over the exact details. Pinky will be here to supervise."

"Right." Lucy's face flamed at the mention of his name. Luckily, Snowy didn't notice. She nodded at Lucy's mug of cocoa. "Shall I make one for his nibs or will I disturb the muse?"

"Hugh's gone out," replied Lucy. "He's started going for long walks in the morning. Comes back around midday. Says it helps him think."

Snowy looked surprised. "I thought he worked on his pharmacy leaflets in the mornings."

"He's been let go." Hugh had said they should sit on his bad news, but Lucy failed to see the point. "They made cutbacks at short notice. Last in, first out. Don't worry, we can still cover the rent. He... we have savings. No need to tell the owners, is there? No antique tea strainers to flog on eBay as I recall."

Snowy gave her a long, searching look. "None of mine, at the end of the day. I'll get on. I'm taking a nozzle to the pelmets in the living room and your bedroom. Could be nests of mice up there. That's a joke," she added grimly and bustled away.

Lucy finished her drink, brooding. Hugh was still badgering her about the seance, increasingly excited by the idea. "We could hold it in the acanthus room. That seems to be the centre of spooky operations. Could be the room Phineas leapt from."

"I don't like that room. It gives off a bad vibe."

"My point exactly. Negative energy."

"A seance is also against Church teaching."

"So was eating fish on Friday until recently."

"Hardly the same."

"Jeez, Luce, you'll be wearing a hair shirt and showing me your stigmata next. Look, if we reckon the spirits of this house are already raised, it's a bit late to go putting genies back in bottles, so why not ask what they want? Where's the harm in a quick chat on the astral plane to explain that we come in peace? I'm willing to risk it for the sake of my book." He'd turned sheepish. "Goes without saying the words aren't exactly flowing."

"Yeah, I kind of guessed."

She didn't want to put obstacles in the way of his own creative flow – of course she didn't. But wasn't a seance akin to poking a bear?

"Not if it's done properly," he'd insisted. "Like I said, we'd be careful. Take precautions."

"Such as?"

"Sprinkle some holy water about? Snowy must have gallons of the stuff. You could scrounge a few drops off her. Or scoop some out of the font in Sowersby."

"Very respectful of the spirit world. Not. I won't be doing either of those things."

But she was still, officially at least, considering the seance, if only to delay the inevitable row when she cried off.

Despising her cowardice, she rose from the kitchen table and washed her mug in the sink, imagining Snowy's horror if she discovered what they were contemplating.

And Pinky... how would she look Pinky in the eye when he arrived with the plumber?

She went up to the attic, trying to catch a glimpse through her mind's eye of the painting yet to take shape. But the seance thing kept intruding.

Maybe Hugh had a point about soothing a raised spirit? For years she'd tried to invoke her mother through the pencil or brush in her hand, pouring love and longing into shape, colour and texture. But the harder she'd tried to recapture her mother's essence, the fainter it grew.

If she *could* accomplish this painting, would she be honouring or summoning the dreaming, benign spirit of Rosa in a finished portrait? Was the act of painting her own version of spirit-raising?

She strode to her easel and concentrated on thinking like an artist, not a shaman. First consideration; should she work from a photo or the deepest recesses of embellishing memory?

Her colours were nearly chosen, lined up and ready on the draining board in metallic fingers. Thrilling orange was already bent at the knuckle from getting knocked about in transport, and seemed to beckon her. Orange and black – the ideal background?

The sharp rap on the attic door came just as she'd nearly, very nearly, touched a charcoal tip to cream paper to make an initial sketch.

Sighing, she opened the door, surprised to see Snowy standing there, twisting a duster through her fingers with uncharacteristic unease.

"There's a noise in the acanthus room," said Snowy straight off. "If you don't mind and you're not too busy, I thought we'd check it out together."

Lucy hid her surprise at Snowy's obvious discomfort. Hadn't she walked these rooms plenty of times alone?

She set down her piece of charcoal. "OK, let's go. What do you think it might be?"

"If I knew that, I wouldn't be seeking company."

"Maybe we should call Pinky."

"He's in York today."

Selling his poached produce, no doubt. Lucy hesitated. Snowy's jumpiness was contagious. "I can call Hugh to come back from his walk."

"I don't think we should wait."

Lucy followed Snowy down the stone staircase, along the landing and past the bathroom to the acanthus room. As they approached, they could hear a soft *whump!* beyond the shut door. It stopped for a couple of seconds, then resumed.

Just as hairs rose on Lucy's arms, she heard a harsh, guttural caw from inside the room and Snowy relaxed. "Sounds like a jackdaw."

"How'd it get in? The window's shut."

"Down the chimney. They shove sticks down to test for nesting spots. Must've tumbled down with his stick. Probably inexperienced and over-eager."

"I thought they looked for nesting sites from April onwards, not this early in the year."

"This one didn't get the memo." Snowy tucked her duster into the waistband of her trousers and put a hand on the doorknob. "Ready?"

She threw open the door to find the jackdaw perched on the windowsill, sheeny black feathers contrasting with the silvery elegance of its swivelling head, vivid blue pupils set in pale cream irises. Its eyes were curiously human, its gaze insolent, reminding Lucy of the man glaring out from the living room portrait with mockery and defiance.

The bird had left winged soot marks on the wallpaper. Lucy had a horrible flashback to magazine articles about the aftermath of Hiroshima, human beings reduced to expressive pavement stains by an atomic bomb.

Snowy, back to her assertive self, stalked to the window and tugged the sash up, grunting. The sash yielded with a squeal of protest that set Lucy's teeth on edge, the jackdaw merely sidling to the far end of the sill.

Snowy turned back into the room. "There's your so-called 'ghost of Belle Napier screaming' right there," she said, gesturing to the sash. "I remember now. The window in this room always made a racket. Right, you stupid thing." She clapped her hands at the bird and pointed through the window at the bare elms. "Yonder."

The bird tilted its head to examine Snowy, then rose on silent wings and vanished through the open window. Lucy found its silent exit almost as unnerving as its direct gaze.

Snowy lowered the window with another eerie screech, just as Lucy heard a freshly soft *whump!* and turned to see a small, complete human body fall into the fireplace, round blue eyes staring out of black and brown soot, arms and legs raised at stiff, unnatural angles.

She screamed.

"What the...?" Snowy approached the fireplace, chin trembling. She bent to examine the 'body' but didn't touch it. "A ruering doll."

"A what?" shuddered Lucy.

Snowy plucked the duster from her waistband, spread it out and rolled the 'doll' into the cloth by its edges, then lifted the whole cloth up, determined not to touch its contents. "The word 'ruering' means 'crying' – a bairn's crying. You'd make a doll out of scraps and put it in the crib to comfort a ruering bairn. But then such a doll took on a different meaning."

"Like what?"

"Take a closer look." She held out the doll; Lucy reluctantly approached.

Close up, it was a crudely-made rag doll fashioned from tightly wound strips of cloth – perhaps an old pillowcase – with scorched button eyes that reminded Lucy of the jackdaw's. It had been stuffed lumpily but sewn up with surprising care.

Four stumpy limbs protruded from a vaguely round torso. Its mouthless, noseless face gave the eyes a melancholic expression. It looked very old; the fabric stained with ancient soot and fire-blackened down one side.

It must be years, thought Lucy, since anyone lit a fire in this room.

Snowy drew her attention to a long, tarnished hairpin sticking out of the rag doll's belly. The pin had a blackened head in the shape of a star.

Snowy didn't touch the pin but said: "A woman with an unwanted pregnancy might make a ruering doll and wedge it up the chimney for the stork to take away the bairn rather than deliver it." She paused. "Sometimes, the woman might drive the point home into the doll's belly; mebbe just make a slit with a butter knife."

"That's horrible!"

Snowy chewed her lower lip. "Reckon it could be the handiwork of one of the maids Ezra accosted. Poor young things. Would only take a moment for a maid laying a fire of a morning to slip the doll from under her apron and slide it up the chimney."

"Was this room anyone's in particular back then?"

"Probably a guest room, given its size."

Lucy inspected the star-headed hairpin. "Would a maid own a fancy, decorative hairpin like that?"

"Plenty were light-fingered. Or ladies dropped their hairpins and forgot about them, a maid keeping what she picked up."

Lucy wondered whether a young housemaid's despair still festered in this room, the source of its 'vibe'. She imagined some illiterate, underfed country girl making a doll in moments snatched alone, then stuffing it up the chimney the first chance she got, an old folk tale her only hope of avoiding misery and disgrace.

Lucy shivered. Then a fresh thought occurred. "You don't think it was *Marianne's* hairpin and doll?"

Snowy shook her head. "Not a chance. Marianne was as carefully chaperoned as a princess with a duty to the realm. No man interfered with her on Ezra's watch!" She regarded the doll with open distaste. "We can't leave it here. A ruering doll is meant to burn in the flue. If it comes back down the chimney, it must still be burnt. I'll put it in the Rayburn."

"Hugh might like to see it."

"What on earth for?"

"Inspiration."

"If you say so." Snowy bore the doll out of the room, hammocked in the duster. "I'll leave it on kitchen table. But don't forget to burn it up after I go, hairpin and all. Still got a sharp tongue, that pin, I reckon. It's bad luck *not* to burn a ruering doll and you've had enough of that already today. A bird has been in the house," she added, when Lucy looked at her blankly. "And I wasn't referring to myself."

19

"A what?" Jude asked, passing her cigarette to Hugh. They were lying in the double bed of their usual room at The Grange.

Hugh told her about the ruering doll he'd come home to the day before. "A fascinating piece of old folklore. Lucy was repulsed, but intrigued too. Could see it on her face. It came down the chimney in that room I told you about. She insisted we burn it, unfortunately. Wish I'd taken a photo to show you."

"The room that might as well have a pentangle on the floor?" Jude sat up. "You think Chucky falling down the chimney might be enough to tip Lucy your way about the seance?"

"I dunno."

Jude pouted. "Honestly, I can't believe anyone would kick up a fuss if you looked for this mystery room behind the wall *or* held a seance."

"If Snowy hasn't got eyes on us, Pinky has. Can't afford owners giving us the elbow."

She tilted him a sloe-eyed look of her own. "Because your book would stutter even more if you were cast out on your ear?"

"Yep." He didn't tell her that he'd had a sort of breakthrough with the book. Thanks to Phineas's coat.

One arm behind his head, he gazed at the ceiling and blew an inept smoke ring at the light fitting.

He'd told a rapt Jude about Lucy's recent experience in Napier's Wood, a strange interlude possibly brought on by warning signs of a migraine. They both agreed that Lucy was the probable lightning rod for 'spooky' occurrences and therefore essential to the seance. Apart from anything else, Lucy also claimed to have heard that 'weird scratching', despite Hugh never hearing a thing.

He'd only been half-serious about the Birds staging ghostly charades to get Rook House on the cheap. For a start, there was no way Pinky or Snowy could've engineered his 'nightmare' in the attic. It couldn't be a coincidence that he'd experienced it after putting on the greatcoat.

"Who d'you think might answer if you did put in a call to the other side?" asked Jude.

Hugh considered. "Ezra's our best bet. Everyone claims he never left."

"Would you ask him why he's hanging about?"

Hugh grunted. *Were* ghosts guided by a sense of purpose? Unfinished business? Hamlet's father's ghost, certainly. *Avenge me.* "Maybe just ask him to ease up on the chain rattling while I'm working," he joked, thinking of the coat.

He'd put it back in the shed, bundled around the axe. It was there should he need it again. Should he dare to.

His rational left brain still insisted that the whole 'encounter' in the attic had been a nightmare while he was fast asleep. The creative right brain buzzed with an alternative explanation: the coat had lured Ezra out of spectral hiding and, in the process, unblocked Hugh. At least temporarily.

The day after the nightmare, he'd filled two pages of his turquoise notebook with his recollection of the experience and the possible words 'Ezra' had spoken – his grim insistence there would be no discussion, followed by the imperious demand: "Did he understand? Did he?"

The way Hugh saw it, Ezra could've taken him for Phineas in that coat and tried to reason with his son or lay down the law. Perhaps it was the tail-end of a circular argument between the two of them about – what? Phineas going off to war? Phineas returning from war to mope about the house with a death wish? Phineas yearning to know more about his mad, dead mother?

Hugh was excited about where to take the 'story' next.

He could trim away the fat of hearsay and speculation to expose the raw meat beneath: maybe a father-son clash of wills that had brewed for years and culminated in Phineas taking the king's shilling against his father's wishes.

But Hugh was also a hostage to uncertainty and fear. Not of Ezra per se, but of his creative flash flood dwindling gradually to a trickle, then drying up altogether.

It was already happening. He'd gone back to his notebook early this morning and hesitated, fatally.

As for the seance idea, it had flashed into his mind while Lucy was talking about her own experience in Napier's Wood.

What if there was a safe way to conjure Ezra? A seance, after all, was as good as a controlled experiment. It was worth a shot.

Jude rolled on to her belly. "*I* could organise the whole shebang for you. I was a dab hand with a Ouija board at boarding school. We'd scare ourselves daft, then raid the booze stash of the housemistress. It was a right laugh."

Jude made her boarding school sound like St Trinian's. Hugh was still too traumatised from his own scholastic past to trot out comparative anecdotes. As far as he was concerned, his school years were a blur of aggravated violence with Latin verbs. "I'll think about it."

"Don't think too long." She flopped back on the pillows, glancing down at his bare feet. "You have very ugly toes."

"Dropped Dad's toolbox on a foot when I was a kid. Several little piggies squealed all the way to A&E."

"You could write a children's book about that."

"*The Severed Toe & Other Tales*," he nodded.

"You and Lucy want kids?"

"We've never discussed it." Reaching for his jumper cuffs to pull over his knuckles, he remembered he was naked. He was more comfortable talking about ghosts.

"Look, we both reckon Luce holds the key to communing with the other side," insisted Jude. "So work on overcoming her resistance. She's way too uptight. Does her disapproval ever take a day off?"

"You've only seen her in short bursts," he protested.

"Come on, she'd reach for the Epsoms if she saw you smoking that fag. Probably upset her more than the extra-marital."

"Bit harsh. You know very well that a drink-driver left her mother for dead on a zebra crossing and her dad got hitched again, this time to a woman as cuddly as a piece of shrapnel. Be odd if she wasn't 'uptight', as you put it."

"All right, don't air-quote me. I just think she needs to wake up and smell the birdsong occasionally, get with the programme."

"Tune in and drop out?"

Jude poked him in the heel with an orange-painted toe. "Just saying, I think I can help swing her over to our side. The dark side. At least temporarily."

Hugh studied the ceiling, thinking about his turquoise notebook. "How?" he asked.

Lucy went into the study without knocking to tell Hugh that Pinky and the plumber were due shortly. "Snowy texted me a few mins ago."

He shifted his laptop away from her. "I'll let you handle it."

How gracious of him. Itching to get on with preliminary sketches for her painting, she hurried into the kitchen to make a pot of tea and plonk Mr Kipling's finest on a plate.

The plumber, a cheery Londoner called Jamal, arrived with Pinky in the latter's spluttery truck.

"Blimey, mini Battenbergs!" grinned Jamal. "Always wondered who lives here. I'll take my vittals upstairs and crack on."

Lucy led both men up to the bathroom, wondering when Pinky would speak.

Jamal stirred the shards of disturbed plaster with a boot tip, then dropped to his haunches. "Right, let's see what we've got." He opened his black metal toolbox. "Depending on what we find, I might have to use a drill."

Lucy nodded, watching him dig into the damp wall behind the sink and make a hole just big enough to shine a torch through. She held her breath as he peered in.

Jamal eased back on his heels and trained his torch beam round the back of the toilet pedestal. "Yep, your fill valve's dripping good and proper. You'd have been smelling damp for a while."

"What did you *see* through the hole just now?" wondered Lucy impatiently. "There was talk of a space behind there, about the size of a small room."

"Definitely a space of *some* kind," Jamal shrugged, waving his torch at her. "Here, have a look."

She got down on her knees to shine the beam through the hole, illuminating a rough wooden floor. She flicked the light up, picking out a low, stone ceiling.

It *was* a tiny room, of sorts; maybe a large crawl space, high enough for a young child to stand up in, though an adult would have to stoop. It was empty.

Then the torch settled on a rough protrusion in the ceiling. An air vent.

She held the torch out to Pinky. "You may as well take a look as well."

To her surprise, he turned and walked out of the room. She heard him heading down the stairs.

"What do you think that space is?" she asked Jamal, handing back his torch. "It's kind of small for a room that you'd want to spend any time in."

"You'd get architects who'd put follies inside houses, like a tiny room or passage behind a bookcase," he replied. "Wouldn't have to lead anywhere. Just be a diversion or talking point."

"You mean, the opposite of a priest hole or panic room?"

"Exactly. Just my opinion, though."

"*Could* it be an early type of panic room?"

"Possible," Jamal agreed. "You'd have to look out the original plans. There was that woman who built the Winchester house in America. Lots of corridors leading to dead ends or sheer drops to fool the ghosts coming after her. In her case, all the ghosts of the people killed with her husband's invention, the Winchester rifle."

Lucy nodded. "Back in a minute," she said, and hurried after Pinky.

He was in the kitchen, staring out of the window.

She closed the door. "Would you thank your mum again for the delicious apple tart she gave us?"

He turned with a sigh. "Yeah, OK." He nodded down at her leg. "Knee seems a lot better."

"Yes, it is, thanks. Healed up quickly. Flesh wound, like I thought."

"Are you friends with the Hollenbecks?" He jerked his chestnut head towards the study. "Both of you, like?"

"Well, we had dinner at The Grange recently."

"You want to be careful there, Lucy." His tone was sombre. "That woman, especially, is not what she seems."

"Oh?" Her Spidey senses tingled. "Do I detect a touch of offended masculinity? Something you want to get off your chest about Jude the Jezebel Hollenbeck?"

She wasn't aware she was holding her breath and combating a wave of misery until he looked at her in surprise and asked: "Like what?"

"Maybe she threw you over or rejected your advances and you've had it in for her ever since, denouncing her to newcomers."

"Me? Take up with that one?" His brows rose into his hairline. "My, my, 'rejected your advances'. You do have an opinion of me." He shook his head more in sorrow than in anger.

"Why, what's wrong with Jude?" Lucy demanded. "She's gorgeous, sassy, rich... I imagine that's every bloke's type if he's got a pulse."

"And don't forget, she plays hard to get," he snorted. "I'm being sarcastic, in case you didn't twig. She's not renowned for rejecting anyone's advances, as you so quaintly put it. In fact, she likes to make the first move."

"Are you *slut*-shaming her?"

"She's married," he said stubbornly. "Which doesn't stop her seeing what else is out there. Who else, I should say. *I* was never on her radar, by the by. Too tough a nut to crack." His cheeks flamed. "Probably said enough."

"Yes, you've been very clear," said Lucy with heavy sarcasm. "Crystal, in fact. You're saying that Jude's after anything in trousers and my weak-willed hubby's next in line, have I got that right? And unlike you, he's bound to be a very crackable nut."

Pinky shrugged, looking as miserable as she'd been made to feel by this whole ridiculous exchange. How had she let it get out of hand so quickly?

"Damned if I do, damned if I don't," he muttered, then raised his eyes to her. "Just a friendly warning, is all. You know Hugh better than I do. About whether or not you can trust him."

She felt as though inner heat was choking her. "Thanks for the heads up about my own marriage!"

He squared his shoulders and moved to the back door.

"Need some air. Tell Jamal I'll be back in about an hour."

"Wait! If we're getting things off chests, I've a question. Are you after this house? Is the plan to get it on the cheap by ramping up the haunted house theory?"

He stopped in his tracks. "What?"

"I think you heard."

"Right. You think I've a 'plan' to get hold of this rotting hulk on the cheap. Can't say it's ever occurred, sorry to disappoint."

But Lucy wasn't finished. "I've just had another thought. Is Henry Hollenbeck behind any plan to buy and do up this place, sell it on? That could be the real reason you swerved his wife's advances. Might queer the deal."

"Deal? First a plan, now a deal. Right."

"I'm talking about any cut Henry gives you for helping him buy this place for a song. You did imply both the Hollenbecks are not what they seem."

Pinky shook his head. "With an imagination like that, you should be the writer in the family." He put his hand on the back door handle. "Maybe go easy on the cheese, though. Or whatever it is you're smoking."

"I barely drink, let alone take drugs!"

"The fact that you were staggering about the wood the other day would suggest otherwise."

"Staggering?" Tears of rage and humiliation burnt the back of her eyes. "I fell over a tree root in a dark wood! FYI, a drink-driver killed my mother, so I take a zero-tolerance approach to booze hounds and drug fiends! Now get. The fuck. Out!"

For the first time, she saw that she had him on the back foot. "I spoke out of turn then, and I'm sorry." He paused, stubbornness etched across his face. "Your go now."

She hauled back her tears before they escaped to undermine her righteous anger. "*I've* nothing to be sorry for and I just told you to fuck off!"

"OK, I guess we both know where we stand." He opened the door. "Pass my message on to Jamal."

"I will. And from now on, keep your opinions to-"

He'd gone through the door and slammed it shut before she could harvest the final word.

She waited until she'd calmed down before stomping back upstairs to Jamal.

She gave Jamal Pinky's message and sought out Hugh. "You're on duty from now on," she told him curtly. "I've done my bit. Jamal might need a tea top-up soon. If you're quick, you can peer into the space behind the wall before he mends it. I'll be in the attic."

She left the study before he could answer.

A couple of hours later, a sulky Hugh came to find her with a progress report. Jamal had replaced the fill valve, plastered over the damp spot and replaced the tiles. "Bloke like that is gold dust. I got his business card before he left."

"Good." She ran a brush under the sink tap, braced for him to ask about raised voices earlier in the kitchen. "Anything else?"

"Nope. Ole Pinko turned up to collect Jamal. Was his usual charming self."

"Let's hope that's the end of the damp problem. I must get on, Hugh."

He left her to it and went to sit in the kitchen with a glass of wine. He'd earned it, the drink his reward for a few hours of fruitless struggle at his desk and a substitute for the coke, which his twitching synapses had started to crave.

Maybe the struggle to write was a good sign? His dad had told him to distrust anything that came his way too easily – an unearned promotion, a beautiful woman, a six-figure advance (chance'd be a fine thing).

Right now, he'd kill for a killer idea. One with 'legs'. Yeah, he'd got a couple of great pages under his belt about the 'coat incident', but since then, zip. And what he did have barely amounted to a coherent plot.

The seance was a possible route to replenishing the well, but he needed Lucy the way a water diviner needed dowsing rods. Or a coal miner his canary. He pushed that thought away.

But still, it was the seance or try the coat again. He'd prefer to keep that as a last resort.

He threw back the wine in one go.

He'd followed her suggestion to look through the hole in the bathroom wall before Jamal filled it. Not much to get excited about. Just a dank, narrow space with freezing air gusting through it. Unusual, though. No reason for it to be there. Funny it was there at all, exactly where Lucy claimed she'd heard scratching. You couldn't pin its existence on the Birds, although it was suspicious that Pinky had been so eager to uncover it.

His phone buzzed with a text from Jude: "*Need u to confirm date for u know what. Tomorrow night good for me. After dark to generate atmos. Mrs Moral Majority onside yet?*"

He texted back, "*Stand by*", rose unsteadily and went to the bathroom to brush his teeth, then returned to the attic, going straight in without knocking.

Lucy turned in annoyance, dragging her easel out of his line of sight. Like he cared.

He decided to put her on the spot. "The seance is on for tomorrow night. Jude's coming over to take part."

"Jude?"

"We discussed her involvement."

"Did we?"

"I met her on one of my inspirational nature walks and ran it up her flagpole. She's taken part in a few, so thought she'd be handy to emcee events. Plus, she said three's a better number for contacting the spirits."

Bullshit, but Lucy didn't call him on it.

"I didn't agree to it yet, Hugh."

"You didn't actively *dis*agree. And Jude knows her spiritualist onions."

"Letting the dead speak through her, presumably? The Madame Arcati of the Yorkshire Moors."

He went on stubbornly: "I thought we'd set up in the acanthus room, as also discussed. It's closest to the hidden room. Plus, you found the spooky old doll there."

Lucy fiddled with her gold locket. "I'm still not keen."

"You said you'd keep an open mind."

"And I am! But you're blindsiding me."

"My book-"

"Oh, for God's sake, Hugh, you can't keep playing the book card. You're supposed to be a writer, so why can't you just invent spooky stuff instead of focus-grouping the nearest bunch of ghosts?"

He reeled back. "Jeesh, didn't know you held me in such low esteem."

"I'm not happy that you discussed any of this with Jude."

"Look, I've been reading up on this stuff. Ghosts hate to be ignored. A lot of stuff they do is attention-seeking. Let's give them some attention and they might go away."

"Or call in reinforcements."

He clenched his jaw. "Jude's coming. You can duck out if you want. We'll be in the acanthus room tomorrow night if you decide to join us." He turned on his heel.

"Just don't let Snowy find out," she called as he strode from the room.

"I won't tell if you won't. I won't disturb you again today, Madame Artiste."

Unfortunately, due to its silent hinge, the attic door was the one door in the house that never delivered a satisfying slam.

Lucy watched him go, then fell into the ladder-back chair with her head in her hands.

So, he'd met Jude on one of his "inspirational walks". Would Jude really make a pass at Hugh? How would he respond?

What if they'd met more than once on his walks, Hugh dangling the old "my wife doesn't understand me" line?

He and Jude were so not each other's type, but that might be the whole point, of course. Anyway, Lucy couldn't be sure that Hugh had a 'type' other than available and as bored as he was. Let's be honest, she'd just intimated to Pinky that Jude had all the necessary qualities to draw the wandering male eye. Plus, Hugh was becoming increasingly furtive, even creeping downstairs at night for yet another nightcap, once he thought she was asleep. She could smell the stuff coming out of his pores.

But here was a thought. The seance, despite her qualms, would allow her to see the pair of them up close and draw her own conclusions. Then decide how to act.

Sitting up, she gazed at her easel, the appetite to work leaking away.

She waited an hour, then went downstairs to tell Hugh that she would join the seance after all.

He looked up from the kitchen table, too delighted to notice her stony delivery. "Why the turnabout?"

"You made a good case, on reflection. Sorry I was snippy about your writing. I – I hate it when we argue."

"Me too."

"Yet we seem to do nothing but," she added sadly.

"Yeah, well, we've been under a lot of pressure, what with one thing and another. But are you sure about this, Luce?"

"At the mo, I am, so let's leave it there. If I feel differently tomorrow, I might still back out, OK?"

He nodded. "Fair enough. Jude reckons it could be... illuminating."

"OK. And listen, Hugh, maybe ease back on the fermented grape? Not just tomorrow night, but it'd be a good place to start."

He smiled tightly. "I will. Seeing as it's you who's asking."

20

Jude arrived just after eight the following night, announced by her throaty little car.

Hugh, stirring soup on the Rayburn, left off to open the back door.

"Brrr!" Jude tumbled into the kitchen and shucked off her cream wool coat. "Something smells good."

Hugh hung her coat over a chair and returned to his soup. "Your idea, Jude, that we eat properly beforehand."

"Oh yeah, I did say that, didn't I? *The condemned spiritualists ate a hearty meal.* Joke!"

They exchanged such a blatantly conspiratorial look that Lucy caught her breath. Maybe they assumed that she was too stupid to notice.

Jude had dressed for the occasion in a witchily black, off-the-shoulder T-shirt exposing a sherbet-yellow bra strap. Black nail polish too and heavy on the eyeliner. Boy, did she fancy herself or what? Lucy set out soup bowls. "I gather you're the expert in this field, Jude?"

"I wouldn't go that far, but given all Hugh's told me-"

"When did he tell you, exactly? We'll get to 'what' he told you by and by."

"Met you on one of your morning walks, didn't I, Hugh? And here's *what* I know, to satisfy your curiosity, little Luce."

She reeled off all she knew, Lucy stunned by Hugh's

indiscretions. He'd told Jude about the ruering doll, her experience in Napier's Wood, and even her history of migraines. Thank goodness she'd said nothing to her husband about finding herself 'inside' the hidden room behind the wallpaper. He and Jude would've had a field day with that.

"It's fascinating, right?" Jude ended triumphantly. "The migraines could make you receptive to ghostly transmissions, Luce. You're on the right frequency, so to speak. Next stage could be a third-level encounter."

"What's that?"

"I'll explain in a bit."

"Soup's ready," announced Hugh. "Luce, would you hand round the buttered bread?"

Moments later, Lucy pushed her spoon through thick mushroom soup. Her stomach rose to reject it.

"I've got everything in the car," said Jude, dipping her own spoon. "Ouija board, card table – just need a paper cup or plastic beaker. You don't want to use glass."

"Why not?" asked Lucy.

"Had an incident at school once – the glass flew across the room and shattered on a wall. One bit ricocheted and nearly caught a girl in the eye."

"What's a third-level encounter?" Lucy pressed. "Though I can probably guess."

"There are three phases to a haunting," Jude said. "First, smells and noises. Second, objects moving and, finally, a full manifestation. Like your sighting in the wood. Only, you glimpsed a ghost without encountering it. Interaction is also key to the third level."

Lucy snorted. "Never heard such bollocks, to be brutally frank."

Hugh said hurriedly: "*I've* been reading about the stone tape theory. It started out as this idea that the past was absorbed by the stones or bricks of buildings in the form of sounds or visions-"

"Oh yeah, I know this one too," interrupted Jude. "It's reckoned that events are stored in the fabric of a place and play back as if on a loop. Like the sighting of Phineas jumping from an upper window. Or you glimpsing Mickey in the wood, Lucy. An invisible video recorder plays back the image."

Lucy frowned. "Are you saying the trees absorbed past events, just like stones and bricks? But if it's a recording on a loop, why don't we see Phineas, over and over, falling from a window? Or Belle being dragged out of the house?" She shuddered. "Not that I want to."

"Maybe conditions aren't right," said Jude. "Or the Rook House ghosts aren't just images, they're actually here. And they want something or want to tell us something." She scraped the spoon around her bowl in defiance of any listening ghosts. "All grist to our seance mill, I'd have thought. I'll fetch my stuff from the car."

"I'll go out with you," said Hugh.

"I think I can walk three paces there and back without being menaced by a headless horseman."

When she'd gone through the back door in a blast of cold air, Lucy asked Hugh: "Do you know who she contacted in her previous dabbling?"

"Oh, that was schoolgirl stuff and nonsense," he replied, gathering the bowls. "You didn't finish your soup."

"Ate most of it. Tasted funny. And it's still all bollocks. How *does* the stone tape theory explain me seeing things in the middle of Napier's Wood? You just said the images were absorbed into the fabric of buildings."

"Luce." He stacked the bowls, regarding her anxiously. "Honestly, tonight could help us decide whether to stick or twist. Don't you want to get to the bottom of the rumours about this place?"

Did she? It occurred to her that previous tenants had lived here peaceably enough without rocking the boat. She merely shrugged in reply. Too late to back out now. Apparently, she was part of tonight's 'experiment': crucial to it, according to Jude.

Jude returned carrying a small cardboard box, a folded-up table wedged beneath her arm. "Had a devil of a job finding all the bits in the first place. Wish I had an EMF meter for measuring electromagnetic fields."

"Like they had on *Ghostbusters*?" laughed Lucy.

"Luce, if you're not going to take this seriously…"

"How can anyone take this seriously?"

Jude tipped her head towards the ceiling, unfazed by Lucy's persistent scoffing. "Let's get on with it. I'm dying to see this fabled room anyway."

Jude switched on the light in the acanthus room and shivered. She strode across the floorboards, heels snapping like gunshots, setting Lucy's teeth on edge.

She and Hugh were in their usual thick-soled socks, preferring to glide about the house without advertising their presence.

Jude touched the radiator under the window. "Ouch! That's roasting."

"Heating this room makes no difference," Lucy shrugged. "A cold-spot room. Spookology 101."

Jude peered out of the uncurtained window into the blue-black night, the glass reflecting their distorted faces. "What's the view out there in daytime?"

"An old shed and a sightline of the ridge leading up to the wood."

"Cool," nodded Jude in the tone of a Californian teen. "Whole vibe's already fantastically creepy."

She turned and took the box that Lucy had carried up for her, setting it down by the fireplace. The flue made its obligatory sound of pursed lips round a bottle rim, Jude taking a step back as a rush of air teased her heels.

Hugh asked where she wanted the card table.

"Just here in the centre of the room. Lighting's all wrong with that unshaded bulb, though," Jude frowned. "We'll use the candle I brought. But first, this." She pulled a slim, wand-like object from the box. "Shut the door and turn off the light, Hugh."

He obeyed and they were plunged into blackness. Lucy suppressed the urge to scream.

A purplish-blue light pooled over the fireplace, directed from the wand in Jude's hand. "Ultraviolet light pen," she explained. "Absolute must if you're staying in a hotel with fewer than four stars. Shows up marks on walls and floors that you can't see with the naked eye."

The ominously coloured light roved about the room in sync with Jude's creaking footsteps. She stopped. "What's *that*?"

Lucy examined the blurry outlines of wingtips on the wall-paper. "Jackdaw got trapped in here, the same day the ruering doll fell down the chimney. What about the floor?" she asked impatiently. "Train that light on the floorboards, near here." She pressed a hand over the wallpaper, close to the imagined outline of a wardrobe.

Jude flicked the light downwards, showing a mishmash of footprints on the bare boards.

Lucy realised that her alleged handprints from days ago were now buried under layers of restless pacing.

Jude tossed her UV light pen back into the box and unfolded the card table, while Hugh flicked the overhead light back on. "Wish I'd brought a tape recorder to record any unusual sounds," Jude sighed. "Oversight on my part."

"You'd have to clear it up afterwards to filter out the non-stop creaking floorboards and moaning wind," Hugh replied. "Know how to do that?"

"No," Jude admitted. "Let's stick with what we have. I'll light the candle and away we go. Anyone got an issue with kneeling on the floor?"

The candle, black as obsidian, was shoved into an open-necked bottle, Jude igniting it with a lighter. "All you really need for this activity," she said, "is a table, a sheet of paper tacked to a piece of cardboard and a plastic tumbler like so instead of a la di da planchette. Et voila."

As they knelt around the card table, Jude pointed to her homemade Ouija board. "I've included the letters of the alphabet, numbers one to nine and the words 'yes', 'no' and 'farewell'. Everyone ready? Hugh, overhead light off again, please."

As soon as the light went off, the serpentine coils of the acanthus leaves formed new tendrils behind the candle flame. Lucy stared into the flame until her eyes hurt. This was a bad idea.

"Door open or left closed?" asked Hugh.

"Closed, I think. Creates a tightly defined space."

Once Hugh had reclaimed the floor, Jude turned the tumbler upside down so that its rim sat in the centre of the numbered and lettered board. "Just put the tips of your index fingers on the tumbler's base but don't press down or make any attempt to move it. Got it?"

Outside, the wind picked up. Candlelight traced the outlines of furled leaves on the wall. Lucy sat with her back to the black maw of the fireplace. She felt sleepy and hyper-alert at the same time. She felt like giggling and rolling on to her back for a tummy tickle. She felt like throwing up.

Jude began in a deep, serious voice: "We are aware this room may have witnessed certain events in the past. Can someone who once lived in this house tell us more?"

The tumbler didn't move.

"I think it has to start out less specific," said Hugh. "Like, is there a spirit nearby who would like to make contact?"

The tumbler trembled and slid diagonally to the word 'yes'.

"Holy hellfire," gulped Hugh. "I said that as a 'for instance'. Didn't know they'd take me up on it."

Jude shushed him. "What is your name, spirit?"

The tumbler circled 'yes' uncertainly, then moved towards 'no' and hovered over it.

Jude shut her eyes. "No, you don't have a name or no, you don't wish to share it?"

The tumbler moved to the letter 'S'. Then it was off again, Jude reading out the letters as the tumbler circled, danced and hovered: "P, I, R, I, T, N, E, A, R, B, Y"

"That confirms their presence!" whispered Jude excitedly. "Pretty unequivocal, that. Who are you, spirit? Can you tell us your name?"

The tumbler made several new moves. They stared at what it spelt out: "Y, O, U, A, R, E"

Lucy had a sudden realisation. "They're repeating back some of your words, Jude. Like an echo. 'You are' is a reversed echo of 'are you?' And before that, Hugh asked if there was a spirit nearby. Th-they're toying with us."

She recalled the echo she'd heard in the wood, her own words boomeranging back with a seam of mocking malice.

"Luce could be on to something," frowned Hugh, annoyed at the spectral cheek of it.

"Spirit, we only wish to make contact," said Jude solemnly. "And to ask what it is you seek or why you stay in this house."

The tumbler was off again: "W, H, A, T, Y, O, U, S, E, E, K"

Lucy took her fingers off the tumbler. Now it was more than a mocking echo – it was a dig at them for holding a seance in the first place as a form of morbid entertainment.

"Lucy, you're breaking the circle," snapped Jude.

"Don't care."

"This won't work unless we're all on boar-"

"Are you spelling out these words?" she asked Jude.

"Of course not."

"Well, I've had enough. I don't like this. I-"

A noise like a pistol crack made them all jump. It seemed to come from a long way away, yet resounded throughout the room with sharp clarity. The candle flame bent sharply before fluttering upwards again. "What was that?" asked Jude hoarsely.

"The portrait in the living room, I think," croaked Hugh. "Probably fell off in a sudden draught. See the way the flame wavered just then?"

Lucy sat tight. She'd been about to go downstairs and leave them to it, but now she was terrified of going it alone.

"Let us proceed," said Jude. "Lucy, put your fingers back on the tumbler."

Lucy debated telling Jude to take a running jump, then reluctantly obeyed.

"Spirit, are you Belle Napier?" Jude intoned. "Or her son, Phineas? Are you Ezra?"

The tumbler trembled but didn't move.

"One of the servants? Am I getting warm? Wait! That's it, isn't it? You're a servant girl who died a lonely death in this room from TB or scarlet fever."

The tumbler shot off once more on its travels. This time it spelt out: "G, E, T, T, I, N, G, W, A, R, M"

Lucy felt acid reflux bubbling. She peered from Hugh to Jude and back again. Was one of them orchestrating this?

"Hang on," said Hugh suddenly. "Don't you get it? They're *all* here. The ones who never left."

The candle blew out, guttered by an audible breath tinged with mocking laughter.

In the darkness, Lucy saw an outline rear up, a fourth at the card table.

She yelled in terror and rocked back on her heels. In the same instance, the tumbler shot off the table, flew across the room and hit the tiled fireplace.

Lucy tried to stand up and reach for Hugh, but she was pulled back towards the fireplace by questing fingers on a long, elastic limb that coiled round her neck. She couldn't breathe.

The same 'hand' had grasped her arm in her 'dream' of being inside the hidden room. She remembered its icy-hot grip.

She tried to claw the limb away, slicing through black mist knobbled with invisible bone. She tried to scream. She tried...

21

"My dear girl." A face swam into my vision. A face with penetrating blue eyes and a thick handlebar moustache. "My dear girl, whatever is the matter now?"

I pulled my hands from my throat and gulped down air, looking around. It was daylight. A hazy summer sun latticed the rich rug on the floor. I was lying in bed; my comfortable, canopied bed overlooking the tunnel of elms at the front of the house.

The sheets had been changed, of course. More than once this past week. Ezra sat on the counterpane, regarding me with concern and something else – predatory inspection. It matched the mocking hauteur of his tone. "Another nightmare?" he asked.

I nodded, my throat still raw from where I'd clutched it in my sleep as I imagined an unseen force doing the same.

"You must take care of yourself. For obvious reasons." He laid a hand on the counterpane to touch my violated belly.

I shrank from the brazen intimacy of his touch. My husband's touch. I tried to meet his eye, but quailed at the last moment. I could not endure another day in this house with this man.

"Where is my son?" My voice a mere shadow of itself.

"*My* son, my dear Belle. He's with his wet nurse, as he should be."

I tried not to tremble but it was no good as I forced out the next words between chattering teeth: "Did you, did you really?" Or had I imagined what he'd done? Oh God, I hoped so.

"I've already explained the price of your treachery," he replied mildly. "I did what I had to."

And then I wished I *had* been strangled inside a dream.

I turned my face into the pillow with a cry of despair: "I hate you! I hate you!"

He slapped me across the face. Not hard, but hard enough.

I gasped at the outrage. For all his coldness, he'd never struck me before.

"You will behave, madam," he said, "for the sake of appearances. Naturally, I shall never touch you again or allow you to be touched. You are wicked, tainted, diseased in mind and corrupt in body." He added calmly: "Now you must rest. The doctor was very clear about that."

I touched my burning cheek and forced my gaze to meet his. "What do you intend for me?"

"You'll attend the christening of my son, as befits Mrs Ezra Napier. The boy will be called Phineas after my father. Shortly afterwards, you'll remove to Eastbourne for your health and express a desire to remain there. I'll divorce you, quietly, and remarry if I choose to do so. You will do as you're told if you wish to retain a small allowance and a roof over your head far from here."

"But my son…"

"I may permit him to visit you when older, if you are obedient and play your part." His voice turned icy. "Do you intend to play your part?"

I nodded, still clutching my cheek.

"I should like to hear you say it."

I struggled upright on my pillows. "I-I shall be a model wife to you, sir."

He snorted. "I think that ship has sailed. You have besmirched the word *wife*. I require only your assurance that you will behave."

My ragged fingernails curled around the counterpane. "I-I will."

He slid off the bed and moved away. Oh, the relief.

"I should like to get up today," I murmured. "Take a short walk outside."

He gazed down from on high. "The doctor advises against."

"But the fresh air and some exercise may restore my spirits more quickly. For the sake of appearances," I managed to add.

I could see him weighing it up. He was a proud man and he hated me. What could I do about that when I hated myself as much as I loathed him?

"Just a short walk," I repeated, wheedling.

Shrewd, piercing eyes flicked over me. "Is that wise?"

"I would only go as far as – perhaps the pear orchard?"

His gaze held me, his solicitous smile just shy of mockery. "Not the wood? Or the sunken lawn? Perhaps the rose garden, so fragrant at this time of year. Just as when you came here, a fresh, innocent bride."

He was taunting me. Somehow, he knew it all.

"Oh, the pear orchard would suit me better, I think. I'll bring Darrow with me," I added quickly. "I have no intention of, of…"

"Wandering off to speak to those you shouldn't? Very well. I'll have Mrs Tankerton order Cook to prepare breakfast for you in the morning room. But no walking. Myers will take you to the orchard in the donkey trap. The climb is quite steep and you are hardly fit to tackle it. You may bring your maid."

I nodded. I dared not ask where Mickey might be. I hadn't seen him for weeks past, long before my confinement. But Darrow might know his whereabouts.

And Darrow was still my maid, so Ezra hadn't marked her out as complicit in my deceit, and for that, my grieving soul rejoiced. I was glad now that I'd kept her at a certain distance.

Pride had played a part, of course; in the end, I'd preferred to let her imagine I had a lover rather than rely on her discretion too completely.

But concern for her had stopped me too. The less she knew, the more convincingly she could protest her innocence, if called to do so.

"I hope to see you downstairs in due course," said Ezra with something approaching civility and I nodded absently, forgetting just for a second that he was my jailer from now on. And something worse I could not even put a name to. Not then.

Did his cold rage absolve me of all that I'd done? Was his cruelty to me now a vindication of my loathing for him or a justified response to my betrayal?

Once he'd left, I stumbled out of bed, wincing, tiptoed to my wardrobe and eased open its door, my movements slow and cumbersome.

Darrow came to dress me. "Here, let me, marm." She gently pushed away my hands as I fumbled with hooks. "You're still weak from the birth."

"Have you seen the child, Darrow?"

She shook her head. "But the wet nurse has gone below stairs to heat milk and says he's as bonny as his mother."

I brooded. Confined to this room for days, I had no idea what she and the other servants knew or didn't know about events as they'd really happened. I knew so little of anything.

Perhaps it was the mention of the wet nurse and milk that caused a sudden, embarrassing leakage from my bosom. Wordlessly, Darrow fetched a towel to dry me before she continued to help me dress. "That will happen from time to time, marm. We must find a way to conceal it."

She was a good girl, stout of frame and character. I'd raised her up from nowhere to be lady's maid, telling Ezra that a good lady's maid was hard to come by. That had been a 'warning' to keep his hands from straying to her underskirts.

I'd seen the wreckage he left in his wake. Half the county talked of it.

Once, I even spied on him on the back stairs, little Angharad the Welsh scullery maid pinned to the wall while he juddered and shook against her, thick moustache scouring her small white face as he ordered her to "say my name in that Welsh lilt of yours, my little chapel bell! Let me ring you."

He'd rung her good and proper and I'd guessed the result before she did, poor innocent, watched it push out her apron until she was tossed aside with the meat bones and cabbage stalks, dismissed as a silly, ruined girl who couldn't keep her legs together.

Maybe she'd gone back to Wales? I'd asked Darrow to find out, but word came back that Angharad had been seen begging at the crossroads and then not seen at all. Only my status had so far spared me the same fate.

Now Darrow walked to the window, drew back the curtains fully and gazed at me in consternation. "Your face!"

I raised a hand to cover the stripe of bright red still glowing above my cheekbone. "It's nothing." My frenzied gaze roved the room, dismayed at how little of value I owned. If only I could buy a ticket, take my son, escape from here to... where?

"Mr Napier thinks Eastbourne may agree with me, Darrow, especially at this time of year. I plan to travel there soon. I hope you'll come with me."

Darrow nodded, gaze now averted. "I'll fetch down your valises, marm, and check what's in the laundry room, ready to press and pack."

Then everything went white and I sank to my haunches.

Darrow rushed over. "Let me get you back into bed."

I let her help me up, then shook my head. "I'm to go down to breakfast, then you and I will go as far as the orchard in the donkey trap."

We can talk properly there, I stopped myself adding. While old Myers dozed over his pipe stem and the donkey munched grass in the shafts, I'd step down for a walk and finally take Darrow more fully into my confidence.

It was time and I had no other recourse. I'd ask her to get word to Mickey to meet me as soon as possible in our usual place.

He could not fail me once he learnt the full horror of what Ezra had done, a truth I intended to share only with him. For now, I'd only reveal to Darrow that I had a matter of the utmost urgency to discuss with Mr Nellis and that I must send her to ask him to meet me in our 'usual place' at midnight this very eve.

So far, Ezra hadn't locked me in my room. Should I continue to 'behave', there was no reason for him to doubt my utter capitulation to his will. Of course, that was assuming I'd find the strength to climb the ridge and walk into the wood tonight. But this morning's walk could prepare me.

"The pear orchard, marm?" Darrow was looking at me askance.

"To take the air." I moistened cracked lips. "I've seen so little of the outside world these past weeks. What of the servants, are they all well?"

"Millie has the toothache, so Cook has sent to Lowmorten for oil of cloves. Mrs Tankerton complains of rheumatism in her wrists again, despite the fine weather."

"And what of the gardeners?"

"I'm sure they're busy, marm."

"Have you seen Mr Potts and Mr Nellis?"

Darrow nodded without (perhaps) realising how much depended on her answer. "Seen them both in the distance, marm, when I've gone to and from the ice house. You can't miss that foot on Mickey Nellis."

Which was true, and brought sweet relief. Ezra hadn't taken revenge on Mickey – at least, not yet.

And how could he do so, without advertising the probable cause or at least fanning a rumour?

I pressed Darrow's arm gratefully. "We'll take the air after my breakfast, Darrow. You're a good girl. I can depend on you, can't I?"

"Of course, marm. Always." Her gaze was clear and untroubled. My good Darrow.

I felt a ray of hope. Once Mickey knew what Ezra had done, he'd stop at nothing to get all three of us away from here: me, him, our son. Mickey loved me, I knew he did.

But then that little ray of hope melted away.

What *could* he do? Mickey was a groundsman with a deformed foot and a rudimentary knowledge of letters and numbers; Ezra a gentleman with riches, a cruelly agile mind and a deep wellspring of malice.

I shook as Darrow buttoned me up at the back. "You're sure you wouldn't rather go back to bed, marm?"

"I'm fine, thank you, just a little unsteady."

How could I get to my son? How would Mickey? What if I shouted the truth of the child's parentage from the rooftops or threatened to? Might that be enough to shame Ezra into cutting his losses?

I'd said nothing to Mickey as I realised my condition, with no way of knowing *then* who the father might be. I'd decided to let nature take its course, especially as Mickey had made clear he wouldn't run away with me. *Then.* Above all, I'd simply allowed events to develop because there was nothing else I could do.

Oddly, for all my panic, the pregnancy had been the most tranquil period of my life.

I'd told myself that if I didn't know who the father was, how would Ezra?

In the highest flights of fancy, I'd convinced myself that all this had happened for the best, hastening the fulfilment of my purpose as Ezra's wife.

Best of all, a delighted Ezra had kept a respectful distance, cosseted and fussed over me, sent to York for delicacies and heaped my plate with nectarines dipped in sugar.

Never for a moment had I felt sorry for him, knowing his delight might be unfounded. I only thought of him as a dark 'thing' in my life, a presence I had to endure. Which was all he deserved, having reduced me to a brood mare.

But now that the truth was known by at least three people – myself, Ezra and Doctor Shaw, who'd attended my delivery – I knew I was in a terrible bind.

What if Ezra took my son – Phineas – away from me *forever*? He might've spun the Eastbourne story to keep me in the dark until he could sever me completely from my son.

I turned to Darrow. "I want to see the baby before we set out for the orchard. Have the wet nurse bring him here after I return from breakfast."

"Yes, marm."

Even if I couldn't flee with him at this very moment, at least I could hold my son. He'd learn my smell and the sound of my voice and know at once that I was his mother.

I took Darrow's arm to leave the room. My good girl. Whatever discretion held her back from voicing it, she had to be aware of Ezra's cruelty. She must have seen other maids turned out of the house for the disgrace pushing at their aprons. And she must have realised I'd protected her from such a fate.

"Do you – do you have a little money put by from your wages, Darrow? Mr Napier has always been generous to you, I believe."

She nodded.

"I may beg to borrow a little from you, in due course."

Her silence signalled her amazement.

"My pocketbook is a little light at the moment, you see, and I don't wish to trouble Mr Napier. I'll repay you, of course."

"You don't need to explain owt, marm." And she squeezed my elbow in what might've been an over-familiar gesture in any other circumstance.

But I'd just asked to borrow money off a servant. And shortly, I'd ask this same servant to carry a message to the under-gardener who dragged his foot and whistled out of tune.

Beyond the room, the landing sloped away from me, at once alien and familiar. I groped my way towards the staircase, wondering which shut door my baby lay behind. If only I could hear a cry. But then, I knew I'd rush in there, weak as I was, scoop him up and never let him be prised from my clasp again.

At the top of the staircase, I gripped a carved pineapple instead, almost hard enough to break my fingers. How would I make it to the wood tonight in darkness and find the path to our secret bower? But I had to. I had to.

"Marm..."

"It's only a little dizziness, Darrow, nothing to alarm. Go to the wet nurse this very moment to relay my request about bringing my son to my room."

She nodded but went on watching me as I descended the stairs on trembling legs, anxiety etched on her broad, kindly face. She only hastened away from the top of the stairs once I'd cleared the final tread.

The morning room was empty, thank God, so I could sit and eat alone. But the few mouthfuls I managed tasted like sawdust.

Millie came and served me coffee, one hand raised to her

swollen cheek. We had something in common, then. "Have you taken the oil of cloves yet, Millie?"

"Still waiting on it, marm. Cook says a tot of brandy may do just as well. I can't abide the notion of pulling but Cook says if I don't leave off blubbering, she'll tie a piece of string to the scullery door and yank it out herself."

Poor mite. A replacement for Angharad, she was too red and cracked from skivvying to catch even Ezra's wandering eye. She didn't know that her plainness was a shield against ruination.

The coffee was good, hot and restorative. Perhaps enough of it would clear my thoughts and soften the edges of my despair. Once I spoke to Mickey tonight – and I *would* get to our bower in the wood – he could go into Lowmorten first thing tomorrow and look up train times to London via York. He might have to purchase the tickets himself before I secured Darrow's loan.

As for tonight, I could creep down the back stairs when everyone was asleep, then slip through the passageway that ran along the back of the log store and led to the log shed outside.

How to leave here undetected with my son in my arms, once Mickey had secured our tickets, was a harder puzzle to solve. I'd need Darrow again, for sure.

I ached for Mickey in body and soul. Once I'd begun to show, Ezra had forbidden me to walk further than the sunken lawn, and then only in clement weather, always accompanied by Darrow.

But it seemed obvious to me that, once Mickey heard of my condition from other servants, he'd have wondered whether the coming child was his.

Then again, fear of that possibility would've kept him away from me at all costs.

And what if Ezra did risk turning Mickey out of his job, beggaring him in the process? Mickey had told me often enough that employment was hard to come by. Ezra had only to fault his work and dismiss him on the spot.

And even when Mickey did learn the truth – the *whole,* terrible truth – no one would believe it, or offer him work once it was known.

Ezra held all the cards.

London, then, was our only chance. A chance to start over.

Sitting there, the hard chair digging into my aching back, I dared to open a door into my mind and peek inside, hoping to find respite in the memory of my first meeting with Mickey, his fingers touching mine as he handed me an apricot rose.

But instead, memory served up my first meeting with Ezra in Grandfather's drawing room, a great black corvid hovering over my wrist, cold lips grazing my skin while colder eyes scrutinised me as a shopkeeper might assess his stock or a horse breeder follow the lines of a flank.

"Yes, she will do very well," he had the temerity to say to Grandfather in front of me. "She's just as you described, Sir Noah. Quite fetching. But is she wilful?"

"Sir," I'd said archly, extracting my hand. "You should address such questions to me."

"There's your answer," my grandfather had grumbled. "No doubt the country air will knock off her corners. Or you've ways and means yourself, Mr Napier?"

"I've broken in many a filly," Ezra had observed, but when he'd smiled at me, for a fleeting instant, I'd seen something else – a capacity for passion that made my pulse quicken.

I believed that he genuinely loved me in that moment, as far as he was able to – or at least, had genuinely wished to possess and cosset me, as long as I played by his rules.

But I'd shattered those rules and there could be no going back, for either of us.

The deal was soon made. Grandfather laid out his debts to me (perhaps he exaggerated to gain my acquiescence?) and warned that we'd both be on the street if I did not "see things through".

He stressed that Ezra was a good man, "a member of White's like myself. Impeccable breeding. And looking for a wife of the same."

I was married to Ezra Napier a month later.

A brief honeymoon at a respectable boarding house in Dawlish; he was gentle with me, much to my surprise. But even then, he was brusque with servants and ready to raise his whip to a stable lad before the ostler stepped between them.

I bonded with the cheerful young maid who brought a pitcher of fresh water to our rooms each morning. One morning, after Ezra had left on a walk, the cheerful young maid came in with downcast, red-rimmed eyes that refused to meet mine. When she set down the pitcher by the washstand, her cap slipped and I saw what looked like fresh teeth marks on her neck.

"What has happened?" I asked, horrified.

It took a while to coax the truth from her. She was a local orphan sent into service at the boarding house aged 13 and ill-used ever since by the landlord and his wife.

She was 18 now and, though she longed to leave, feared to lose her home and receive a bad reference.

"They have no right to gnaw you like a bone!" I'd gasped indignantly.

"Oh marm, don't say owt or it'll go worse for me again."

I promised her I'd say nothing, but I did tell Ezra when he came back. "I suspect the marks I saw on her body were few among many."

He seemed indifferent to the girl's plight. "What would you have me do, rescue every urchin from here to Exeter treated harshly by their employer?"

"Rescue, yes! I'd have us rescue her! She's been beaten for years probably, Ezra, but bears it all with good cheer before the guests. Her courage deserves recognition and reward. Think of it as a wedding present to me," I'd added, pleased with my diplomatic skill. "We can take her back to Rook House with us. I'm sure they could use one more servant about the place and you see that she is pliable and hardworking."

"Well," he'd said, gathering me up, "I cannot deny my bride on her honeymoon. I'll speak to the brutish landlord and see what he has to say. No doubt he'll agree to part with her for a compensatory sum."

Was Darrow the last true gift he had ever bought me?

There were trinkets certainly. Before we left Dawlish, he bought me a set of long hairpins decorated with green tourmaline stars. Back at Rook House, he'd sometimes dismiss Darrow to affix them himself, once or twice jabbing me in the skull as I sat before the mirror, then apologising for his clumsiness while smiling and kissing my neck and holding my gaze in the silvered glass.

His interest in how I presented myself extended to what colours I should adopt for the season or weave into my needlework. I'd thought such interest proof of passion at first, before I saw it for what it was – throwing golden reins over his broken-in filly and pulling on them whenever she grew too mettlesome.

And I'd learned how easily he could turn, like a Devon fishing sky. I came to understand that his calm voice and measured words were often just brooding skies before the storm crashed in.

I closed the door firmly on such memories and looked at the clock ticking on the far wall of the morning room. I had no idea where my gold timepiece was. As I wiped away the last crumb with my napkin, Mrs Tankerton the housekeeper sailed into the room, all black bombazine and cold disapproval.

I told her I'd go upstairs to prepare for my visit to the pear orchard.

"Of course, marm. Shall I see you up the stairs?"

"I'm not an invalid!" I snapped, then thought better of antagonising her. Tankerton had always played her cards close to her chest. I'd no idea if she was Ezra's familiar or an impartial bystander. "Thank you for the offer, Tankerton, but the doctor said I should use my limbs as much as possible."

"Of course."

At the top of the stairs, I paused. All was quiet, slumbering in the drowsiness of a summer's day. I reached my bedroom, pausing breathless at the door. Was my son already inside, waiting for me?

I shut my eyes and grasped the doorknob.

The door wouldn't open. I rattled it. Was it stuck?

Footsteps approaching; I turned, identifying the white apron of Darrow and ready to ask: "What is the meaning of this?"

But she wasn't alone. Ezra had her elbow gripped in a vice-like hand. His smile was almost ecstatic beneath his cold blue eyes. "I don't think that room is suitable for you any longer, my dear. You'll be good enough to follow me."

Darrow wouldn't meet my eye, her red, puffy gaze cast to the floor.

I tried to push past him, back down the stairs, only to have Tankerton block my way, resplendently awful and festooned with keys.

Ezra released his grip on Darrow, who scuttled away down the stairs, not once looking back.

He picked up my hand and gently kissed it, his eyes never leaving my face. "Come along, my dear. I've arranged for you to be very comfortable and untroubled. Because you've been deeply troubled, haven't you?"

He turned slightly and I saw that Doctor Shaw had appeared behind Tankerton.

"I wouldn't be doing my duty if I didn't look after you properly and take the very best care of you that I can. Will you let me do that?" Ezra pleaded. "I see that you won't," he added with sad patience as I tried to struggle out of his clasp.

Doctor Shaw advanced, holding a syringe that I remembered from my confinement. He'd taken it from a box where it lay alongside two hideous metal needles. Now he raised the syringe and I saw a flash of silver-coloured metal. "Please, Ezra, my son..."

"*My* son will want for nothing. I'll see to it."

He drew my hand deeper into his grasp, rucking up the delicate voile of my sleeve and offering my outstretched arm to Doctor Shaw. The needle went in with a pain and violence that made me scream, dizzying black stars blooming behind my eyes.

The darkness... please! Help me, anyone, help me...!

Hate, hate, hate coursing through me with the black poison syringed into my veins! And rage – against Ezra and my conniving grandfather, against Doctor Shaw, even against Mickey... men who'd imprisoned, demeaned, destroyed and ultimately abandoned me.

I reached out for that unflinching blue eye, longing to claw it from his face, uttering a screa-

22

"Luce!" Hugh twisted away from Lucy's flailing arm as she lunged at him across the card table. "Luce. Lucy?" Despite the room's darkness, he snapped his fingers in front of her face, then turned an accusing glare on Jude. "What was in that stuff?"

"Not enough to knock out a baby. You did distribute it the way I said?"

"Of course I did!"

"Well, look at us, totally unaffected. She must have a lower tolerance."

Hugh pulled Lucy towards him and tried to soothe her. "Yeah, well, she's really out of it, Jude. Glassy-eyed. And babbling away about Ezra and some other names I can't catch."

"This could be one of the levels of haunting I didn't address. Possession. I'm not sure what to do if that's the case."

"That's just great, Jude!"

"I'm not serious, you twonk!" Jude crossed the room to snap on the overhead light. "Whole thing was getting weird anyway, the way the candle went out, then she yelled and jerked back like that. We're in the clear unless she starts levitating and spewing green bile."

"Shut up!" hissed Hugh, now holding Lucy's wrist. He knelt by her and folded her hands into the lap of her juddering body. "Mouse, it's me, Hugh. You're safe here, with me and Jude. There's nothing to be afraid of."

"Wouldn't be too sure of that," muttered Jude.

Lucy refocused and gazed around the room. "Wh-what happened?"

"You tell us," Jude snorted. "You went full padded cell there for a few secs, shrieking and waving your arms about."

"Don't exaggerate, Jude. You were a bit out of it, love. What do you remember?"

Lucy rubbed her eyes. "I think I had one of those weird episodes again. Like a dream but not a dream. It's all hazy and jumbled... there was another figure at the table and then I felt someone get hold of me, so I lashed out-"

"That was me, love. You tried to claw my face."

"God, did I? Sorry."

"It's all right. Must've been pretty scary."

Lucy bit her lip until a bead of blood popped out. "I *told* you this was a bad idea."

"Got results, though," said Jude. "Those words spelt out by the tumbler and your reaction to them, going full tonto on us."

"Jude!"

"Everything's a game to you, isn't it?" Lucy croaked. "You don't care who you hurt in the process!"

"You're not hurt," replied Jude evenly. "But you nearly took a chunk out of Hugh."

"I didn't know what I was doing or where I was for a few seconds." Lucy blinked at Hugh. "We should've left well alone."

Hugh glanced at Jude. "I'm starting to think you're right."

Jude strode out of the room, her heels clacking along the landing and down the stairs. She threw light switches as she went, daring any ghosts to tap out Morse code through flickering sockets.

"I'm absolutely knackered," said Lucy, chin dropping towards her chest. "And I feel a bit sick. I don't want to see her again tonight. Can you get rid of her while I go straight to bed?"

"Of course. I'm so sorry for this, Mouse. Should've listened to you all along."

He put her tenderly into bed and drew the duvet up to her chin, then switched off the light and hovered in the open doorway of the bedroom, looking back at her.

Lucy was about to let herself drift off when Jude joined him in the doorway, sipping from a glass. "Gone beddy byes, has she?"

"Sssh, keep your voice down!" Hugh peered back at the bed where Lucy lay with tightly shut eyes. "Wish you weren't so blasé, Jude. What if she's had an allergic reaction, like you read about when someone takes ecstasy? She said she feels sick and she's a weird colour."

"Calm down, panicky Pete. Stuff I gave you was organic and far less harmful than Es. Soup would've diluted it anyway. Plus, studies say shrooms are good for headaches. You wanted a reaction, didn't you? That's what we got."

"From using psychedelic drugs!"

"Don't be so dramatic. I told you, it was organic. Barely a magic mushroom to begin with."

"Tell me truthfully, Jude, did *you* spell out any of those words?"

"No. Did you?"

"No. And I'm sure Luce didn't."

"Are you? She could've been channelling a spirit without realising it. Anyway, I've been thinking about the words and they *could* be a message. *Spirit nearby you are what you seek getting warm.*"

"What sort of message is that?"

"Dunno," admitted Jude. "But it's almost a sentence. We're close to something, I can feel it. This wine tastes horrible, by the way. Maybe a ghost has gobbed in it to teach you not to buy screwtops or keep booze in the fridge." She turned towards the landing. "Anyway, I'll take my box of tricks and get out of your hair. Let me know if she remembers anything else when she wakes up."

"At this point, I'd settle for her waking up without brain damage."

"Oh God, dramatic, much?"

Hugh's reply was lost on Lucy as he followed Jude out of the room, closing the door softly behind him.

Lucy opened her eyes and stared into darkness.

If proof were needed of a haunting at Rook House, the odds were stacking up.

But if proof were needed that Pinky's ominous warning held a ring of truth, it seemed a stone-cold certainty that something had already begun between her husband and their nearest neighbour.

Lucy woke to pale lemon light seeping through a gap in the curtains. She'd slept right through the night.

Alone in the bed, she stared in bewilderment at the water-stained ceiling rose. Hadn't she slept in a different bed just a few hours ago? A much narrower bed? She spread her arms and legs to make sheet angels, luxuriating in the space she occupied.

Instinctively, she rolled over and touched her back, feeling gingerly for – for scars along her spine. But the skin was smooth.

She sat up and the room tilted. Suddenly nauseous, she leapt out of bed and ran to the bathroom in socked feet, making it just in time to throw up. She stared at the cloudy, mushroomy contents of the toilet bowl.

Something nagged at her, tugging with softly urgent claws deep in her Mariana Trench.

Not claws, but words, floating to the scummy surface of her

purged body and mind – *She must have a lower tolerance... You wanted a reaction, didn't you?*

She washed her face and went back to bed.

Ten minutes later, footsteps on the stairs announced Hugh, who appeared in the room with a steaming mug and a plate of buttered toast perched on a tray. "Thought I'd let you sleep in, but it's gone nine, so sprang into action when I heard you moving about. Even cut the crusts off. How'd you feel?"

"Bit delicate. What happened to me last night? Don't remember much."

He sat on the bed and put the tray on her lap, watching solicitously as she bit into a triangle of toast. "You had the strongest reaction of all of us to the Ouija board. As Jude reckoned might be the case." He reminded her of the words the board had spelt out. "You kind of flipped and went mentally AWOL for a few seconds."

She frowned. "Seemed longer than that."

"So you do remember?"

"Not really. It's all in a locked vault and I don't have the key. It's like, my mind's trying to protect me from revisiting whatever happened. So I'm guessing I wasn't in a good place. Literally."

He nodded. "I'll text Jude and tell her you're OK. We were both worried."

"Think I'll get up in a bit and walk as far as the pear orchard. No need for the donkey trap."

"What?"

She blinked. "Dunno why I said that."

"Ezra's portrait hadn't fallen off the wall, by the way. Jude and I checked on her way out last night. No idea what that thunderclap was. Maybe we imagined it."

"Can I ask you something?"

"Go for it."

"Was there something in the soup we had last night? The

condemned spiritualists ate a hearty meal," she reminded him dully.

At once he looked cornered. "Luce, I... it was just a few shrooms to mix in with the shredded portobellos. Quality stuff, Jude assures me."

"So you and Jude decided to drug me?"

"We all took the same amount! It was just to... to heighten the experience, Jude said."

"Then why not tell me in advance?"

"Didn't think you'd go for it."

"So you dosed me anyway. After I'd told you about my migraines and that certain foods can trigger them."

"*Micro*-dosed you. Come on, it was just to make everything more 3-D and Technicolor. Like I said, heightened."

"Or make us – me – susceptible to imagining a load of old cobblers!" She thrust the tray back at him, nearly spilling its contents. "You can take this away. Might need to hire a poison taster from now on."

"Luce – Mouse – this is ridiculous! It was about the same as taking a slightly hot chilli. You didn't kick off that time we went to that cantina in London and the chef admitted later to slipping a couple into our sauce."

"I didn't end up tripping from a slightly hot chilli."

"Maybe that was just blind luck, given what you've said about your migraines. Still think you're overreacting."

"I know you do." She flung back the duvet. "I'm going for a walk and then I'm going up to my studio."

"The studio I'm renting for you."

"Excuse me?"

"All courtesy of my parents' ten grand, lest we forget."

"Fat chance of that."

"They want to firm up a date for their visit, by the way."

"Are you seeing Jude, Hugh?"

A small silence wrinkled the air. "Define 'seeing," he said at last. "I've met her a couple of times on my walks. So what? Am I forbidden to fraternise with the natives now?"

"You've given her a lot of intel: shared some long, cosy chats."

"What, exactly, are you accusing me of?"

She passed a hand across her brow. "I'm talking about trust, Hugh, the cornerstone of any lasting relationship, let alone a marriage."

"Thanks for the update," he said sourly. "Jude is the only other person I talk to apart from you. If I've over-shared with her, it's the cabin fever talking. She just got invested in the Ouija board thing and wouldn't leave it alone."

Lucy was suddenly exhausted and didn't want to go there. He'd either flat-out deny an affair or, worse, make a craven admission and expect her to be the bigger person and understand.

Poor Hugh. It was Luke, her ex, all over again, a victim of *issues*. Men and their excuses; their casual entitlement and, yes, their instinctive cruelty.

"Told your parents about your redundancy yet?"

"One thing at a time."

"Well, maybe you should break it to them before they schlep all the way up here. Might put a dampener on their holiday vibe."

"I'll leave you to it," he said, and left the room with an air of wounded dignity, taking the tray.

As soon as he'd gone, she grabbed her soap bag off the dressing table and hurried back to the bathroom.

Once dressed, she ran out of the house through the front door without even glancing towards kitchen or study. She didn't give a toss which room he was lounging in, doing sod all except feeling sorry for himself.

She paused by her car.

Stuff going for a walk, she'd get clear away from Hugh and Rook House, and drive into Lowmorten.

23

Head still fuzzy from last night's *drugging*, she drove with extra care, wondering whether her stomach would tolerate a cappuccino and croissant at The Little Red Cooking Pot.

All the while, her mind circled back to Hugh dosing her with magic mushrooms, then watching the effects play out.

Moving here had been his idea. The seance had been his idea. Had she asserted her will about anything? And now – now her innards twisted and roiled as if trying to expel the final vestige of last night's 'poison', bleakly concluding that no, she *didn't* trust her floppy-haired, wryly amusing husband of seven months and counting. How could she, after last night's stunt? Elena's words returned yet again to haunt her more persuasively than any ghost: *how well you know this man?*

Hardly at all, Elena. How about that?

She pulled over on to the verge, stopped the car and wept.

After a few moments, she sat up, wiped her eyes and tried to pull herself together.

A truck rattled past her, slowed down and drew on to the verge ahead.

She groaned. Pinky bloody Bird!

He got out of the truck, hitching up his long black coat. She clambered out to meet him.

"Car trouble?" he asked.

"Marriage trouble," she snorted, then wished she hadn't.

"Right," said Pinky, unfazed. "Want to come back to Ma's for a hot drink? She's doing the church flowers this morning."

Lucy wiped her coat sleeve across her reddening nose, gazing at a landscape she'd once hoped to capture in vibrant colours. She shrugged.

"Fall in behind, then." He ambled back to his truck.

Too sure of himself, that man.

She followed his rear lights before she could overthink it, determined to tease out any more info about Jude and Hugh that Pinky might be sitting on.

She parked up behind him, outside the slate-roofed cottage.

"Here we go." He unlocked the front door and ushered her inside. "No bandy tart knocking about but I can do a buttered pikelet if you're peckish. My speciality."

"I'm not hungry, ta. You live here as well, then?" It was possible she already knew the answer and had temporarily forgotten.

"Yep, got to keep an eye on Ma." He peered at her doubtfully. "Don't want to sound *like* Ma, but you look as if you could do with a square meal. Any road, I'll put kettle on, soon as you tell me how you take your tea or coffee. I like mine with the spoon standing up. Sit."

She claimed a chair at the kitchen table, finding his gruffness soothing rather than imperious.

The cottage felt less cosy in her present bleak mood, its black beams knotted together like furrowed brows, the Brown Betty on the worktop thin-spouted with hands-on-hips disapproval.

Pinky plonked a mug of tea and two hot, buttered pikelets in front of her. "Took an exec decision and made you a couple anyway. Get that lot down you and you'll be right as rain."

"You think?" She sipped her tea. "Along with the cure-all cuppa, a national cliché."

He sat opposite her with his own mug. "So."

"So." She was surprised to realise he was nervous. It gave her a little spurt of confidence. "Look, if I implied you were up to no good with Henry Hollenbeck, I accept your denial."

"That your way of apologising?"

"I suppose so. I wanted to... look, you implied Jude was casting her eye in Hugh's direction. But do you know if anything has actually happened?"

She gripped her mug, hiding a dizzying sense of panic at what he might say. Proof of Hugh's infidelity would also be shattering proof of her stupidity: her total lack of due diligence.

"I don't *know* anything, but if it looks like a duck and walks like a duck, etcetera." He dropped his gaze to the table. "Not sure you want to hear any more, Mrs D."

"Bit late to go putting genies back in bottles," she said, quoting Hugh. "And call me Lucy."

His pinky-ringed finger inched across the table and hooked around her own little finger.

She didn't move away.

"Whatever I say next, Lucy, I'll sound jealous. Cos I am. He punched well above when he landed you but he's too arrogant and self-pitying to own it. You ask me, wherever you ended up together, he'd have found a Jude, because he's that type. Give him jam on his bread and he'll say he wanted strawberry 'stead of raspberry."

Lucy blinked down into her tea. "Very poetic."

"Thank you."

She laughed, then stopped, mortified.

"Anyway, it's that thing about shooting the messenger." He unhooked their fingers. "I've no evidence of anything and Ma would skin me for putting a spoke in, but can't help it. Can't help it cos you deserve better."

She raised her eyes. "You, presumably?"

"Oh, don't worry, I'm not daft enough to believe I'm the best thing since sliced pikelets. But since I first clapped eyes on you

in that kitchen, ready to ward off intruders with a butter knife..."
His sudden smile caught at her heart. "You've been on my mind.
I've thought how I'd look after you properly. Cos you need look-
ing after, Lucy."

"Because I fell over in the wood that time? And you reckoned
I'd been crawling about on the landing of Rook House? Up to
that point, you had me down as a lush."

"That was before I knew about your mother."

Lucy shrugged. "It is what it is."

"It's a hard hand to be dealt, that's what it is. My dad went
from cancer, but at least we were prepared. Scattered him off
Roseberry Topping, like he asked. I'll take you there some time.
You'll need proper boots. Any road, what happened to Rosa and
to you and your dad stinks."

Tears beaded her eyes. Yeah, it did stink.

"I'd kill the bastard responsible if you asked me to," he said.

Lucy gazed at him. "You actually mean that."

"Don't say owt I don't mean."

"Everyone else I've ever met reckons violence is never the way."

"Wait till they're on the sharp end of it."

Lucy nodded. She felt the same and wasn't ashamed of it.

"There *is* a smoking gun," he blurted. "About Hugh and Ben
Hur in high heels. If you're interested. He smells of her fags. And I
reckon they do a few lines together. Probably back at The Grange.
Possible that one thing leads to another, as things tend to."

He let that sink in. Lucy was appalled to think of an obvious
signal she'd missed, a smoke signal no less, her senses blunted by
Hugh's top notes of Chilean Malbec.

"Like I said, he wouldn't be her first," Pinky added reluctantly.
"She's got a pattern. A dependency and not just on coke. Uses
men as crutches. Cos she's damaged but, like Hugh, she can't or
won't own it."

Lucy knew she should go, but her legs refused to work. Only

her tongue seemed capable of independent movement. "I'm damaged too. I must be. Isn't everyone?"

"Up to a point. Not everyone uses it as an excuse for bad behaviour."

"Forget about Hugh and Jude for a moment," she murmured. She told him of her episodes inside and outside Rook House. It was a relief to let it all tumble out. "First there was the scratching, then I imagined myself in the tiny room behind the wall *with someone else there*, then I thought I saw Mickey in the wood, and last night, when we held a seance – Hugh's idea with Jude as cheerleader – I felt again that someone else was in the room with us. I think it was Belle and she wanted to show me her last days in the house."

She omitted the part about her disorientation and lashing out at Hugh. "Thing is, Hugh's admitted to putting shrooms in the soup last night before the seance, although I'm the only one who had a weird experience. And before those other incidents I've just told you about, I felt the warning signs of a migraine, though I didn't actually get one."

She paused, heart racing. "So, what do you think? Did I hallucinate stuff because of chemicals in my brain going off-piste, or might I have built-in ghost-dar? Or am I just nuts?"

Pinky's darkly handsome face stiffened as he rubbed his stubble. Lucy suspected that he was the sort of man who grew a five o'clock shadow at noon.

He asked slowly: "How'd you know it was Mickey you 'saw'?"

She explained about the dragging foot. "Snowy said you were born the same way, but it's easily corrected now." She blushed at this breach of his privacy.

"Wait here," he said, got up and ran up the stairs.

He returned moments later with a photo album, sat down and flipped through tissue-lined pages to a photo at the very back. He swivelled the album round to show Lucy. "This is a photo taken just after Belle arrived at Rook House. Can you ID Mickey?"

She pored over a sepia photo that was clearly a group shot of the staff at Rook House, which loomed in the background.

It had been taken on a sunny day, which meant that many faces were steeped in shadow, others hidden under peaked caps.

Yet her trembling finger found its target quickly. "That's him." She pointed to a strapping bloke holding a rake. He wore baggy trousers and coarse boots, shirt sleeves rolled up to his elbows. His peaked cap hid the dark hair she'd seen, but his strong jaw was familiar from the profile she'd glimpsed. "That's the man I saw. Looks a bit like you."

"Yep, that's Mickey Nellis," confirmed Pinky, shuffling his chair closer to hers, his own blunt finger moving along the row of figures. "That one chewing a wasp is the housekeeper. These here look like men who'd help bring in the harvest, so the photo was probably taken in autumn. Ezra Napier owned a lot more land than Rook House lays claim to now. Then we've got the maids..." His finger found a young woman at the opposite end of the row to Mickey. "This here is Mickey's future wife, Susan. Tough and clever little thing. She's the one put fire in his belly to pool what money they had, leave service and open a hardware shop in town."

He sat back. "So do I reckon you were part of a spectral show and tell in the wood? I wouldn't dismiss it. As for the rest of it... hell, I dunno. One thing I *do* know is that you're not nuts. You're brave to live there in the first place, IMO. I wouldn't be caught dead in that house overnight," he added unexpectedly. "Ma wants you to move on. Already spelt that out, she says, but you want to finish some painting first."

"Not *some* painting, one that might actually have some merit. You see, Hugh is blocked, but living at Rook House has loosened creativity in me. I can't explain how or why."

"I'm building my own place three mile yon," he said next, pulling the album away but not looking at her. "Builders will be breaking ground soon. I could put in a studio built to your own spec. I'd do anything for you, Lucy."

Lucy's insides curdled with a mixture of joy and panic. It was the sort of thing teenage boys said earnestly to girls they really *really* liked rather than just fancied: *I'd pull down the moon for you, I would.* Pinky Bird, an old, romantic soul. Who'd have thought?

"Jump from the frying pan into the fire, you mean?" She flinched, realising what she'd just admitted about her marriage.

Pinky waited a moment before he spoke again. "You might think you've found inspiration at Rook House, but at the cost of finding what else? That creativity you've awakened could be a side effect of whatever the house is triggering in you or channelling through you. It's not a healthy house. Never was, never will be. Your visions or whatever you want to call them are proof of that."

"You've just spelt out your own reason for wanting me to leave, Pinky." Did she mean the house, her marriage or both?

"Vested interest, they call it," he admitted. "Yes, I want you properly in my life. How about calling me Jerome? Not a name I'm over-fond of but all mine."

"After St Jerome?"

"Yep. Ma's idea. I lean towards Pinky for everyday but sometimes Jerome suits the occasion. Your pikelets are getting cold."

She chewed her food in a mutually tense silence, conscious of swallowing too loudly in the thickened atmosphere. "Please don't tell Snowy about the seance. Doubt she'd approve."

"*I* don't approve," he observed, "and I've barely seen the inside of a church since I was an altar boy, but fine, it's none of my beeswax. Apart from being pissed at Hugh for the shrooms. Ever occur to you that the house could be working on him in a different way, bringing out the worst in him?"

Lucy thought of Hugh's drinking. "No. And you don't know him."

Elena snorted in her head, *while you only know him a little bit!*

She stood up. "I'd better go. Thank you for being so direct. Believe it or not, I prefer that to blokes spouting poetry or comparing me to a summer's day. But we hardly know each other. You say you want to care for me, but maybe that's your thing, rescuing. We all have a thing."

"Be great if yours was being rescued."

At that, she had to laugh out loud. "Ironically, I think it used to be. Up until this very moment."

"How'd you know I don't just know what I want?"

"Nobody knows that!"

She shook hands with him in an awkward formal gesture, then almost ran out to her car.

She sat at the wheel composing herself, trembling in the aftermath of her draining exchange with a man who didn't beat about the bush or expect her to.

He'd said he wanted rather than loved her, a verb that spoke of possession; to have and to hold. *But if you break her, consider her sold.*

He might not even 'want' her for the long haul. Yet the prospect of being possessed and later discarded didn't bother her as much as betrayal inside marriage. To want was to express an unmet appetite, not to make promises beyond that.

She started the car and drove back to Rook House.

❦

24

Hugh was waiting for her in the kitchen. He wanted to talk. He'd given up shaving, she noticed, a wispy 'tache sprouting unattractively above his lip.

He apologised again for the shrooms, an apology that sounded like a justification.

"And yes, the book is holding out on me," he went on glumly. "I've made stop-start progress with too much stop. Don't want to be seen to fail, Luce, having to creep back to London, book unwritten, money burnt through. I know I said my parents are happy to sub me, but it's different now. I'm supposed to be a responsible, married adult."

She noted the preponderance of "I" and "me" over "you" and "us".

"So it's all my fault."

"What? No, where'd you get that from? It's just, I'm supposed to be taking care of both of us."

"Because your parents only signed up for bailing you out, not your layabout, skint wife. Just to remind you, I offered to look for a job here."

"You're twisting my words again."

"Maybe *I* should be the writer if I'm so adept at word-wrangling."

He gave her a look of solid hatred. "Low blow. I'm trying to sort things between us."

"I'm going up to the attic."

She'd handled that badly. She'd handled everything badly. Really, prolonged backbiting was the only growth industry in their marriage. They were moderately successful in that regard; could stage an off-Broadway two-hander, as Jude might've said.

She sat in the ladder-back chair and did nothing beyond pick at the skin round her nails. After a bit, she went downstairs to find Hugh.

He was sitting glumly at his desk, gazing out at the elms.

"Hugh, I think we have to consider that we're not working. And it can't just be the house's fault. Or anyone's in particular," she added as he drew breath to be offended. "We gave it our best shot and it hasn't worked out. We should never have married. Should've just moved here as friends with benefits. Don't you think?"

He eyed her narrowly. "You want me to agree we're a lost cause so you can feel better about calling time?"

"I'm not... I'm trying to talk it through. We *could* try to go on as we were before," she said desperately. "Move back to London, get a flat, go out to work every day, have things to talk about in the evenings." Her heart ached with the finality of this proposition. What about her painting?

"My parents-"

"Your parents what?"

"They warned me not to rush into anything. If we split up, I'll just be fulfilling their prophecy."

"That's not a good reason to stay married or stay here. Who cares what they think? You're drinking too much. I worry for you."

"Oh, really?" He swivelled on the listing chair. "That's very touching. An hour or so ago, you more or less accused me of an affair with Jude."

"That's immaterial now. You're not yourself. This house, the drinking..."

He turned abruptly back to his desk, fingering the edges of his turquoise notebook. "I need to think over what you've said. If we do leave here, I don't think we should stay together at all. Too much water under the bridge. You're right to say it doesn't matter what my folks make of it. They'll get over it. They always do."

"All right."

Exhausted, she left him to it, grabbed her coat in the kitchen and walked as far as the wood.

What were she and Hugh becoming to each other? Strangers, she thought. Strangers who resented each other's differences.

They'd started off in a rush of joyful intimacy, but now their true apartness was leaking through. And they were both guilty of failing; partners in the crime of rushing their fences, depressingly unoriginal in their failure. They'd simply been too immature for the big step of marriage.

Perhaps she should go easier on him. And herself. It didn't mean that she was running off into the sunset with Pinky Bird. Jerome. She should try that name for size, treat him as a fellow grown-up.

She tipped her head back to follow a plane contrail, its pure white tail feathering a carbon-grey sky.

Then she looked at the wood and decided to plunge in, following thin shafts of wintry sun briefly illuminating the damp ground. But this time, no searing sunlight and plenty of fluting birdsong. She walked under the trees without any sense of direction, pausing to anchor her heels in the earth, closing her eyes to let her remaining senses take over.

Smells: the cloying, fissured soil, hard-packed in places and loosened in others by water-filled ruts that would freeze after sundown.

Sounds: small, muttering birds and the wind rolling under needled branches.

Tastes: she stuck her tongue into the wind and lapped its

loamy edges, seasoned here and there with scattered essence of distant hedgerow.

Textures: she opened her eyes and bent down to feel the rough bark on a nearby trunk.

No sign of mushrooms, poisonous or otherwise, this early in the year.

Conscious of getting lost again if she wandered too far, she retraced her steps, the path revealing itself willingly enough, glimmering among fallen pine needles. Reluctantly, she headed back to the house.

She'd sit down yet again with Hugh and try to help him see that their apartness was nobody's fault, it just *was*. If Rook House hadn't bested them, their own immaturity would have done for them anyway.

They'd discuss where to go from here, even if meant separate ways spiced with the memory of once belonging to each other.

It would be sad and it would hurt, but someone had to spell out the bleak truth of their disintegrating union. If he confessed to a fling with Jude, she'd salute his honesty, but it didn't really matter because she didn't love him, and he couldn't break her heart.

But she *could* be grown-up, civilised and even kind as they finally broke apart. And she hoped he could be the same.

After Lucy left the house (destination unstated), Hugh got up and walked out to the woodshed, ignoring the biting wind.

He picked up the coat and unravelled it from the axe, holding its musty thickness close to his chest.

He was about to fail at everything. He'd been warned and would now be unmasked as the dewy-eyed fool/cock-eyed optimist he'd been all along.

His parents would welcome him home and regret his short-comings behind his back, Lucy moving on (she had no other choice), while he'd remain a blocked writer in his childhood bedroom, the whispered "could've been a contender" stalking him like Ezra Napier's footsteps on a spiral staircase.

Ezra Napier was the key, his only remaining chance to forge something from his doomed stay here. If he could make contact again, through Phineas's coat, he might reignite that spark of imagination that had already filled two pages of his notebook.

A closer encounter, while awake, could even be enough to fire him up like a blast furnace for the duration of a whole book. He needed more than an idea. He needed an entire narrative.

He twisted the coat between his hands.

Relying on the ghost of Ezra Napier was a huge risk, no point pretending otherwise.

Should he succeed in summoning Ezra again, he might come to depend on 'It' in ever larger doses to feed his craving, his writing habit. He might be helpless to prevent what he'd summoned from invading his dreams, ensuring they became nightmares, unable to separate wakefulness from dreaded slumber.

That might all happen. Yet it was his last throw of the dice.

He slipped on the coat as he walked back to the house. It flapped around him with satisfying substance. The coat was real, even if his expectations of it might be rooted in dangerous wishful thinking.

Inside the house, he stood in the hallway, just as he had on his first night here.

Outside it was daylight but the windowless hallway was always gloomy.

The stairs creaked invitingly. He started to climb.

On the landing, he paused. The wind tapped along the wall and a door banged gently in its frame up ahead.

He answered the summons, pushing open the door of a room they rarely entered.

It was a large, empty bedroom with the obligatory sash window. Funny, he'd come to think of the acanthus room as the centre of spectral operations.

He stood at the window, bracing his wrists against the sill and staring out. From here, he could just make out the ridge and the dark arrowheads of evergreen treetops.

The pane was filthy with stains and cobwebs. He spread his fingers on the sill and examined the pale crescents of his nails, aware that his hands were shaking.

Behind him, someone had stepped into the room.

He whipped around.

No one there.

He laughed unevenly at his jumpiness. What he wouldn't give for a top-up – the glass of red he'd finished this morning was still tucked behind his laptop.

He turned back to the window, raised the sash and peered over the ledge to check the drop. Yeah, could've happened at this very window, a straight drop to the driveway, nothing to cushion the fall.

About to draw his head back in, he noticed a rusty, bent nail sticking out of a brick just under the sill. A thought ran through him like khaki thread and excited him. He leant out further to take a closer look.

What if Phineas had snagged himself on the nail after jumping, hanging there for a few agonising seconds with time to change his mind, before the nail ripped through cloth and he plunged to his death?

Careful to keep his balance while leaning out, he raised both coat sleeves to check for tears, but they looked intact.

Of course, Phineas probably hadn't been wearing this coat when he-

A heavy paternal hand landed on his shoulder. A mouth came so close to his ear, he could feel the tickle of a handlebar moustache. "What are you doing up here?" Ezra asked.

Hugh froze, his head still ducked out of the window. He began to talk out of the side of his mouth, careful to keep his head absolutely still: "I'm not... I'm only..."

"I only wanted what was best for you. But you wouldn't listen. You still won't."

Phineas's tears pricked Hugh's eyes. "Papa, what if I stay like this? The wind never changes its direction when it moves around this house."

"What are you babbling about now, you damn fool boy?"

"They say you shouldn't pull a face in case the wind changes and you're stuck like that. But I want to change and I can't, I can't, I can't." He began to shake uncontrollably.

Tom said: "It's probably shell shock, then. Has he ever seen a therapist?"

"Damn fools, those doctors," Ezra replied. He turned to Phineas. "It's your mother all over again. You're a disgrace to my name. I should never have-"

Tom interrupted: "But speaking out of concern, he seems to be drifting."

Phineas sobbed and shook. "I can't go on like this."

"No more than any of us can," Ezra muttered.

"Tread carefully," said Tom. "Bottling things up never does any good."

"Papa..." pleaded Phineas, starting to pull in from the window. "The wind – is it about to change? Look at the trees. Not the elms, but further up in the wood. Do you think-"

"You're not my son," said Ezra in weary disgust, shoving the shoulder he still grasped.

As Lucy skittered down the ridge, the sun emerged fully from cloud cover and struck her between the eyes. She raised a protective hand to deflect its sudden glare. Drawing closer to the house, its windows seemed lit up, molten fire sparkling off every pane of glass.

But something was wrong.

A thin spear of darkness fissured the pools of light bouncing off glass. She stopped and gaped.

Phineas Napier hung from just below a bedroom window, floating eerily like a high-wire kestrel, the folds of a coat flaring out behind him.

Then the figure swung, legs flailed, hair flashed in the light... she began to run, screaming his name.

Hugh, dazed with terror, stared intently at the unravelling cuff of his favourite old jumper poking from under the coat sleeve, the rusty nail snaring and tearing softly through baggy wool.

He gazed up, but no cold blue eye looked down from the window to taunt him, no palms slapped together above him as if dusting off a crushed fly.

Perhaps that was the final blessing, though it left him with the dull certainty that he'd only himself to blame. As usual. He could've been a contender.

He was held above the world by a filament of fabric spooling away from him, brightly coloured wool unwinding the 'stone tape' of his too-short life.

A scream beneath him.

He looked down. The last thing he saw was Lucy running towards the house before he fell to earth.

PART THREE

25

Lucy sat untidily on a plastic chair in a hospital corridor, waiting for Hugh's parents to arrive in York. She'd rung them while waiting for the ambulance to reach Rook House, gabbling out the situation with Hugh's head cradled on a pile of towels she'd fetched from the house.

Frances had become hysterical, Tom distantly calm. They'd be here in a matter of hours.

She had knelt there on the driveway in the bright afternoon with Hugh a stick of chalk under her touch, his eyes shut, mouth agape, hair revoltingly sticky.

Her phone buzzed now in her coat pocket, where it lay alongside Hugh's phone, the house keys and her newish purse.

It was Jude. "What's happened? Overheard someone in town say an ambo came out of your gates, flashing blues and twos. Everything all right?"

"Hugh's had an accident."

"What do you mean; what sort?"

"No time for this, Jude."

"But..."

Lucy rang off. Let her stew. This was partly Jude's fault. If she'd left Hugh alone, if she hadn't twisted his arm about the seance...

Moments later, a call from Snowy. "Lucy, what's happened? People are saying all kinds. Are you both all right?"

Lucy supplied a deliberately vague account of Hugh's 'accident', settling for the key info that he'd had a fall or what she euphemistically termed "a slip". If she threw a fall from a *bedroom window* into the mix, the rumour mill would implode. Besides, she didn't know what had really happened. "Hasn't regained consciousness," she informed Snowy. "Due to have a scan. Probable bleed on the brain."

"He hit his head badly, then?"

"Yes."

"Those stairs, I always said they should be carpeted! You're in York? You went in the ambulance with him?"

Lucy nodded. "I mean, yes, I'm in York."

"How are you getting back? I'll have Pinky come pick you up."

"No, it's fine. I'll wait here for Hugh's parents and the outcome of the scan. Um, will I have to let the owners know what's happened, or will you?"

"I'll take care of that. Just look after yourself and that husband of yours, Lucy."

"I will. Thank you, Snowy."

Ending the call, Lucy bit down hard on her lip.

She was dreading the arrival of Tom and Frances. They *did* know that Hugh had fallen from a window, details to follow. She'd better prepare some.

Hugh had poked fun at his parents' 'ways', but fondly. "Works for them," he'd said of his mother fussing that everyone use a coaster and his father vanishing on solo expeditions to a greenhouse, carrying a portable radio.

Tom had said that he'd book a York hotel as soon as he got off the phone, keeping a cool head despite a son at death's door, a wailing wife, and a dazed and incoherent daughter-in-law.

Now she faced the ordeal of telling them face to face all that she knew (the *little* that she knew) of Hugh's 'accident'.

She must've dozed off on her plastic chair. In her dream, she was pacing the light-filled rooms of Rook House on a bright winter's day, Hugh's fingers click-click-clicking on a distant but audible keyboard, like a blackbird breaking a snail on a rock.

A hand touched her shoulder and she jerked awake, to find Pinky leaning over her, face blanched with concern. "What are you doing here?" she asked angrily.

"Ma thought you needed moral support."

"I already told her... oh, never mind."

A man in green scrubs approached, frowning at a clipboard. "Mrs Driscoll?"

Lucy leapt to her feet, Pinky moving to a discreet distance.

The doctor introduced himself. "Your husband has a bleed on the brain, a shattered pelvis and a leg broken in three places. He's going down to surgery shortly. Depending on how that goes, we may have to put him into an induced coma until the swelling on his brain reduces."

"Will he – will he survive?"

"We're doing all we can."

"Can I see him?"

"He's still unconscious and will be for some time, including after surgery, but you're welcome to sit with him when he goes to the recovery room after his operation. We'd also like to, ah, go over the details of how you found him." A flip of the paper on his clipboard. "You said he fell from an upstairs window?"

Pinky's head jerked up.

"Er, yes. I was walking back to the house when I saw him... hanging there, before he fell."

"Hanging?"

She swallowed. "I think he may have leant out for some reason, I don't know, slipped and grabbed hold of a bit of brickwork to try to stop himself falling."

"His blood-alcohol level was quite high."

Lucy saw where this was going, the thought having already

occurred to her. A drunken Hugh leans or climbs out of a window, loses his balance and falls.

But why? If he'd needed fresh air, he could have opened the back door.

And then there was the coat. Why'd he been wearing that rancid old thing? She thought he'd thrown it away.

"He's been drinking more than usual for the past few weeks," she admitted. "He's had, um, pressures."

The doctor nodded, expression inscrutable. "As I say, surgery is the next step. In the meantime, if you live locally, you may like to go home, shower and eat. You'll be no use to him out on your feet."

This was a standard speech to next of kin, Lucy knew. She nodded, thanked the doctor and reclaimed her chair.

Rook House was a considerable drive away, so she may as well stay put.

Pinky shuffled over. "Doc's got a point. Could be here a while. This is your chance to hit pause and take a breather before his parents pitch up."

"I'm staying put. I must ring his parents now with the doc's update about his injuries and the induced coma."

"Lucy." Pinky looked earnest. "The police may come asking questions too. He fell from an upstairs window. The fact it sounds like he was pickled should put you in the clear."

Lucy rounded on him. "I was outside! I saw it happen *from* outside!"

"Just beware what you tell the plods if they come on the sniff. Don't go into unnecessary detail about any bad vibes between you and Hugh."

"Hang on. You think... you really think I could've left yours, gone back to the house and demanded to know for definite if he was sleeping with Jude, then flipped and shoved him out of a window?"

"Of course I don't believe that, but it doesn't matter what I think. That's my point. Stick to the facts, volunteer nothing. Look, once you've updated his parents, can I drive you back to Lowmorten? Ma thinks you should stop with us for the foreseeable."

"I just told you. I have to stay put. I must be *here* when his parents arrive."

"If it's not for a few hours yet, I can drop you off at Rook House to collect a few essentials before we head to Lowmorten. Grab a bite to eat at ours and I'll drive you back here."

She shook her head. "Can you go now, please? I'd rather you weren't earwigging when I ring his parents with an update."

If Pinky was offended, he didn't show it. "If you change your mind, I'll be outside for a while yet. You can't miss the truck."

"I know you mean well, but just go away, Pinky. Please."

She watched him walk off, shut her eyes briefly, then faced the inevitable and jabbed the number for Hugh's parents. She just hoped that Frances wouldn't start wailing again.

The air outside the hospital was like a wet sheet hitting her in the face. Pinky was still there, leaning on a pillar, examining a fingernail moon scraping the last filaments of light from a dusk sky. She was surprised to find that it was evening. Both time and the air itself seemed to hang suspended inside the hospital.

"How'd it go with updating his folks?" Pinky asked.

"How you'd expect," she shrugged, reluctant to elaborate.

"You're shaking, and not just from the cold." He started to slip off his sandalwood-scented coat.

"Don't get all gallant on me, don't you dare!" she hissed. "I'm sticking around."

She turned back towards the entrance.

"OK," said Pinky. "But howze about we bust out of this joint for just a bit and grab a bite to eat locally? Already checked out the hospital caff and it lacks... privacy."

She glared at him, then stalked past him. "I don't see your unmissable truck, so you'd better lead the way."

"I don't think his parents ever approved of me," she admitted, her decaf latte and tuna melt barely touched. She and Pinky were the only customers in a York café well off the city tourist trail. "I was never part of their grand plan for him, which I'm also guessing didn't include a stop-start writing career."

"Parental approval is overrated," said Pinky, who'd finished his BLT. "Ma thinks I should be winding down a few of my own ways. Marianne Napier knew that some parents live to be disappointed."

Lucy glanced upwards as if expecting to see a water-stained ceiling rose. It always came back to Rook House. "D'you think the house had anything to do with Hugh's accident?" she asked.

"Not directly," said Pinky. "I think living there might have caused the drinking."

She pushed her fingers through tangled hair and gazed out at a near-deserted street. "I don't get it, any of it."

She'd kept quiet about the coat but she knew that Hugh had definitely been up to something in her absence. She just couldn't figure out what, and perhaps never would. "You said before that the house might've brought out the worst in him, but he never seemed *afraid* of living there."

"Hardly admit it, would he?" shrugged Pinky.

"But you said you wouldn't be caught dead there overnight."

"Unfortunate turn of phrase. I've never felt at ease there, even on short visits. Ma's the same but hides it better."

Lucy thought of Snowy's jumpiness that time she'd heard a noise in the acanthus room. "You talk as though you think the house has a character all of its own."

"Don't you?"

She sipped her latte while she reflected. "Yes. I felt from the get-go it was deciding whether or not to tolerate me. I'm not sure acceptance was ever on offer."

She checked her phone for a text from Frances or Tom to say they'd arrived in York. Still nothing. She placed the phone face down on the table. "Look, talking of the police coming on the sniff, I should probably tell you, I once implied to the Hollenbecks that you were a coke supplier." Her face flamed. "I only said it to wind Jude up."

"But you don't think it now?" he asked, apparently unfazed.

"It doesn't seem you, somehow. I'm only mentioning it because, if the police do start wondering how Hugh came to fall out of a window, they might not stop at the alcohol in his blood. They might start wondering about any other habits he could've developed. You seemed to think it was possible."

Pinky sat back. "You're right, drugs aren't my scene. Nor is booze, really. Like I suggested, if Hugh was smoking fags and doing the odd line, it would've all been courtesy of Ben Hur herself, over at The Grange. She's probably flushing stuff down the bog as we speak. Don't sweat it, Lucy. I'm not offended. I know you've got enough on your plate."

"Thanks... Jerome. My given name is Lucia," she revealed suddenly. "But when I started nursery school, a couple of other little girls ragged me about it, calling me Lootchy Loop and so on. I told Mum I wanted to be known as Lucy to attract less attention. Isn't that awful of me?"

"No, you adopted camouflage for protection, little kids being what they are, so kind and accepting of each other's differences."

"Mum said they were just jealous of my beautiful name."

"Makes sense."

"But I must have hurt her, don't you see? Ditching the name she chose that kept a link to her heritage. Maybe I've never made a mark with my art because I've always been confused about my identity."

"Don't overthink it. Tell me, what was the name of the scumbag who killed your mother?"

She gasped. "Why ask me that?"

"We're naming things. Ancient cultures believed that knowing a person's name gave you power over them. For curses and so on."

"I never know whether you're winding me up or not."

"Not, I promise."

"Nathan Stelley." She spat out the name like a grape pip. "I don't like to say it aloud because it's etched on my heart, like Calais was for Mary Tudor. He's going about living his life while Mum is – while Mum is rotting underground, all that beauty and kindness and potential wiped out. Oh God!"

"Lucy... Lucia."

She shook his hand off her wrist, refusing to be comforted. "I must get back to the hospital."

"Finish your food first."

"Lost my appetite."

"Look. I hope Hugh recovers, but I doubt it'll make any difference to your marriage. It's not as if doing a Flo Nightingale number at his bedside will suddenly make him more appealing or less of a dickhead."

"OMG, do you have to be so matter of fact about everything?" She pushed back her chair. "There is such a thing as too much reality, Jerome."

"Not really. Facing things head on is bracing, like being up on the moors on a raw day and sitting there still as an angler, watching for a hare's ears or a sight of its haunches."

"I've behaved badly towards Hugh."

"How?"

"I just have. As my dad liked to say, actions have consequences."

He'd first said it when she returned in disgrace from an Easter egg hunt at a classmate's house, a year after Rosa's death. Defying instructions to return to the house as soon as she found a gold foil bunny in the garden, she'd gathered up as many as she could, locked herself in the hostess's bathroom and scoffed the lot until she was sick.

Hadn't looked at a chocolate bunny since.

"Acting out," she now knew it was called, thanks to several therapists she'd seen in her 20s (and kept quiet about).

Wicked, Elena had called her when she'd scrawled all over her new stepmother's clothes with a tube of Rouge Noir liberated from Elena's handbag. "This child is wicked, David. Feral. You ever think of boarding school?"

Despite knowing the official psychological term for the way she'd behaved all those years ago, the word "wicked" still resonated.

"Are you saying you've behaved badly, simply by hearing me say my piece over the buttered pikelets?" Pinky asked earnestly. "Give yourself a break. You've far less to apologise for than Hugh. Besides, all relationships are transactional and therefore consequential. I'm guessing you already know that."

"I can't deal with this now." She stood up. "Will you drive me back to the hospital?"

He left her at the hospital entrance. "Call me when you're leaving again," he urged. "I've put my number into your mobile and added your number to mine. Did it when you were in the ladies at the caff," he clarified. "Your phone was unlocked. Wherever I am, I can be here in a jiff when you ring."

"Thank you," she said stiffly. "For the lift."

At the hospital reception desk, she learnt that Hugh was just out of surgery.

She hurried up to the recovery floor – to find Tom and Frances Driscoll occupying hard plastic chairs of their own.

Tom spoke first. "We thought you'd be here, waiting."

And I thought you'd keep me posted on your ETA. "I just popped out for fresh air," she replied defensively. "How are you both doing?" She regretted the question immediately, knotting her hands loosely in front of her. Thankfully, there seemed no appetite on either side for hugging.

"We're hoping to sit with him soon, though he won't know we're here," sighed Tom. "I don't imagine we can all be by his side at the same time."

"I suppose you take priority as his *wife*," hissed Frances.

Lucy glanced at her. Frances was rail-thin and white as an ice chip. Sharp enough to cut on contact. "I... really, if you two want to go in first..."

"What did I tell you?" Frances snorted bitterly to her husband.

"Have you checked into your hotel yet?" Lucy asked, head starting to buzz.

"Dropped off our case, then drove straight here," replied Tom. "Oh, there's that nice nurse who brought us the hot chocolates, Fran. Let's ask if she's got an update on the swelling."

Lucy could feel herself being edged out. In a way, she'd be grateful to hand primary responsibility for Hugh to his anguished parents. Should she mention his drinking or had the docs already filled them in?

She jolted out of her brief reverie to focus on what the nurse was saying: "Still some concern about the swelling... induced coma... take it one step at a time... too early to say..."

Lucy watched Frances get thinner and whiter in front of her eyes.

Then the room went spinning and Lucy was being helped into a chair by the nurse, who regarded her anxiously. "Are you OK, Mrs Driscoll? Shall I fetch you some water?"

Lucy shook her head while Frances said angrily: "Making it all about *her*."

"Shush, Fran."

Lucy let them go into the recovery room first to visit Hugh, who was hooked up to bleeping machines.

Frances came back clutching a hanky to her face. Lucy rose on trembling legs. She didn't want to see him but had no reason not to.

Once alone with Hugh, she shuffled her chair close and stared at his wax-like face, all its features over-prominent and girded by tubes and IV lines. His head was swathed in a thick white bandage, one lock of hair escaping to cover his forehead.

She took his hand, which felt cold and smaller than her own. "I'm sorry for what I said this morning." Which already seemed a lifetime ago. "If – when you get better, Hugh, we'll sort things. I want you to be happy. Anything I said in haste about your work, I didn't mean. Yes, you and Jude shouldn't have micro-dosed me behind my back..." She trailed off, wary of straying down familiar, churned-up paths. "We've both said and done things we shouldn't have. Your parents are here, I'm here and we all love you and are rooting for you." She touched the lock of hair. It felt brittle and not really part of him. "Just rest now, darling." The word was exotic on her tongue. Melodramatic. "I'll be here when you wake up."

She nodded off with her hand still cradling his, a different nurse coming to tap her on the shoulder. "Your in-laws are waiting outside. They'd like another word."

Lucy rotated her stiff neck, thanked the nurse and went out to deal with the latest.

"You should go home. We'll hold the fort," Frances said. "Also..." She glanced at her husband. "I'd like to go to Rook House and see where it happened."

Lucy panicked, trying to recall whether there was blood on the pile of towels puddled under the window. "Right. I can go ahead and give you a ring when-"

"I'll drive us there now," interrupted Frances. "We're in the hospital car park, obviously. If you came by ambulance with Hugh, I'm guessing you don't have your car with you. The one he bought you," she added snidely. "Tom will stay here with our son and wait for my return. You will remain at the house."

Lucy stared at Frances Driscoll, coaster freak and 'functioning' alcoholic of the parish. "You know Hugh was pissed when he fell, right?"

"Probably because of living with you!" sneered Frances.

"Fran! Girls! Come on."

"*Probably* because he'd been let go from his day job and his new book was going nowhere," Lucy retorted. "Neither of which were my doing. I tried to offer encouragement from day one."

"This isn't helping Hugh," frowned Tom, then sat down, suddenly overcome. "Go to Rook House if you want, Fran, if you think it will help. I told you I've no desire to."

Frances glared at Lucy with malicious triumph. "Shall we go then, Lucy dear?"

26

On the way out of the hospital, Lucy spotted a shop about to close, one that sold last-minute gifts, cards and other essentials to frazzled visitors. "Just going to get a bar of choc," she told Frances. "Haven't eaten much today."

"I'll wait outside," muttered Frances. "I couldn't eat at a time like this."

Frances's driving technique was not dissimilar to Jude's. "I'm guessing Tom drove up from Surrey?" asked Lucy, fingers clamped to the edges of her seat as Frances ignored speed limits and potholes flashing up in her headlights. "I mean, you both reached York in one piece."

"Tom drives like an old lady," snorted Frances. "With all due respect to old ladies, most of whom are probably more daredevil than my husband."

Seeing Hugh's mother in a whole new light, Lucy murmured to the dashboard: "I hope *you* haven't been drinking."

"Not touched a drop since the call came through that you'd struck a blow for women's lib by trying to off my son."

Lucy sighed. "Frances, we must talk and behave rationally. Tom's right. No point in fighting like cats in a sack when we both want the same thing: Hugh's recovery. So what's your theory, that I snuck up behind him and pushed him out of a window?"

"Only got your word for it that you were outside at the time, conveniently too far away to run into the house and pull him back."

"You don't know me," said Lucy coldly. "If you did, you'd realise how daft you sound. Daft and cruel."

"He'll be leaving here for good and coming home with us when he pulls through. You can go where you like."

"I'm sure Hugh will want his say when the time comes."

She directed Frances through the pillared gates of Rook House and up the pitch-black driveway, the elms managing a stiff bow in a chasing wind.

Frances finally fell silent, perhaps regretting her mission.

Then Rook House came into view, crouched silently under a dark blue sky rich with stars.

Frances parked up behind Lucy's car.

Lucy shivered and fished out her house keys. "I'll get a torch before I show you the spot where he... Are you sure you want to do this?"

Frances nodded, jaw tight.

Lucy unlocked the back door, snapping on the kitchen light. The house was cold, the Rayburn long gone out.

Frances came in behind her, hugging her elbows.

Lucy found the rubberised torch in a kitchen drawer and led the way to the front of the house, tripping over the towels in the dark. She stood on them to hide them better. "It was here." She trained the torch beam on the window above, which was still open. "The sun was very low, now I come to think. Might've blinded him for a second or two and caused some disorientation."

Although, no, wait. That didn't make sense. The light had been in *her* eyes, not shining into Hugh's.

Frances said nothing and walked back into the house, turning on the hallway light. She plonked down on the bottom tread of the stairs. "I wouldn't put a dog in this house."

"For Hugh, it was – is – atmospheric."

"Not even a year," said Frances softly. "In less than a year, you've managed to meet, marry and nearly kill our son, after taking him away to the other end of the country."

In the weak light washing over them both, Frances's skin had turned the colour of bone broth. Lucy felt obscurely frightened, as though Frances was still sitting out in the car, or even back in the hospital, and she had brought her shadow walker into the house.

"I wish you'd stop pretending that Hugh had no agency in any of it," she murmured. "This house was always his idea. As was marriage, actually."

"But you went along with it all."

"What do you want me to say?"

"Did you ever love him?"

"I thought I did. We thought we loved each other. I'll show you our bedroom if you'd like to help me pick out toiletries for him."

"I'd rather do that alone."

"I'd rather you didn't."

Frances regarded her curiously. "*Did* you try to kill him?" She turned and gazed up the shadowy treads. "A scuffle up in that room, things getting out of hand-"

"I would never harm Hugh! You heard the docs. His blood-alcohol level was high. He, he leant out of that window for fresh air, the sun in his eyes, got dizzy..."

Upstairs, a door creaked, a doorknob rattled. Frances jumped off the step. "Is someone up there?"

"It's the wind." Lucy hoped. "Come on, we'll go up together to pack stuff for him."

There was no one upstairs to disturb them.

Lucy switched on the light in her and Hugh's bedroom. Frances looked at the Strawberry Thief wallpaper and began to cry, arms dangling uselessly at her sides. Lucy froze to the spot. The last thing Frances would want was her touch.

"If I'm honest, Frances, Hugh and I should never have come here. We were together 24/7 in an isolated house, bickering over stupid stuff, like who'd let the briquettes get low in the basket without restocking. I mean, I did suggest day trips to York and stuff, but he worried about being self-indulgent. He didn't see this as a holiday. He was very conscious of your and Tom's generosity towards him. Towards us both. He didn't want to let you both down."

She realised how that sounded. "I'm not for a minute saying that you and Tom put pressure on him. I know you said a while back that he's not a 'sticker', but Hugh is very driven. His default is to put pressure on himself."

To her surprise, Frances stopped crying and nodded. "That was my father's accusation, never mine. Yes, his drive is his main flaw as well as strength. He gives off this air that everything comes easily and he's not too bothered either way, but I suspect you know that's far from true. I remember when he was learning to ride a bike. After coming into the house with grazed knees and elbows, he declared he didn't care either way about riding a stupid bike. But early next morning, while Tom and I were still getting up, I raised a curtain and spotted him creeping down the driveway, wheeling his bike to the rec. He only came back a couple of hours later when he could cycle up the drive."

Lucy was touched. It was the first moment of bonding she'd shared with Frances; the first time she'd seen her in 3-D. "Look, when we get back to the hospital-"

"I'm going back alone. No debate. Tom and I would like time alone with our boy." She widened her eyes at Lucy. "You understand, don't you?"

"I... shouldn't I be there?"

"We both know you'd be relieved to stay away for a bit." Frances gazed around the room. "Even if it means staying alone in this creepy old mausoleum. I'm right, aren't I?"

Lucy swallowed. It was a devil or deep blue sea choice. "I'm not sure the hospital will let you stay all night. Think we've long exceeded chuck-out time for visiting hours."

"Tom and I will take our chances. Can you fetch Hugh's electric razor, comb, toothpaste and brush? Plus a couple of T-shirts, socks and fresh underpants for when he wakes up? Slippers and dressing gown, if he has them."

"Boxers, not underpants. Hugh is a boxers man."

She rounded up the requested items and brought them to Frances on the landing, folded up and placed inside a carrier bag.

"I want to see the window where it happened."

Lucy nodded and led her into the rarely visited bedroom, the raised sash admitting a wind that sounded like Lucy's old maths teacher whistling through his dentures.

Her hand went to the light switch.

"Leave it," ordered Frances, preferring the room to be lit by a spill of ashy light from the landing.

Frances put down the carrier bag for a moment and leant out of the window, her thin, shaking arms braced on the sill.

"Careful," said Lucy instinctively.

Frances drew her head back in. Lucy couldn't see her expression in the dim-lit room.

"A steep fall," Frances observed.

"Yes." Lucy hesitated. "Lucky to survive it. Shows his strength. His fighting spirit."

Frances pushed past her with an unnecessary shoulder barge. "I'll be on my way."

Lucy followed her down to the kitchen, Frances turning at the back door. "You'll put in an appearance tomorrow, I imagine."

That bonding moment was already fading. "I think you'll find I'm required to be there as his next of kin for any paperwork that needs signing. And I still care for Hugh deeply. I *want* to be there."

"Do as you wish. One more thing. His phone. I assume you have it? You won't know most of the people in his contacts who'd like to be kept in the loop, but I do."

Silently, Lucy drew the phone from her coat pocket and handed it over. It felt like a defining ritual in the severing of marital bonds.

Lucy waited until Frances had flicked on her headlights and reversed into the gloom. Then she locked the back door and stood in the kitchen, listening to her heartbeat. She had never been alone here at night.

The house had never had her all to itself before.

And then a shriek rang out. She gasped involuntarily before recognising the eerie ringtone of the green Bakelite phone.

When she picked up the receiver, silence pulsed down the line.

"Hello?" She gripped the serpentine phone cord, anticipating a Napier crackling through the static of years, a reverse-charge call from a stone tape, fizzing with unintelligible words and manic laughter.

But when the voice finally spoke, it belonged to Jude. "So you're there. I've been trying your mobile. Going frantic here. What's the latest?"

Lucy was vaguely aware of several missed calls on her mobile from Jude. Her reply emerged more sharply than intended. "It's late and I'm tired. How'd you even get this number?"

"I noticed the number on the dial when I visited."

"Of course you did."

"Well?"

"Broken bones and surgery for a bleed on the brain. Been placed under sedation while the swelling goes down."

"Oh my God!"

"It's not an anecdote in the soap opera of your life, Jude. One to save up for your next visit to your colourist or manicurist. The one who doesn't trim hooves."

"Cheap shot, Lucy. I'll let it go across the bows, given the circs."

"I don't have the bandwidth for you at the moment. Bye."

"Wait! OK, OK. Did they say anything at the hospital about... you know. The shrooms?"

"Not to me. Maybe the alk had washed it all out of his system. Your concern for Hugh is duly noted."

"Oh, get off your high horse, Lucy. You were up for the se-ance too! We all were. And we didn't take enough stuff to knock out a baby. You were different, granted, but maybe you had an upset stomach or something beforehand? It was just a bit of harmless fun. I said so at the time." Jude's voice dropped an oc-tave. "Listen. Keep my name out of it, will you?"

"No can do if the police come knocking."

"Why would the pol-"

"Goodbye, Jude."

She hung up with a spurt of satisfaction. It was only on her walk back to the kitchen that dizziness nearly floored her.

How long had she been up? When was the last time she'd eaten or drunk, despite Pinky pestering her to do both?

She was just grappling half-heartedly with the Rayburn, her coat still on, when her mobile rang. It was Snowy. "Lucy, where are you?"

"At home. Going back to the hospital in the morning."

"At Rook House on your own?" Snowy was appalled. "You can't stay there!"

"It's where I live, Snowy."

"I'll send Pinky to fetch you back to ours if you're not up to driving."

"No thanks. Honestly, I'll be fine." Fingers crossed.

"What about food? I can have Pinky do a shop."

"Thanks for your concern, but I'm *fine*. I'll call if I need you, I promise."

"How is Hugh?"

Lucy updated her wearily. This time, there was no reason to be evasive about Hugh's fall. Pinky was bound to tell Snowy about the plunge from the window, if he hadn't already.

"But Lucy, are you sure ab-"

"Thanks again, Snowy. I really mean it. I just need a good night's sleep now. Bye."

She gave up on the Rayburn and made a cup of tea with milk already on the turn, pulling her coat cuffs over her knuckles as she sat at the kitchen table, scrolling through her phone for who *she* might need to update on Hugh's condition.

Pretty much nobody. She was struck by the extent of her unpeopled life, its vast, unpopulated blankness. What did that say about her? Nothing flattering.

Hugh had two parents and a bunch of mates from university. Some were no more than casual acquaintances these days, but a hardcore handful remained regular callers and texters.

By contrast, she lived in a Saharan landscape strewn with the bleached bones of abortive friendships and unsatisfactory hook-ups. Other than Snowy and (wince) Pinky, Elena was the sole constant in her life.

Elena, of all people!

She paused when she found her last contact number for Elena. She knew it would get through to her because she'd contacted Elena on this number to tell her about the wedding (and, by implication, invite her to attend it).

She'd sworn to herself that hell would freeze over before she contacted Elena again for any reason. But now, gazing at her stepmother's name, she succumbed to an impulse she expected to regret, and stabbed the number.

Her call went to voicemail. Closing her eyes, she gabbled

an edited account of Hugh's accident, ending with: "You may recall, we moved to Rook House in Yorkshire after the wedding? Anyway, you're up to speed. No need to worry unduly. If indeed, you ever did."

She rang off.

Right. Hardly the sort of message to soften Elena's stepmotherly heart, assuming one beat beneath that dead polecat coat or whatever poor creature it was made from.

Before removing her own coat, she delved into the fluff-filled Mariana Trench of her pockets to hook her purchase from the hospital shop, a packet of over-the-counter tablets to help you sleep, bought in expectation of the night ahead. She read the tiny writing on the back of the box. The tablets contained 'organic properties' to help you drift off. Allegedly. They weren't real knock-out pills. You'd have to see a GP for those.

OK, she was exhausted enough to go out like a light without any pills, but the house might have other ideas, so any port in a storm...

She moved to the fridge, extracting Hugh's latest bottle of Chilean Malbec.

Probably a bad idea to mix booze with shut-eye pills, even organic ones, but she'd earned the right to indulge.

She swallowed two tablets with two big gulps of wine and carried the bottle across the hallway, pushing open the door of the study, imagining for a second that the empty swivel chair drifted round to face her. Fanciful stuff. Neurotic.

His laptop was switched off with the lid still raised. She lowered it and spotted the empty wine glass tucked behind, sides stickily red. Exhibit A, m'lud.

Picking up the glass, she noticed the turquoise notebook sticking out of a half-open desk drawer. He'd been fiddling with that more than the laptop recently.

She washed the glass in the kitchen sink and decided to take the notebook up to bed, along with her phone. Not forgetting the bottle of wine. She might read the notebook if she lasted that long. Things were already becoming pleasurably woozy.

By now, it was so late that she didn't even bother checking her watch as she undressed and crawled into bed without brushing her teeth, shutting the bedroom door but leaving the light on in the room and the curtains ajar to capture the first rays of morning.

Propped against pillows, she opened the notebook, taking a few more swigs of Malbec.

Lots of doodles and word play on the first few pages. Then a couple of tightly scripted pages that required close reading, words thrown down in a frenzy as though he'd lassoed these wild black stallions before they got away, intending to tame them later. She did get the gist... the coat was mentioned. A scare in the attic. Barbed wire. Lice. A cold blue eye.

But it all added up to an idea or the start of an idea known only to Hugh.

Tucked into the back of the notebook she found a shred of yellowing paper containing handwritten words smudged darkly with red wine. Had she smudged them just now or had Hugh a while ago?

She peered at the smeary words but couldn't make them out.

Eventually, she laid the notebook on the bedside table, next to the bottle.

It seemed that he'd been wearing that mouldy coat as a source of desperately sought inspiration, one half-formed image tumbling over another, trying to think himself into a character – perhaps the character of Phineas newly returned from war.

Behind all those wild black words, with their blotted exclamation marks and staccato gear changes, lay a possible echo of the disturbed war survivor who'd roamed Rook House a hundred years ago, mumbling one word, shouting another, chasing in vain the last remnants of his fleeing sanity.

How it might have all hung together like the folds of a coat, only Hugh would *ever* know.

She slid down the pillows at an awkward angle, knocked sideways by fatigue that swept over her in a sudden, huge wave. A "gnarly", surfers would've called it. Her mouth fell open as her eyelids fluttered shut. Her last waking thought was that she must remember to pick up the towels from under the still-open window. Nothing should've woken her for hours.

But the house had other ideas.

27

She woke in the deep stillness of night, heart thumping to warn her that something had just happened – someone had just come into the room.

She lay ramrod-still, straining her eyes towards the curtains. They were now tightly shut and the room lay soaked in sable black. But hadn't she left the light *on*? She turned her head towards the door, unable to make out if it was open or still closed.

Shutting her eyes, she counted slowly to ten, retreating into the void behind her lids.

It was that old game you played as a kid, pretending that others couldn't see you if you couldn't see yourself.

The bed dipped as something sat down beside her, bringing an icy draught. She fumbled a hand towards her mobile phone, which must be inches away on the duvet, aiming to switch on its torch.

A finger of ice touched her exposed wrist. "Mouse..."

The voice was thick with the buzz of swarming bees, yet also light and mocking, like the echo she'd heard in the wood. It spoke her father's nickname for her, later echoed by Hugh. But this voice didn't belong to her father or Hugh. It wasn't a human voice at all.

Her phone slid down the bed, her trembling fingers chasing it. She finally swept it up, switched on the phone torch and angled its thin beam towards the voice, braced to release the scream lodged in her throat.

Nobody there.

She flung watery legs out of the bed and ran across the room, flicking the main light switch back on, flooding the room with a harsh yellow glow that only served to expose the shadows lurking under every angle of furniture and within each fold of drapery.

Creeping back into bed, she sat upright against her pillows, scanning the room like a lookout from a crow's nest, jerking back to wakefulness whenever her eyes grew heavy.

At one point, she woke in a darkened room again, senses temporarily scrambled. The curtains were ajar once more, blue-violet shadows leaking in. What else was different? Hadn't she left the light *on*? Opening her eyes wider, a coat-shaped figure reared up at the foot of the bed. She dry-screamed.

But when she looked again, it was just the outline of her dressing gown, which she'd left hanging on the back of the wardrobe door.

She got up again, wrapped herself in the dressing gown, shoved her phone in her pocket and opened the door to the landing, glad she wore socks in bed. Without looking right or left, she ran out of the room and along the landing to the spiral staircase, racing up to her attic.

There, she turned on the light, closed the door behind her, wedged the ladder-back chair under the doorknob and sat on the floor with her back braced against the sink, waiting for sunrise to christen the slanting window. It couldn't be long now, surely? A glance at her watch. 5am. Another hour or so of vigil on the night watch.

All she had to do was stay awake.

But the house had other ideas.

She felt herself drifting off. A hand tightened on her upper arm, a black tourniquet she 'saw' in a dream as the boneless spread of smoke fingers, tugging at her urgently. *Look, look! You can't look away now! You can't!*

I woke in a narrow bed in a small room filled with the blue-violet shadows of a long, unending night. I seemed unable to move more than my tongue, slowly, around the roof of my mouth. The doctor's sedative appeared to have stricken my limbs but I tried, feebly, to break free of the paralysis.

The door opened and Ezra came in. This time, he stood over me, since there was no room to perch on the narrow bed frame. I was able to turn my head just a little to look up at him. He loomed before a blue-tiled fireplace.

I knew this small room. It was a rarely used guest room. Apart from the bed I lay in, the sole item of furniture was a large wardrobe against the wall.

This seemed to have been moved away from the wall slightly. Ezra noticed me noticing the gap behind the wardrobe. He pulled it away further to reveal the outline of a low wooden door set into the wall.

"There's a space behind that door," he said in his usual cold, polite tone. "I'd quite forgotten about it. I remember my father telling me that it was intended as a hiding place during some imagined emergency, easily obscured behind a piece of furniture. The architect who built this place was so taken with his own ingenuity that my grandfather let him add it to the plans."

"Do you intend to put me in there?" I asked. But my lips, floppily swollen and useless, refused to form words.

"You won't be able to speak until the sedative wears off entirely," he said languidly. "And you may be given more, depending on your behaviour. I shall come back later."

Horrifyingly, I was so isolated in my terror that I didn't want him, its instigator, to leave me here alone. "Darrow?" I tried to ask.

But he left and I *was* alone.

I drifted in and out of sleep. In moments of lucidity I resolved that I would indeed 'behave' when the drug wore off. It would buy me time and perhaps what remained of Ezra's civility. That was all I could hope for. He lacked a conscience I could appeal to.

But the next time I drifted up to wakefulness, it was to feel another sharp pain in my wrist. I opened my eyes to meet the blank gaze of Doctor Shaw.

I struggled and shouted, but in vain, my wrist growing black from the deepening bruise of continued piercing.

Shaw stepped back from the bed with distaste. "There," he said to someone behind him. "You may wash her, change the sheets if needed and when she wakes again later, administer a little water or soup. She should be quite safe for several more hours."

He snapped shut his black box of horrors and left the room, and I saw it was Darrow who'd stood behind him, eyes still downcast and red. A ray of renewed hope shone through my fog of despair. "Darrow! How long have I been here? Have days passed or merely hours?"

She leant over me, carefully. "Oh marm, whyever did you do this to yourself?"

"Mickey!" I croaked, desperate to get my words out before the fresh sedative took effect. I had not succumbed instantly, so Shaw must have given me less than before. "It's not too late to get a message to Mickey, Darrow! You must tell him what the master has done here. *I* must tell Mickey what Mr Napier has done to his son!"

I couldn't tell if my words were making sense or not, but Darrow frowned. "It's a wicked enough thing."

I tried to nod. "Yes, but it's not too late. It can't be!"

She took my hand from the coverlet and squeezed it till the bones protested. "A wicked thing you've done, marm. In the months before you birthed, I said nothing of your antics as you sloped off to the woods, thinking yourself so clever. Oh, but I knew. And when you asked me but yesterday if I'd seen Mickey Nellis and then asked me for money, likely for the purpose of running away with him and taking the bab with you..." She shook her head sorrowfully. "Oh marm, even then you wouldn't give him up. You as had everything. You needed teaching that life don't work that way, even for the likes of you."

The fog still sat heavy on my brow, but her words broke through.

She had betrayed me to Ezra! While I'd sat at breakfast making plans to escape, she must have gone to Ezra and scuppered them. But why? Why now?

"He killed my secondborn child, you stupid, ungrateful slut!" I shouted uselessly, my limbs, bones and mouth as floppy as a rag doll's. "The boy born a few minutes after Phineas! Ezra saw his turned-in little foot the second I did, and he *knew* without doubt. He nodded at Shaw and Shaw took my little boy aside and covered his face with a sheet... but the child cried, Darrow, I heard him! I heard him cry for his precious little life before it was snuffed out of him!"

Darrow patted my trapped hand. "You're not making any sense, marm, and shan't again from what we hear."

"Please help me, please!"

I could forgive even this betrayal if she'd help me; if she'd yet show a morsel of compassion.

She leant in close then, her eyes as wide and shining as her broad forehead and she said, in a chilling mimicry of her master's voice: "Twins, madam, but as you clearly saw, one of your bastards had a deformed foot. I've put him down as I would any limping whelp. His brother's fate I've yet to decide. It depends whether your – rustic paramour – ever learns the truth and finds the courage to claim that he sired your bastards. If he values his own and the surviving child's life, I think not."

I don't know if she understood every word she'd overheard, but she had recorded them like an attentive polly singing for its seed. They were words I'd done my best to shut out.

"You listen at doors," I realised. "You listen and scheme accordingly. Just as you followed me towards the wood when I'd thought myself safe."

Bravo, I might have said if her stealth had served my interests.

"You shan't have Michael Nellis," she told me now in her own voice, breath stale with onions and determination. "Not now and not ever. You had more than any woman could want and still took from them as had nowt. Leading a good man astray! A man too good for the likes of you! You're a wicked woman what's done wicked things and will go to Hell for it as surely as the master will for what *he's* done to that bab. As if I'd care if I bore Mickey a child with a sticky-in foot, poor mite! He'd be loved just the same. As for the living child you bore, he can stay here, and Mickey shall be none the wiser for any of it. I'll make sure of it. Now then. D'you hear... marm?"

How long had she set her bonnet at Mickey, I wondered? Had she merely seen me go into the wood and drawn conclusions from a distance, or spied on us in our bower and waited to see what came of it and how she could thwart the affair? Had she been 'comforting' Mickey these past weeks while he lay beyond my reach?

I bit down on her cheek.

She drew back and howled. I was pleased to see I'd drawn blood.

She rushed from the room clutching her cheek and I sank into my damp pillow, filled with murderous rage. 'Loyal' Darrow had betrayed me to Ezra in pursuit of her own base ends.

When I got out of here, I would rain down vengeance like a dragon scorching the townsfolk from its smoking lair. I would... I would...

I would do nothing, it soon became clear.

I sank into a deep sleep I could no longer hold at bay. It might have been an hour or three days later – I lost track of time – when I awoke to find that Ezra had returned. No sign of Darrow. But he'd brought Mickey.

I heard the dragging foot before I saw him. He held loose serpentine coils in red-veined hands. Then I saw what those coils were. Leather straps.

I tried to scream his name. I tried to scream for his help. A strand of hair caught in my mouth and nearly choked me.

Ezra removed the strand tenderly and told Mickey: "As you can see, she's beyond the power of coherent speech. She's also become dangerous. You saw what she did to her maidservant. Proceed as I told you."

Mickey trussed me in the straps as tightly as any partridge fettered to a belt. Three straps in all; one across my chest, one across my knees and one across my ankles, lifting me up each time to secure the strap beneath me with a thick metal buckle, and not once meeting my wild, rolling eye.

He tried to ensure that the buckles were not digging into me, but over time, as I moved in my shackles, the buckles would move too, sharp points digging welts out of my spine. The buckles would never move far enough to come within reach, however.

Mickey made sure of it.

To give the man his due, he always shifted the straps to less painful positions when he came to wedge a pot under me or feed me spoonfuls of thin soup. He bathed me sometimes with a wet flannel, his kindness and sadness like a burning ember.

He was my designated jailer now; Ezra's ultimate revenge on us both. Shaw continued to sedate me so that I was never able to form words and sentences in Mickey's presence. Mickey would never know that Ezra had killed one of his sons and claimed the other.

It was my husband's exquisite revenge on his adulterous wife and her lover. And it broke me.

But Ezra was not quite done yet.

Sometimes it amused him to sit by my bed and watch me scrabble at the leather straps like a furtive animal digging a burrow. One day, he said: "You're disturbing the household, even now."

And he moved my bed himself into that windowless cubby – it was not a room worthy of the name – set into the wall behind the wardrobe, where I had no light or hope and only freezing air for company.

He locked me in there for hours at a time. "No one enters but myself and anyone I choose to send."

I was to be spoken about from then on, rather than to. I was reduced to a household object or a donkey in the shafts.

He sent Mickey less and less once the dark cubby became my new resting place. Perhaps he knew that Mickey's soft heart might break apart at my increasingly callous treatment, though so far, his heart had stood fast in obedience and deference to his powerful employer.

Gradually, my sole attendants became Shaw and a reluctant Mrs Tankerton, who whisked in and out of my oubliette with a rough flannel and a high temper at being called to such duties.

I gave up any thoughts of fire-breathing dragons and dwelt more on men left to die on battlefields, cut to ribbons by cannon fire but unable to see their own wreckage in the darkness and filth, looking up at the stars and murmuring: "When I get out of here, I shall do this and that."

Would I ever get out of here or die slowly on this hellish battlefield?

And all the time, I dwelt too on Mickey and Darrow, Darrow and Mickey.

To him, she'd have been "Susan".

"My own Susie," perhaps. "My best lass."

Susan Darrow, my little protégée, the wounded bird I'd rescued. She had pretended to yield to me while hiding her true, cunning nature. She had bested me.

Mickey had explained Original Sin to me once. "We are all of us born with the sin of the first man and woman who disobeyed our Lord."

"When Eve gave Adam the apple?"

"That's it. An' we must be cleansed of it in baptism."

"So you people believe that even an innocent baby can be born wicked?"

"Not knowingly, but we must all be cleansed and born anew."

Shackled in my cell, I thought of the child Ezra and Shaw had murdered and disposed of, denied both Christian baptism and burial or a name to call his own. What would Mickey have said to that?

I still worked on the straps in my darkness behind that wall. I'd proved I had bite. If I could apply my frayed mind in lucid periods between Shaw's hideous ministrations, I could yet bite and chew and claw my way out, flee this place, find people who'd heed me, comfort me, march on Rook House, demand justice and-

She woke to a room filled with the blue-violet shadows of a long night, jerking upright when she sensed something different about the attic and the atmosphere in the rest of the house. The light was no longer on in the room. And a thunderous knocking was coming from downstairs.

It sounded like – like furious knuckles rapping on the polished wood of a dining room table. Or a portrait lifted by its edges smashing repeatedly into the living room wall.

Until the sound rang out once more and Lucy realised its true provenance: the lion's head door knocker reverberating throughout the house.

It wasn't going to stop.

She pulled herself upright on stiff haunches, moved the chair away from the door and opened it, shaking.

The spiral staircase had never looked steeper and, when she crept down the treads, the landing had never seemed darker. She fumbled for a light switch, the overhead bulb stuttering reluctantly to meek life. The main staircase lay cauled in shadow.

The door-knocking *had* stopped now but whoever was out there still waited. She could sense it in the silence filling every space inside and outside her head.

I won't go down, I won't go...

Another thunderous knock, followed by a flurry of knuckles and a voice calling, faintly but audibly: "Hello? Any bodies in there?"

Lucy blinked. In this case, she knew the speaker didn't intend a tasteless pun. At least, she didn't *think* they did.

She ran down the stairs and crossed the hallway to stare at the massively solid front door. Suppose she was wrong?

"Hello!" shouted the voice again. "You do know it's freezing out here?"

Lucy reached out and drew back the bolt, then opened the door, expecting it to creak.

But it yawned smoothly and the night caller stepped smartly through the gap, pausing to shake out the lapels of her white fur coat.

"I come," announced Elena.

28

"Chickens," said Elena, "always come to roost – isn't that the expression?" She'd come to roost.

"They come *home* to roost," clarified Lucy, bleary-eyed in the kitchen's cold, early morning light. "Rook House isn't your home."

"Nor yours," Elena pouted. "Maybe I count my chickens then. Only here, it would be sheep. So many sheep as I drive here. More than people, I would think. Like Australia or Wales."

"Have you been to those places?"

"I read. I watch TV."

Lucy had no idea of Elena's nationality, Elena herself coy about it to the point of paranoia.

Hugh reckoned she was Interpol's most wanted: "Got a safety deposit box with at least four passports, couple of burners, cyanide capsule and pearl-handled revolver to stick in a stocking top. Married your dad for cover and sleeps with one eye open for an Albanian hitman."

"What you smile about?" Elena asked, watching Lucy crank up the Rayburn.

"Nowt. Not a lot to smile about at the mo." Lucy poured tea and tried to get her head round her stepmother's sudden appearance. Elena's smart suitcase was still in the middle of the kitchen floor and Lucy was still in her dressing gown.

"I get your voicemail," explained Elena. "Bernard look up Rooks House on the Google. I tell Bernard I will come."

In the past half hour, Lucy had heard a lot about Bernard: "The first man I love since my David."

Elena lived with him in a Docklands penthouse. She'd literally gone up in the world.

Lucy had decided against making this joke. Elena had been puzzled enough when Lucy's dad used to joke that her shoe habit was her Achilles heel.

"Bernard didn't want to come with?" checked Lucy as her phone warbled in her dressing gown pocket.

"He get car sick."

"Hang on." Lucy recognised the number on her screen as a local call. "Gotta take this."

She stepped into the hallway, pulling the kitchen door shut behind her.

The caller was a police detective from Sowersby. She wanted Lucy to drop by the station later today: "Just a few questions about your husband's accident. Or I can come over to Rook House if more convenient?"

"I'm due back at the hospital this morning, detective. I'll try to get over to Sowersby by, say, late afternoon?"

They agreed on 4pm. Detective Goldring added good wishes for Hugh's recovery and hung up.

Lucy tapped her chin with the phone, recalling Pinky's warning to volunteer nothing. Did the police really suspect foul play?

Back in the kitchen, Elena was pouring her cup of tea down the sink.

"I haven't got a room made up for guests, Elena. If you're stopping, you'll have to book into the pub in Lowmorten."

"Why the police want to see you?" Elena asked. "I hear you call someone 'detective'," she shrugged.

"It's standard procedure when someone dives out of a window," said Lucy, instantly regretting her choice of words. She felt herself growing hot and wondered whether Tom and Frances had urged the cops to investigate a domestic scuffle theory. Detective Goldring had sounded suspiciously unsuspicious.

"I go with you to hospital and to see police," offered Elena. "And I don't mind sharing a bed. What do they call it, top and tail?"

"God, no, on all fronts!" Lucy headed back into the hallway. "I'll phone the hospital to see if there have been any developments, then head there on my own."

"Surely they would call you if something change?"

"I'll see you later, Elena. Maybe. Have a look at the pub in Lowmorten. It's called The Rusty Nail. They might even have a cocktail of the same name."

It was the start of a long day dashing to and fro, barely giving Lucy time to think, absorb, digest.

Or reflect on last night, alone in the house.

Last night... *had* there been someone in the bedroom with her? Then, up in the attic, she'd fallen into the bottomless well of a richly textured dream that eluded her in the light of day.

No migraine warning or shrooms this time to stimulate her unconscious mind, but she had taken those two 'organic' pills and hefty slugs of wine...

At the hospital, Hugh remained in an induced coma. She sat with him as before, aware that she'd run out of things to say. "Oh, you might get a kick out of Elena turning up out of the blue. Who'd have thought that she'd be our first proper guest at Rook House? I've suggested she book a room in Lowmorten if she wants to hang around, but I reckon she'll soon get bored of pretending to be supportive and bog off. Reckon she only came to show off to this Bernard bloke, pretend she gives a toss about her ingrate stepdaughter."

She had, with great reluctance, loaned Elena the spare set of house keys that Pinky had surrendered a while back.

She passed Tom and Frances in the corridor as she left. They exchanged brief, colourless words about Hugh's condition and she explained that she had to go into Sowersby but would return for an evening visit. "Don't rush back on our account," muttered Frances. "Or Hugh's."

Lucy glanced at Tom but he looked away quickly.

Back at Rook House, she discovered that Elena had indeed driven into Lowmorten, but only to buy a folding bed, pillows and linen, setting up camp in one of the spare bedrooms. "Not in that small room with leaves on the wall. That is *cold*."

Also, luckily, not in the room that Hugh had fallen from. Lucy went in there to shut the window. Before doing so, she poked her head out and gazed down at the trampled towels beneath. About to pull back in, she noticed a rusty nail sticking out of the brickwork beneath the sill, fluttering a tiny streamer of wool.

So Hugh had caught his sleeve on the nail and hung there. He'd have *known* he was going to plunge on to concrete and gravel below.

Swallowing a rush of saliva, she drew her head in and slammed the sash down.

On her way downstairs, she poked her head into the room Elena had requisitioned. Her half-full suitcase sat on top of the folding bed, her impractical shoes ranged alongside.

Lucy went down to the kitchen and asked: "Where'd you park the white coat?"

"Your wardrobe, of course."

"Right."

"I cannot throw on floor!"

"Sure you want to stay here, Elena? It's not very comfortable."

"I read about Rooks House on my phone while you are gone. This is my first haunted house. I expect great things."

In fact, with Elena's presence, the house already had a lighter atmosphere, its usual febrility banished by her outspoken belief in the supernatural. Perhaps, with no one left to convince of their presence, the ghosts were taking a breather.

Not even the portrait of Ezra bothered her. "A handsome man," she declared, staring him out as she and Lucy stood in front of the stone mantelpiece.

"Really?" Lucy shuddered. "You don't think he looks cruel?"

"Handsome men often are."

Lucy sniffed the air. "You can't smoke in the house, Elena. Feel free to use the extensive grounds."

Elena rolled her eyes, then turned from the portrait and clapped her hands. "I come to see police with you. Moral support. I will not take no for my answer."

Wearily, Lucy agreed, still puzzling over Elena's real agenda for coming to Rook House. Morbid curiosity? Hoping to leave with a few heirlooms stashed under the dead polecat?

Abandoning pointless conjecture, Lucy hurried off to (finally!) deal with the pile of muddied towels under the window before Elena truffled them out and started pressing for the gory details of Hugh's fall.

So far, she'd exhibited surprising restraint on the subject, willing to accept Lucy's threadbare version of events: that Hugh had leant out a bit too far for fresh air, been blinded by the sun and accidentally toppled forward. Even to Lucy's ears it sounded lame.

But she could just imagine Hugh snorting: "Perhaps she's a honeytrap specialist who'd lure a dissident to a Moscow high-rise and watch a couple of heavies heave him out the airlock. Might even have tipped a few out herself. Wouldn't put it past her."

Then Lucy felt an irritating stab of guilt. It was equally possible that Elena was a victim of human trafficking who'd fled a lock-up with her organs just about intact. You never knew, did you?

At half three, she drove herself and Elena to Sowersby police station, the turquoise notebook in her cross-body bag.

Should she have left the window open and the towels in situ? Christ, there was a thought – she'd put her fingerprints all over the window sash. What if the police came to take a recce of the scene and drew highly implausible conclusions?

Especially as Lucy only had that equally improbable 'leaning too far out of a window' explanation for his fall. The alcohol might clinch it, though. She despised herself for being soothed by the thought.

At the police station, Detective Goldring led her into a windowless room, leaving Elena perched in reception.

Martha Goldring was a young woman in a velvet Alice band who reminded Lucy of a smooth-haired, coifed figure in a Dutch old master.

"Do I need a lawyer?" Lucy asked, sitting down at a metal desk.

"I shouldn't think so," Goldring replied blandly. "This is just to go over a few points."

Lucy recounted, yet again, the awful, slow-motion seconds when Hugh had dangled from an upstairs window at Rook House. She added her recent discovery of the nail sticking out of the brickwork beneath the sill. "Now I think of it," she frowned, "is there any connection to the fact there's a local pub called The Rusty Nail?"

Detective Goldring flipped open a folder. "The Rusty Nail has had that name for a couple of centuries. I see his blood-alcohol level was high."

"Yes, he'd developed quite a drinking habit. Sadly. Neither of us were used to rural isolation."

"Which you'd both sought."

The implication was clear. She and Hugh were a pair of urban numpties who'd expected to be frolicking in meadows and bottling jam.

"There were also minute traces of recreational drugs in his system," said Goldring. "As I say, trace amounts. Still, not a good mix with alcohol."

"I don't know anything about that. I rarely drink and I've never done drugs, detective. My mother was killed by a drink-driver."

"So *you* never over-indulged, even though you and Hugh were together much of the time?"

"He went for long walks and could be quite secretive about some things. How did you get my mobile phone number, by the way?" Lucy had her suspicions.

Goldring gave a tight smile. "Anything else you can think of that might help us build a picture of Hugh's state of mind? You told his parents that he'd lost his freelance job and was also struggling to write his latest book." She put her head on one side. "Was he depressed? That would certainly explain the drinking and other behaviour."

Lucy made her move and produced the notebook. "He was definitely struggling. He bought this notebook recently. It's full of – well – he kind of rambles in it. Coincides with the drinking, I think. There may be more coherent work on his computer, but I haven't looked."

She felt hot again, this time with disloyalty. But none of it was untrue. And it was crucial to get across that she'd done nothing to push him over the edge, literally.

Goldring took the notebook, shut her folder and placed the notebook neatly on top. "That'll be all for now. Thanks for coming by, Mrs Driscoll. Oh, his clothing will be returned to you as soon as forensics have done their bit. The clothes he was wearing at the time of the... accident," she clarified.

"I wasn't aware you had them." Shouldn't the hospital have told her they'd passed his clothes to the police? "I don't want them back. You can chuck when you're finished."

Goldring nodded without appearing shocked. "The clothes are not bloodstained but I understand your reluctance."

Hardly, thought Lucy. She never wanted to see that reeking old coat again.

She hesitated.

"Something else on your mind, Mrs Driscoll?"

"No. Only my husband." She'd teetered on asking whether the police would be making a dawn swoop on Rook House to seek 'evidence' of foul play, then decided against. The question would only look defensive.

Moments later she was back in reception with Elena, pretty damn certain that Frances or even Tom had been telling tales to Goldring and co.

On the drive back, she detoured into Lowmorten for supplies, noticing a few loaded glances aimed her way.

She grumbled to Elena: "The police might have their suspicions about Hugh's injury because that's their job. But why would strangers jump to conclusions?"

"Because that's *their* job," snorted Elena. "Maybe they already sharpen tridents. Yes, I look them up! Pitchforks too. Remember, every story needs a villain. Better still, a *villana*."

She dropped Elena at Rook House with the provisions (Elena professed no misgivings about being there alone after dark) and drove on to the hospital.

Pinky rang her on the way. "When can I see you?" he asked. "I worry about you in that house on your own."

"No need. My stepma's arrived to offer moral support. I can't talk now, Pinky. I'm not hands free and I'm on my way to Hugh for an evening visit. Just leave things until I call you or Snowy. Please. Oh, and tell Snowy there's no need to come and do any cleaning for a while. Not until things settle down a bit, OK?"

Driving in the dark, fragments of last night resurfaced in her black windscreen: a pressure on the side of her bed, a finger on her wrist – a dead finger yearning to touch a pulse.

She shivered, suddenly glad of Elena's company.

<hr />

The next few days fell into a routine marked by hospital visits, hurried meals and verbal sparring with Elena.

On the third night of Elena's stay, Lucy returned late from the hospital to find her stepmother at the foot of the stairs in the dark hallway, gazing up into the shadows with a firm glint in her equally dark eye. "I intend to cleanse this house of negative energy," Elena declared.

"It's all right, I ate on the way," Lucy said sarcastically, shucking off her coat, footwear and bag as she reclaimed the kitchen.

Moments later, Elena came in, carrying a dark-grey bowl and a rolled-up transparent bag containing what looked like weed.

"Sage leaves," she explained, shaking the bag. "I burn some in each room for good energy. I will use my lighter."

Lucy frowned. "I thought you were hoping to be spooked rather than chasing ghosts away? Did something happen while I was in York?"

"I bring my cleansing apparatus for your sake, Lucia."

"Don't call me that!"

"Oh yes, I am not allowed." Unperturbed, Elena set the bowl down on the kitchen table. "You are not so comfortable here, I think. Me? Pfff. It's the living you have to worry about."

"I told you, Elena, I don't want smoke drifting round the house."

"I will be careful."

"Can't you do it tomorrow? Preferably when I'm out."

"Now is good. We open window in each room. Then I light small bundle of sage, blow out flame and walk around, waving smoke into all corners, inviting positive energy to push out bad. I hold bowl under sage as I walk. This collects ash."

Lucy noted that this was quite a jargon-heavy speech from Elena. "Done a lot of spiritual energy cleansing, I take it?"

"Not when I live with your father. He complain of smell. The smell is good. It gives energy to the soul."

"Think I'll pass."

"Lucy, this is important! I want to do for you. As gift."

"Look, I'm knackered and I don't want you wafting about doing a hocus-pocus number, OK?"

Elena let out a deep sigh. "Very well. OK." Apparently defeated, she sat down at the kitchen table. Her dark eyes still gleamed tellingly. "I went to see painting, in attic. While you were out."

"Did you now?"

"The one you have started. I look more than once. The room is not locked."

An unlocked room being an invitation to enter, of course.

"Are you going to finish it? The portrait is your mother, yes? You paint a black background and she holds a rose. It look familiar. Then I realise why." Elena hesitated, which surprised Lucy. Elena was not one for hesitancy. "You remember, then?"

"Remember what?"

"Come to attic and tell me what you see."

"Elena, what are you talking about? You're making me uneasy, to be honest."

It's the living you have to worry about.

Elena went so far as to put a hand on Lucy's arm. "Please. There is something I must... I must tell you. About your mother. Bernard say I must. That it's good for *my* soul."

Hairs rose on Lucy's forearm under Elena's surprisingly tentative touch.

She flung off the touch. "You can tell me here. Now."

Elena shook her head fiercely. "It concern the painting. Please, come."

Lucy felt her resistance ebb as her unease revved up a notch and verged on panic.

"All right, but I don't like this performative air of mystery. It's all about you, Elena, as per. If you've something to say, you should come out and say it, painting or no painting."

Elena shook her head vigorously like a wet dog, muttered fleeting words under her breath and headed for the hallway.

Lucy followed, reluctantly.

Elena turned to her at the foot of the stairs, eyes darker than ever above stark cheekbones bleached white by the overhead light, now switched on. "Perhaps this is the gift I was meant to give you all along. Come."

29

Climbing two sets of stairs gave Lucy ample time to dread whatever revelation lost to time – *You remember, then?* – Elena was about to fan back to life from grey embers.

In the attic, Lucy switched on the light. Her easel stood where she'd left it, but the pillowcase covering the canvas had been tossed carelessly over the small amount of work she'd completed, all of it done before Hugh's accident.

Elena drew off the pillowcase and turned from the canvas to Lucy. "You see it, yes?"

Lucy gazed at the half-begun outline of her mother's features. One eye was painted light gold, though it was going to be a deep hazel. A suggestion of lacy fingers held the coiled filaments of a pencilled rose that would ultimately match the shade of Rosa's favourite lipstick, Exces de Rouge. The outline of a bird sat on her right shoulder.

Lucy was now working from a photo taken from an album and pinned to the corner of the easel. In the photo, Rosa teased the lens with a direct gaze and an enigmatic, closed-lips half-smile, an unwitting *Mona Lisa*. Or maybe, when the photo was taken (Lucy could only date it to after Rosa's marriage and relocation to England), she'd been musing on Anne Lovell, the lady with the squirrel and the starling.

Now Lucy felt real anger and distress at the notion of Elena coming up here and devouring a hallowed image that Lucy had shared with no one and perhaps never would. "What am I supposed to see that apparently you do?"

Elena pointed at the canvas. "You base this on that other painting with squirrel and ugly little bird, yes?"

"What? How do you know that painting? Talk to me, Elena!"

"I know the lady with a squirrel and a bird because I work, long time ago, in National Gallery. When I first come to London, I work as attendant there. I meet your father in a bar in Soho, but at work, I'm often in gallery room with the lady and squirrel. And your mother – she must find out about me, follow me one day and find out where I work, and after that, she comes and pretends to view paintings while watching me. And some days, she brings you with her. She wants to say, I think: 'Look, he has wife and child. Find someone else, leave us be.' But I can't. I'm now deep in love with my David. But she watches from her eye corner and I can't get up and move because I must sit on chair for precise time and watch people watching the paintings. You see?"

Lucy's legs went from under her and she groped for the ladder-back chair, falling into it. "Oh my God... you're telling me that your affair with Dad was going on *before* Mum died? And that she found out? I thought she took me to the gallery bec-"

"Because she love art and she want you to love art?" Elena nodded vigorously. "Maybe that too. Me, not so much interest. A job is a job. After I tell David about Rosa coming to watch me, he finds me a new job – better job – in the bar where we met. I don't know if your mother stop going to National Gallery after I leave. Rosa says nothing to David about any of it, though he waits to see if she does. When Rosa dies, David is in pieces and says that you are too, so we must wait, wait, wait until time is right. I wait *years*, Lucy, all the while not knowing if my David can be relied on, while my looks and offers from other men, richer men, they slip away. I tell you this so you know how much I love your father and put my faith in him."

Lucy couldn't recall the precise timeline of everything that Elena was referring to, but she was stunned, stricken. She'd been five when her mother died. So – so her father had been cheating on Rosa throughout their marriage or at least for part of it!

All that time spent gazing at, absorbing that particular portrait from an early age, and her mother had probably chosen it because it gave her a good sightline of Elena in her attendant's chair.

She felt sick. She felt robbed. She looked down at her socked feet. "When, exactly, did you and my father start your affair?"

"You were three, I think. He tell me from start: 'I love my wife, I love my child.' Only later, I begin to hope."

"After his wife was conveniently dead?"

"There was no plan, Lucy. I fall for David gradual, at first knowing it is just an affair."

"Until fate intervened on your behalf."

"He fall gradual for me, too. Neither of us want to hurt you or Rosa."

Lucy gritted her teeth. The patronising bitch! How dare Elena talk as though she and David Calland were agonised by the power of their emerging love but unable to resist it!

Why, why, why had her father betrayed every memory that Lucy held precious? He'd always spoken of Rosa as the love of his life, even misting up about the day they met, the light falling on her glossy black hair as she sketched by the Trevi Fountain. Probably all bullshit, the ultimate bedtime story to share with a grieving little girl.

"And you're telling me this now, Elena, with my husband in a coma?"

"Bernard say I must get this off my chest. And this painting give me the chance."

Of course Bernard knew. A stranger knew. Lucy felt like howling, except that her body wouldn't respond. In fact, she felt like she was having an out-of-body experience.

"Right, well, consider yourself unburdened, cleansed even. Now your chakras are realigned, you can bog off back to deluded Bernie and live happily ever after, knowing you've spilled your guts and said your piece. Because it is all about you, as per. Never mind that it might be the last thing *I* wanted to hear at a time like this! Leave now, today, this minute, and never contact me again. We're done, Elena."

"Lucy, I – I am sorry."

"So am I. For a lot of things. I'm sorry for not questioning my father properly when he was alive, asking more about how you two met. But I didn't because I was afraid to lose him completely, which happened anyway. You made sure of that."

"He die of heart attack!"

"But you took him away from me long before that! He didn't want to talk about how he hooked up with you, telling me it wasn't appropriate to ask for details. I got some half-baked bullshit about your eyes meeting across a crowded room at a time and location conveniently post-Mum. And my God, he certainly didn't want to talk about Mum! He made me feel that it was disloyal to you even bringing her up. Though I suspect it was *you* who made him feel like that, you're such an arch manipulator, and probably pathetic enough to be jealous of a dead woman. I never knew men could be so gullible. Though of course, Hugh was the same, falling for Jude," she added to herself. "Probably. Dad was your puppet and I was his. Why do men go for such *obvious* women?"

"Maybe you not obvious enough," mumbled Elena. "Men don't want to read minds or between lines. Men are lazy."

Lucy staggered to her feet, swept the painting off the easel and marched downstairs with it, Elena clattering behind her.

"What you doing with that?"

In the kitchen, Lucy grabbed the bread knife from a drawer, laid the painting on the worktop and started hacking it to pieces.

"Lucy, stop! You hurt your painting!"

Lucy paused, out of breath. "It's based on a lie. Based on a painting I thought meant something to Mum and therefore to me, when all the time, it was just a... a tool she used to go on manoeuvres in an art gallery."

"You throw babies out with bath water!"

"Get going, Elena, please. I'm not myself and now I have a knife in my hand."

Elena backed away, reluctantly, towards the hallway. "You won't like it here alone."

"I may as well get used to it. Everyone I've ever trusted has screwed me over." She slammed the knife tip into the pencilled rose, wincing as the blade slipped and slit the flesh between her own thumb and index finger. "Take your woo-woo sage bundles and Black Opium and your dead polecat coat and get the hell out of Dodge, Elena. You stole Dad, took every penny he had, and now you've stolen my one enduring memory of something special I thought I shared with my mother. Even you must have enough in your swag bag by now."

"If I go, Lucy, I go for good."

"You swear?"

Ten minutes later, Elena clattered her suitcase over the checkerboard tiles in the hallway.

She came into the kitchen and flung the spare keys on the table where Lucy sat motionless, blood dripping from her latest flesh wound.

"We say enough," said Elena with imperial dignity. "Elvis leave building."

Seconds later, the front door opened and shut with a definitive slam.

A snowdrift of white fur went past the dark kitchen window, reversing to stop in front of the glass. Elena tapped on the window and fondled her coat lapels. "Is genuine mink!" she enunciated. Before sailing on her way.

Lucy heard a car start up and listened to it fade towards the pillared gates.

Then she returned to the attic and reclaimed the ladder-back chair, looking out of the slanting attic window into the silent night, unholy night. Let whatever still wanted her seek her out now, be it a ghost or a memory or the welcome oblivion of sleep.

But she sat there, chilled and alert, with only herself for company, unable to stop thinking.

What if... what if Rosa had been brooding on the affair with Elena when she stepped on to that zebra crossing, too miserably distracted to notice the approaching car speeding erratically?

Then an even darker thought. What if Rosa had *chosen* to walk out in front of Nathan Stelley's car, taking care to see the whites of his vodka-crazed eyes?

A low moan started deep in her throat.

And how could her father – who must have been aware of either possibility – have compounded the anguish by continuing to see and then marrying Elena?

A motherless ten-year-old when her father remarried, Lucy had retreated into a mutinous sulk. But her father had treated her as an adult who'd made her own bed and now had to lie in it, instead of the confused, heartbroken child she'd actually been.

Or was she excusing herself too easily for her own mistakes? Like marrying Hugh.

Elena's timeline for the affair also meant that David had started 'seeing' her when he was in his 40s and she was still in her 20s, the old libertine, not content with already being married to a beautiful woman 15 years his junior.

What was wrong with men?

Lucy's chin sank on to her chest, the nails on her uninjured hand scoring deeply into the chair's arm rest, like a faintly chiming reminder of nails clawed to bloody stumps against leather straps.

Shadows massed in the corners of the room and fretted in search of shape. Something came slapping its way up the spiral staircase. Maybe.

Whispers. Sighs. Black fingers on a boneless limb curled over the easel and brushed hair off her forehead, then moved down to play with the gold locket on her throat.

Lucy might've mumbled her mother's name. The fingers pressed a little harder, against the pulse beating in the hollow of her throat. Then tightened around her with frightening suddenness, filled with angry strength. Did this hand want to pull her back into the past again? Or simply to despatch her?

She tried to mumble that she didn't mind, it could do its worst, but she only made a gurgling sound, her hand uncurling but thrumming uselessly on the arm rest, her socks trying to beat the same tattoo on the floor.

The footsteps around her grew louder, things scurrying and hurrying in and out of the room and across its floorboards, stone tape images played on a spool of film she had no wish to see.

Time passed, rewound, passed again.

And then, suddenly, a rougher, jerking motion against her shoulder, an ashen face swimming up close. "Lucy, Lucy, can you hear me? Lucy, wake up!"

30

In Snowy's cottage, Snowy told Pinky to add brandy to the Brown Betty before he poured.

"Think that's wise, Ma?"

"She's chilled to the bone," Snowy tutted. "And lost a fair bit of blood from cutting herself with that knife."

"Which may have been accidental. I told you how I found the painting."

"Yes, all hacked about with a knife she might have ended up turning on herself!"

"Ma..."

"I am here, you know." Lucy struggled upright in a kitchen chair. "I'm sorry for all the trouble I've caused, but I must get to the hospital. What time is it? I can hear birdsong."

"It's gone eight in the morning and you've caused no trouble," said Snowy. "You've been dozing in that chair since Pinky fetched you from Rook House. He's already phoned the hospital and said you won't be going in today, you need to rest."

"What!" Lucy tried to rise from the chair, only to fall back, dizzy from the effort.

"We rest our case," said Pinky, opening the fridge.

"Hugh will think I've abandoned him! As will his parents."

"I've taken care of it," insisted Pinky, making Lucy furious.

"You'd no right to interfere! I'm sorry," she added to Snowy. "Grateful as I am for your care and concern, I'm not sure why

I'm here, exactly, or why you both thought you needed to stage an intervention."

"Isn't it obvious?" asked Snowy sharply. "You were alone in that house, no sign of this stepmother of yours. Pinky fetched up to check things, found blood dripping from the kitchen all the way up the stairs. He were that terrified what he'd find in the attic..."

"Ma, don't exaggerate."

"And there you were, muttering to yourself and thrashing about, one hand cut with a knife. I've washed and bandaged it," Snowy added, Lucy gazing down at her injured hand as if seeing it for the first time. "He had to practically carry you down the stairs. I don't know what qualifies as a breakdown, but all you've been through-"

"Ma, still too full-on," complained Pinky.

"Is it?" Snowy made solemn eye contact with Lucy. "Pinky's told me about the seance and Hugh and that Jude one drugging the soup to get a reaction."

Lucy frowned at Pinky. "Nice one, Jerome. I took you into my confidence."

"Actions have consequences," he reminded her, grimacing.

"I think I'm going to be sick," Lucy gulped.

"Loo is upstairs on your right," Snowy replied, helping her out of the chair. "Can you make it on your own?"

"I'm not an invalid!"

"Right you are."

"Sorry. Sorry, Snowy. I don't mean to snap."

Upstairs, Lucy retched into the toilet bowl for several minutes, then quickly scoured her mouth with tap water, reluctant to leave the Birds discussing her behind her back.

Her right hand had been bandaged expertly where she'd cut it when the knife slipped. They didn't seriously think she'd done it deliberately? Even so, she was conforming to type as the permanently walking wounded.

She went downstairs extra carefully, guided by the banisters.

Pinky was leaning on the sink, sipping tea. No sign of his mother. He nodded at a steaming cup on the table. "Yours if you want it."

"Where's Snowy?"

"Decided to pop up to Rook House to collect a few things for you. How's your hand?"

"Good. It's not even sore."

"Ma's handiwork. We both want you to stay here and out of that place, no ifs or buts."

"You're both taking me over and I don't like it."

"Get used to it." He scratched his stubble. "I mean, try to put up with it for our sake, Mum's especially. She was going spare thinking of you alone in the house. Stopping here would be doing her blood pressure a favour."

"You told her about the seance."

"When I brought you back here a few hours ago, Ma wanted to know what might've put you in this state."

"Apart from my husband hovering between life and death, obviously."

"Apart from that. Anyway, I brought up the seance and the mushrooms. She's fit to kill Jude and she's no fan of your hubby either, give or take his present predicament."

"She still thinks I might've cut myself deliberately with that knife. I didn't! It slipped. *You* believe me?"

"Drink your tea."

"Is there anything else in it, apart from brandy?"

"Like what?"

"I don't know but I don't trust anyone, especially people who claim to have my best interests at heart, as if they know what those are."

"I've put nowt in your tea. Brandy is Mum's cure-all for every type of shock – tips enough of it into her cooking – but I'm not down with all her ideas. Where's your stepma?"

"Cleared off last night. What's the next step, to have me sectioned? No sharp objects in a padded cell, of course. Everything made of rubber, including the food."

"Lucy, come off it." He looked pained.

"I'm being facetious, kinda, but I'm also telling you and Snowy to back off. Are you going to strap me down if I try to go back to the house?"

"Strap you down?" he echoed in horror. "Where did that come from? Look, you're a grown-up free to come and go as you please, albeit suffering from mental and physical exhaustion, in my humble opinion. Look, why not humour us and stay a couple of nights? Ma's already made up the box room, far end of the landing. Just try it for size, the staying here thing."

He jabbed a finger over his shoulder at the kitchen window. "You haven't met the girls outside yet."

"The girls?"

"Catherine, Theresa and Bernadette. Ma's chickadees. Named after saints, to the silent disapproval of the parish priest."

"Maybe later. And stop trying to distract me. Maybe I am out for the count. I dunno. Before she left the building forever, my stepma told me something that broke me into little pieces. Maybe one day I can be put back together and look beautiful in my imperfection, like a kintsugi vase. But not today."

"You're already beautiful in your imperfection."

"Jerome..."

"I've fallen for you. But you already know that."

"You certainly pick your moments. And your women. Fucked-up is your apparent speciality."

Lucy claimed her cooling tea. "I don't know if I've fallen for you. It would be easy to, and that's the problem, especially now. As previously mentioned, my husband's hovering between life and death. I can't think of you that way and it wouldn't be right to."

"No one's rushing you."

"Think I'll have a lie down."

"Yeah, good idea. I've got to go out anyway. I'm meeting my organic meat producer in Sowersby. Don't want to, but can't put him off. Ma will be back soon with your stuff."

Lucy bit back the churlish observation that she didn't want Snowy poking about in her 'stuff'.

Pinky brushed his knuckles against the back of her trailing hand as he passed, just as he'd done on the landing of Rook House.

She pressed back, signalling... what? That he had reason to hope? That she felt the same way? "Jerome, what did you say, exactly, when you rang the hospital to explain that I wasn't coming in today?"

"Just asked them to tell Hugh's parents you'd got a lurgy and didn't want to spread it about. Don't worry, I'm heading there later today to appear on your behalf."

"As what?"

"Mutual friend of yours and Hugh's."

"But you're not."

"Have to go, Lucy. See you later."

"The lurgy excuse is lame. Tom and Frances will think I'm crying off."

"I'll put them right. I can be persuasive when I want."

"You wish."

He grabbed his coat off a hook, took a set of keys from a ceramic dish and strode towards the front door, taking his sandalwood scent and matter-of-fact declarations with him. She'd never met anyone like him. But she didn't know him.

He turned in the open doorway. "If you ever want to talk about what your stepma said to break you..."

"I know, thank you."

But she never would.

When he'd gone, she poured away the rest of her tea and went upstairs to find the box room at the end of the landing, on the way peeking into the remaining bedrooms.

Both had a neutral vibe: magnolia walls, Ikea furniture, scattered toiletries.

She ID'd Pinky's room by the screwdrivers on a bedside table next to some old radio he'd taken apart. She still hadn't pinned down what he did all day beyond the 'poaching' thing; who he really was or might be.

She lay down on the box room bed and stared at the ceiling, counting notional chickens.

By the time she heard a noise, an hour had passed and she'd barely dozed.

She sat up and listened. Someone was clattering about in a passageway at the side of the cottage.

She went downstairs just as Snowy came through the front door, brandishing two full carrier bags. "I grabbed essentials like your toothbrush and dressing gown. Hope you don't mind me going through your things."

It was a bit late in the day if she did, Lucy reflected. "Was that you just now, up the side of the house?"

"Yes, we've got a lean-to there. I was putting my bike away."

"My phone!" gasped Lucy. "Did I leave that at Rook House?"

"No, Pinky brought that back last night, along with your coat, purse, house and car keys. Coat's on the back of the kitchen door. Other bits and pieces are in an envelope in a kitchen drawer."

"Why don't you call him Jerome?"

"Force of habit." Snowy held out the bags and Lucy took them.

"Thanks for all your concern, Snowy, if I haven't said it properly before."

"While I was up at the house, I took the knife out of the painting and left the picture behind the kitchen door. You might want it again, I don't know."

"I won't, but thank you. I didn't injure myself deliberately with that knife, you've got to believe me."

"Is it a portrait of your mother?"

'I – thought it was going to be. I've changed my mind. Pinky's gone out. Says he's going to drop by the hospital later and talk to Hugh's parents on my behalf.'

"Yes, he told me that," nodded Snowy.

"Will he be out poaching tonight?" Lucy added unguardedly.

Snowy blanched. "He doesn't *poach*. The Birds are not thieves!"

"I'm sorry, I didn't mean..."

"No, *I'm* sorry, I shouldn't be snapping."

"Though it's not his land, is it?" Lucy ventured. "When you get right down to it."

Snowy gave her a loaded look. "Sit down, Lucy. It's time you knew."

"Knew what?"

"God forgive me, yet another truth."

Leaning back in a kitchen chair, it took some time for Lucy to process the bombshell that Snowy was the owner of Rook House and the land it stood on. There was no conglomerate that had bought it on the cheap from far-flung Napier descendants.

"So Gymbr Holdings..."

"That's a name Henry Hollenbeck came up with. He helped me draw up the paperwork for the guardianship. Owed me for turning a blind eye to building that monstrosity *he* calls a house. Well, I don't know if 'owed' is the right word, but he understands discretion. 'Gymbr' is a local word for 'lamb', my maiden name."

"Why the need for discretion in the first place? Though I'd call it secrecy."

Snowy sighed. "Everyone around here suspects me of owning Rook House, but I don't go broadcasting it. I told you that Marianne was fonder of my family than her own. She adored Mickey when she was a child and later came to rely on my mother as her daily carer. With no descendants of her own, Marianne probably intended the house and land as a gift for my family to dispose of as they saw fit. It may also have been a final dig at Ezra. I don't know. But she left Rook House to my mother, who in turn left it to me."

"So there were no distant relatives of the Napiers to inherit the house?"

"If there were, none came forward to contest ownership."

"Why not just sell up and bank the cash?"

"That may have been my mother's intention at the start. Then she discovered that she enjoyed the income from renting out the house and selling off land here and there. It was satisfying. I've found it less so."

"So you're really quite rich?"

Snowy shrugged. "I've always been a saver, like my ma before me. Though of course, a house like that swallows up money. And then there are taxes. Plus, I had to give my brother Jack a fair share of the income," Snowy went on. "He went to Canada, died too young, no bairns of his own. Jack and my father never minded that Rook House was handed down through the womenfolk. Lambs by name, lambs by nature."

"So Pinky knows all this?"

"Of course. He's next in line for the house. There's no rule that says it has to go to a woman."

Which might explain the mystery of how Pinky filled his days, Lucy thought. He was actually a landed gent with a major inheritance coming his way!

"But he's keen to sell, hand Rook House off to a hotel chain or some such," explained Snowy. "I've been coming round to the idea for a while. When the last tenant left, I got in property guardians while I chewed it over. Pinky wants to keep the wood, is all."

"But still, why lie to me and Hugh about your true ID?"

"I've always let tenants believe I'm just the gatekeeper, the go-between. Saved me a lot of direct earache down the years, promising to report issues or gripes to the owners and relay the answer."

"Still seems extreme," murmured Lucy.

"I don't normally have so much direct contact with tenants," said Snowy. "And though I told you I heard scratching once and some tenants reported the same, I never set much store by the haunting stories. Until you and Hugh came along." Snowy was silent for a moment. "It seemed like... like the house had been waiting for you two so that something dead could come alive there. Which is why I tried to persuade you to move on."

Lucy gripped the edges of the kitchen table, recalling the 'hidden room' and all that had happened since. Had she released something in that house, like unsealing a vent to let steam escape? The house was pivoting endlessly in time and that hidden room was the fulcrum. She felt ominously certain of it.

"You mustn't go back to Rook House, Lucy, not after what's happened to Hugh. There's already talk among locals."

"That I pushed him?"

"No, nothing like that!" Snowy hesitated. "About the house having its say. I'll be putting it on the market without delay."

Lucy blinked at her. "Meantime you expect me to stay here?"

"I'd *like* you to. For as long as you want."

Lucy let go of the table. "I don't know, Snowy. I just don't know."

She was exhausted, incapable of making a decision about anything. Snowy suggested she take another nap upstairs. "You'll be a new woman by this evening."

Lucy nodded. "Thank you. I'll need my phone, though, in case the hospital rings."

Snowy retrieved the envelope containing her phone and other essentials from a kitchen drawer.

Lucy took it from her. "Thank you again, Snowy, for caring about me. Us."

"Don't be daft. I'm the owner of that blasted house; I've a moral responsibility. And I like you, Lucy. I like Hugh, too, in his way, though he's more of an acquired taste. But then, the men usually are."

Lucy went slowly up to the box room and lay on her side clutching her phone, balefully awake, mind and heart racing, Snowy moving about softly downstairs.

At some point, Lucy drifted into an uneasy sleep.

Around midday, her mobile rang. Snapping awake, she grabbed the phone off the duvet to hear Pinky's voice muffled by traffic and sirens. "Just been inside the hospital but I've come out to the car park to call you. Look, no point beating about the proverbial..."

"When did you ever?"

"I got here just as the docs were updating your in-laws. Hugh's had a setback. Needs another op. Blood clot on the brain."

Lucy blinked at the ceiling.

"Did you hear what I said, Lucy?"

"Is it touch and go?"

"You know what docs are like, erring on the 'wait and see' side of caution, but that's how I read it."

"I'll be right there."

"The Driscolls aren't expecting you. Told them you'd been laid low with a 24-hour stomach bug from all the stress and didn't want to pass it on to them, let alone Hugh. They weren't exactly sympathetic, but they seemed to feel you were doing the right thing."

"I don't care. I *have* to be there, surely you see that? Supposing the worst happens?"

"If you must come, I'll wait here and stay with you when you arrive. Your car... you'll have to take a taxi to Rook House to pick it up. Or I can come and get you."

"No, I'll drive. I'll go and get my car now."

"Have Ma go with you."

"See you soon, Pinky. Thanks for the update. And for God's sake, tell Hugh's parents that I'm on my way!"

She rang off, debating calling Tom and Frances directly. No – Frances might be freshly hysterical and Tom bleary with sorrow. Everything inside her shrank from another encounter with two people who blamed her for their son's condition, but she'd have to face the music. She was Hugh's wife.

Running downstairs to inform Snowy of developments, she spotted a Post-it note on the fridge: *left you to rest, gone out to do a food shop*.

That came as a relief. She could just get on with it.

Easing into her coat, Lucy dropped phone, purse, house and car keys into her pockets.

Leaving the cottage, she hung a left towards the high street. She'd noticed taxis outside The Rusty Nail before. Spotting one parked up, she opened the back door and slid into the seat. "Rook House, please."

The driver put away his mobile, nodded and started the car. He wasn't a talker, thank God. Nor did he seem interested in her destination.

It was a cold, clear afternoon. She felt as though she'd been out of circulation for days rather than hours, re-engaging gingerly with a world of people, movement, noise, decisions and demands. On the drive, the first lambs of spring kicked up joyful heels in rolling green fields. Colour was vivid, her senses heightened.

When the car reached the pillared gates of Rook House, she tapped the driver on the shoulder. "I can walk from here, thanks. How much do I owe?"

31

The day darkened and the wind quickened as she walked beneath the elms into the Rook House microclimate. The elms looked tall and significant; clouds scrambled over each other in their haste to cross the sky. The wind fossicked at her heels and plucked at her elbows – the peculiar, localised wind that funnelled up the driveway and twisted into the house with its own dark signature tune.

When the house came into view, it looked as stark and slab-like as a wind-bitten sarsen in a neolithic field, darkness soaking into its red bricks.

Her car was parked outside. She should just jump in and drive to York.

Instead, she slotted a large brass key into the front door.

The door opened silently. She stood in the dim hallway and felt a foolish urge to call: "Hello?"

As if Hugh might answer: "In here!" from behind the study door.

The intangible smells were still there of coffee grounds and the rich fruit oils once rubbed into polished wood. The house was cold but not freezing.

In the kitchen, she found her painting propped behind the door where Snowy had left it.

It was a shock to see it again, the lightly sketched rose in her mother's hand scored by a blade, her pale golden eyes two blinded pinpricks. Filmed with death, like a rabbit on a car bonnet. Lucy felt sick with guilt at the desecration.

She had two things she wanted to do.

One was to put the other portrait out to pasture. She walked boldly into the living room and reached up to wrench Ezra Napier off the wall.

He yielded without a fight but she still held the painting at arm's length as though he might leap out of the frame and bite her with dripping fangs.

Upstairs, a sound.

She paused. She wanted to put Ezra in the woodshed with the spiders and mouldering logs, where he belonged. But she had that other thing to accomplish first.

Before she could do anything else, however, a white-shrouded figure flitted past the living room window. She just glimpsed it from the corner of her eye, then heard the back door open into the kitchen. She threw the portrait on to the sofa and went to see who it was – who had followed her here. Could it be snow wolf Elena, back for round 102? Though she hadn't heard her car pull up.

It was Hugh. Hugh was sitting at the kitchen table, a blanket heaved roughly over his hospital gown, the white bandage round most of his head giving him the appearance of a half-wrapped mummy. He raised his gaze to her, eyes sunk in bruised sockets. Where the bandage was rucked up, she could see a shaved patch of scalp with a red garland of stitches thrusting through his dark hair like a lamprey's bloody mouth.

"How'd you get here?" she asked, sitting down opposite him. Wary; because she knew he wasn't really there.

"Snuck out when no one was looking." His voice came from a long way away and had a tinny cadence. Like pursed lips whistling round a bottle rim. "Got a bus outside the hospital."

"How'd you pay the fare?" Only mildly curious to hear the

answer (no buses came out this way), she rose and started opening kitchen drawers, keeping her back to him, dismayed to find every piece of sharp cutlery removed.

By Snowy, of course.

That explained the rustling up the side of the cottage. Snowy had decanted every sharp object she could find in the lean-to. Now Lucy thought of it, her returned soap bag hadn't included her nail scissors. Snowy wasn't taking any chances when it came to her self-harm theory.

This was a blow. She'd wanted to arm herself before she went upstairs. Not against Hugh. She hadn't been expecting him and wasn't afraid of him.

"But I cut myself accidentally with the sodding bread knife!" she insisted and turned to show her bandaged hand to Hugh. "Look!"

Her phone started ringing in her coat pocket. She drew it out. Snowy. Must be back from her shopping errand. No doubt she'd call Pinky next. Lucy declined the call and repocketed the phone.

"I'm tired," Hugh sighed, slumping forward with his white head in his pale hands. "Sit with me a while, Mouse."

"All right." Pausing for a final look before she slid shut the last drawer she'd rifled through, she sat down opposite him again. "You're not really here, are you, Hugh?"

He looked up, eyes dark and dead as coal. "I could be."

"Or you could be a fragment of underdone potato." More grave than gravy.

"Or the latest release from a stone tape coming to a multiplex near you," he suggested.

"I don't think so. If that was the case, I wouldn't see a hospital version of you, I'd see the you falling from the window. What really happened there?"

"I... can't say. Because I can't remember. Not yet. Give it time.

What were you looking for in those drawers?" His overstretched smile was a wan, fathomless thing. "Protection against a vengeful ghost? I can't hurt you and anyway, I don't blame you for any of it."

Her hand tightened around her coat sleeve. "I know. I know you wouldn't harm me."

"I tried to love you."

"I know that too."

"You're tired too, Lucy. Can't you feel it?"

"I can, actually." Maybe it was a case of autosuggestion from a persuasive presence, but she lay her head down on the table, exposing the top of it to an apparition of still undetermined motive.

"Mouse," he said fondly. "With this thing wrapped round my head, I'd make a passable Mad Hatter."

She yawned, twitching whiskers that weren't there. "Might have a quick nap. Don't have to rush to the hospital, now you're here."

He didn't answer and she didn't expect him to. Her eyelids fluttered shut.

She wasn't sure how long she dozed. She came to because her phone was ringing again in her pocket.

She drew it out, declining Snowy's latest call. There was also a text from Snowy, more than an hour old: "*Are you on your way to hospital by now? I see your car keys are gone. I've rung Pinky and put him on notice to meet you there.*"

Wouldn't be much longer, Lucy supposed, before Pinky reported that she hadn't arrived at the hospital and Snowy came racing over to Rook House on her bike.

She gazed out of the kitchen window. Light had leaked out of the day. Or been swallowed up by the house.

"Who was it this time on the phone?" asked Hugh, his position unchanged at the table.

"The hospital," she lied. "They've left a voicemail."

"You never told me about seeing those therapists," he complained. "You made out that you thought they were all charlatans, that you'd be better off visiting a fortune teller."

"I stand by that. Anything you say or don't say to a therapist will be used in evidence against you. I don't trust a so-called profession that's based on 'the customer is always wrong.'"

"Noted," said Hugh.

Her phone rang again. She looked at the screen. "Now it's Pinky Bird. Probably checking my whereabouts." Just like his mother.

"Ah. Have you slept with him?"

"No!"

"But you want to?"

"*You* slept with Jude, didn't you?"

"That just sort of happened."

"Shit tends to."

She declined Pinky's call and received another voicemail she didn't play and a raft of texts she didn't open. On her screen, the top one said: "*Where TF are you???*"

The kitchen was almost totally dark now. She stood up, slipping the phone back into her pocket. "Have to get on."

"Don't go upstairs, Lucy."

"I have to."

"Stay here with me."

"I've done staying in this house with you, my love. I'm sorry. Don't you have some other place to be?"

She moved slowly to the doorway leading into the hall. When she turned back, darkness had drained the kitchen of its last shred of daylight, the Rayburn flaunting its bulk but the shadows only Hugh-shaped if she squinted and wanted them to be.

She reached the stairs and started to climb.

The Bakelite phone rang out shrilly. Bound to be Tom or Frances or even Pinky trying the landline out of desperation. Hugh said somewhere behind her: "Stay here with me. Please."

No can do. I told you, I'm sorry.

Besides, she knew the phone caller would be someone at the hospital ringing to say that her husband had died on the operating table a short time ago.

The acanthus room *was* freezing, and dark as Hades.

Never thinking to turn on the light, she sat cross-legged in the middle of the room with her back to the whistling fireplace and addressed the hidden room. "I'm sorry," she said to whoever was listening. She touched her locket and then her coat sleeve. "I'm sorry for whoever you are and whatever you went through in there. I came one final time to tell you."

She sat there for what seemed a long time, though perhaps it was only a few minutes. She didn't know.

It was too dark to see her watch and she never thought of taking her phone from her pocket.

Then she squinted, because the wall appeared to be moving. A door shouldered forward and swung slowly open, revealing a black maw. It seemed to swell and pull her towards it.

She heard it, then. *Scratch, scratch, scratch.*

She gripped the coat sleeve hiding her only protection against whatever was inside that dark space... whatever she'd feared might still be waiting for her when she came up here one final time.

Then a jolt, a buzzing, a flash of pain in her head.

Scritter, scratch, scritter.

Mocking laughter. *You remember, then?* Not Elena's voice. Something older. Not a human voice at all.

The realisation fell on her with awful suddenness.

It all came back to her now – lovemaking in the wood, the twin son that Ezra Napier had murdered when he saw the in-ward-turned foot, Susan Darrow's sickening betrayal, and Belle's banishment to the space behind this small doorway, until she was removed permanently to the asylum in York, screaming an unheeded truth in words that no one cared to decipher.

A voice was whispering from the hidden room, half-crazed with the urgent need to be heard, its truth *finally* heeded.

Lucy crawled closer to listen but it was hard to sift words from another sound, like the thick buzzing of bees. "What? I can't hear you."

She shuffled into the room on her knees. As long as the door remained open behind her, she could escape back into her own world and time.

She was inside the room now. There was someone else here – *Belle* was here – but when Lucy reached out a shaking hand, she touched only air.

Even so, the bee buzz was receding, the whispering voice becoming clearer, accompanied by that *scratch, scratch, scratch* of a trapped animal trying to escape its leather restraints.

And Lucy shook violently, thinking of poor Belle removed from here to the asylum, where she must have been strapped just as brutally to some old-fashioned gurney, with a rag in her mouth and rubberised electrodes Vaselined to her hea-

"The things he said to me!" whimpered Belle, hot breath quivering with bright, shocking clarity against Lucy's ear. "He said: 'You cavorted in the leaves like a sow rutting with its mate! Why shouldn't I throw you out with the scraps to be eaten by the yard dog? I'd eat you myself, gouge you out with a spoon if I wasn't afraid I'd choke on your putrid innards! Say his name again and I'll snap your lying neck, whore.' And with every word, he shook and squeezed me like a terrier with a rat in its jaws. And then – then they came and took me away already in the grip of madness and I died a lonely death, screaming for help that never came."

Lucy felt as though she was suffocating from the weight of these words, each one inflected with a misery tightening around her neck, like the fingers that had coiled around her throat in the attic.

Just as suddenly, air flooded back into her lungs and she fell against the open door, gasping.

Belle, unseen but abjectly present, leant towards her once more. "One chance... One chance... When he comes, take it. End this. You must! Please!" Belle howled very close and yet very far away. Years away. *Scratch, scratch, scratch.*

"I can undo the straps!" gasped Lucy. "I can get you out before he comes back! You can escape, like you always planned to!"

"No!" Belle's blue-black hair tickled Lucy's neck. "No time. He's coming. It's already too late! You must kill him, Mouse, *then* help me escape. It will break the cycle. The loop. Trapped here with him, I wait for him to come and taunt me again and again, seize me, lay out the fate he has planned for me... I want one thing, Mouse. To find Phineas. He's in the house with me, I can feel it. Let me find him and be here with him. But first we must rid..." The words faded out again and Lucy felt her eardrums throb with the effort to recapture them... "him for good. The only way, the only way, the onl-"

Lucy cocked an ear. There *was* a tread on the stairs. Cautious but heavy.

"Getting warm!" buzzed Belle, thick and desperate. "He'll find me, like he always does! You must do it now, now, now. Break the loop now. He does not think me capable of finding an ally after all these years at his mercy. He will not know I found you, brought you to help me. Wait. Wait until he is very close before you strike!"

Lucy froze as footsteps stopped at the top of the stairs.

A word rang out in a deep male rumble. A call or a threat? The distant voice was thick with bee buzzing.

He was coming – coming for Belle.

He was coming towards the dark acanthus room and within it, like the heart of a closed flower, a deeper, darker room. A Mariana Trench scuttling and scratching with all manner of submerged things.

"You have it?" gasped Belle. "You have it, I think? The gift I sent you from ages past?"

Lucy slid clammy fingers up her coat sleeve and found the one object Snowy had overlooked in the kitchen drawers.

Her sole protection against whatever lurked in the hidden room.

And now her way of protecting – freeing – Belle. From the past.

She eased out the cool metal with shaking fingers, the buzzing in her ears failing to block out that awful *scritter, scratch, scratch* of a woman strapped to a narrow bed just inches and lifetimes away. "I keep trying, even now," whispered Belle. "I've worn my nails to bloody stumps clawing. I'd have gnawed through them if I could, like the animal he says I am. Break the loop. Only you... only you can do it, do it, do it."

The door that led into the dark acanthus room from the landing was already open. Lucy heard Ezra Napier come in and stand before the cold fireplace, then move to the window and look out over restless treetops.

He was biding his moment, as perhaps he always did. Enjoying taunting Belle with his presence before he tortured her with his awful words and throttling grasp.

He didn't know that Lucy was here.

Lucy held her breath and imagined him as a great black corvid, bigger and darker than a jackdaw, a mocking eye about to turn in her direction...

"Now!"

She lunged forward silently, seeming to float out of the crawl space and across the acanthus room on winged feet. He turned to her with a look of utter shock on his dark, distorted face, raising his hands to ward her off.

But he was too late.

She thrust her weapon into his chest.

He looked down at it, the once-green tourmaline star blackened by fire on the end of the long hairpin that had skewered him. One of the same hairpins he had stabbed into Belle's head at her dressing table. A hairpin picked up by a despairing maid to pierce the rag belly of a ruering doll.

Now he looked up at Lucy through glazed eyes "Why?" he asked. "How did...?"

He slid down against the wall with his legs splayed in front of him, dark coat billowing out either side.

Lucy's grip slid off the hairpin and she stumbled back with a cry of horror as she recognised him in the dark room; recognised Pinky Bird.

"Fuck's sake, Luce," he murmured thickly. "R-raced here to check if you were... told Mum I'd deal with... saw your car... I called out, chrissake... c-call an ambulance. My God, why did you...?"

His speech was slowing and slurring, his gaze of anguish and – and *disappointment* – dimming in front of her. The disappointment was worse than anything. Because he'd seen something in her worth loving. He'd wanted to care for her.

And behind her, just before a dark doorway in the wall swung shut, a manic curl of triumphant laughter and buzzing words to lodge in her head forever: "You know all about it, don't you, Mouse? The thirst that nothing can slake! You wanted him to be Nathan Stelley. You are what you seek. You are revenge. All revenge. You felt the cold metal in your hand and wanted it to be him. That's why you listened. That's why you came up here one last time. That's why you *heard*."

Lucy collapsed at Pinky's side. "Pinky! Christ, I'm so sorry... don't die, Pinky, please! I'm so sorry!"

But it was too late. Sobbing, she curled up alongside him, tucking one of his hands inside his coat to keep warm and clutching the other, kissing the knuckles, apologising over and over. Promising to fall for him the way he wanted. All useless now.

Everything came flooding back; all the visions that Belle had shown her and what they meant. She remembered and understood when it was all too late. She understood how and why she had become Belle's instrument of revenge.

Sobbing her heart out, she smelt oranges and strawberry penny chews, then felt blue-black hair tickle the back of her neck.

"I didn't know, Mum. I didn't know! I thought he was Ezra. I thought, I thought-"

"Shush, it's done now, darling. You need to rest."

Lucy scuttled round and curled up with her head on her mother's lap while Rosa stroked her hair.

"She tricked me, Mum! She's waited all this time to take revenge on the last of Mickey and Susan's line, Snowy's son. She'll never be free but she waited and waited for me to come; to slake her thirst for revenge. At least for a while."

Because the scratching would go on. Belle's loop would go on playing over and over as long as the house stood and perhaps even beyond that.

As a cool hand went on stroking her brow, Lucy sat up to bury her face in the fragrant depths of her mother's hair. "I didn't know. I'm so sorry. Will Pinky know how sorry I am? Will you tell him? Will Hugh?"

"Hush now," said Rosa. "Sleep now."

"There's waiting and then there's waiting," murmured Lucy, overcome with exhaustion. "You took me to the art gallery and waited to see what Elena would do, what Dad would do, instead of confronting either of them. And then Elena waited and waited for Dad to marry her. But the dead can wait forever."

Her mother didn't answer.

When Lucy drew back to search Rosa's loving face, her mother's blue-black hair had merged with the writhing acanthus leaves on the wall. And a smile beneath piles of soft dark hair was beckoning to her from the leaves.

Lucy got eagerly to her feet and thrust her fingers into the waving fronds, letting them coil around her wrists and draw her into their depths.

Behind her, a noise. A faint, pleading groan, perhaps.

She turned. The leaves were up to her elbows now, weeds choking her remaining strength, but her curiosity was stronger. Perhaps.

"Help, Lu... pl-l-lease..."

"Pinky?" He was alive!

The leaves tugged, indistinguishable from a snare made of black hair, taut as the silken steel of a spider's web.

A susurrating voice urged: "Hush now. Sleep now."

"No!" It wasn't Rosa. Not the hair nor the voice nor the cooling hand on her brow. Another trick the house had up its sleeve, like a black, bent hairpin of tarnished metal.

She wrenched away, falling backwards almost on top of Pinky.

He moved a hand, feebly.

She turned her back on the wall, afraid to see what it might be doing, how it might be coming for her.

She rolled away as far as the fireplace, scrabbling for her phone and punching in 999.

"Hello! Oh, thank God. Yes... man's hurt... Rook House... I'll give the address... yes, yes, he's still breathing... hurry!"

"Lucy." His hand twitched towards her.

She waded over to him on her knees, taking the hand and kissing it again, closing her eyes against the sight of the long, thin sharpness pinning him there, dimly aware of the wall still writhing, its anger palpable at being cheated of another soul, another story to tell down the long years, of death that came for the unsuspecting.

Pinky wheezed, the blood curdling in his chest. "Whatever it... is, whatever you want... to look at... don't." He covered her gripping hand with his own, as though protecting her.

Even now. It cost him every breath he still had.

She'd have howled if she wasn't already crying.

Her phone was still connected to the 999 operator. As the wall reached out smoky limbs of boneless black, she pulled back from its spreading edges and bent over the phone, gasping out all the additional details that she could.

Then she lay beside him and hid her tightly shut eyes in his rattling chest, until blue-violet lights strobed across the uncurtained window and the banshee call of a siren wailed through the tunnel of elms.